CARTEL

Books by Edward Jay Epstein

INQUEST: *The Warren Commission and the Establishment of Truth*
COUNTERPLOT: *The Garrison Case*
NEWS FROM NOWHERE
BETWEEN FACT AND FICTION
AGENCY OF FEAR
CARTEL
LEGEND: *The Secret World of Lee Harvey Oswald*

CARTEL

by

Edward Jay Epstein

G.P. Putnam's Sons
New York

SBN: 399-12086-6

Library of Congress Cataloging in Publication Data

Epstein, Edward Jay, 1935-
Cartel.

I. Title.
PZ4.E6424Car 1978   [PS3555.P652]   813'.5'4   78-7490

For Sansi Duncan

CONTENTS

One: Autumn, 1952

Two: Early Summer, 1953

Three: August, 1953

CARTEL

BOOK ONE

Autumn, 1952

CHAPTER I

THE GROUSE SHOOT

It was an unusually cold September morning, even for Scotland. The mist so darkened the moor that the heather seemed pitch black. The mounds of freshly dug earth, which rose up at intervals of thirty feet, were hardly visible.

Concealed behind each mound, a man with a highly polished gun waited patiently for the weather to clear. Behind each man stood a woman with a card in her hand, ready to mark for the hunter the location of his kill. And behind them both, dogs, alert in every muscle, pawed the muddy ground and sniffed the thin wind.

Just before noon, the sun poked a burning finger through the haze. Lord Crumonde realized that the light would not get much better. Anyhow, it was his moor, and he would have this shoot when he liked. With a shrill blast of a whistle, he signaled for the first drive of the day to begin.

Lou-Anne Bell stood a few feet behind Crumonde, shivering in her sable coat and hood. She couldn't help staring at her host's gnarled legs. His tweed plus fours exposed them precisely at the point where they were most bony. She wondered how such spindly underpinnings could support such a burly body. "This is so exciting," she drawled in her Texas accent.

Crumonde did not answer. He didn't like her, or her husband, and was sorry he had had to invite them. For more than an hour, he had tolerated her annoying questions.

Lord Crude, Lou-Anne thought to herself. That was what her husband, Frank, called Crumonde—and that's what he was. Crude. She hadn't wanted to come on this ridiculous expedition to Scotland, but Frank had insisted. "It's business—important business," he had explained the night before, reminding her, as if she hadn't heard it a hundred times before, "Lord Crude runs Anglo-Iranian Oil, and that means we gotta be very charming to him." Frank always used "we" when he meant her.

"I do declare . . ." she began slowly, trying again to get Crumonde's attention. "I never met anyone like your friend, Nubar Gulbenkian. . . . They say he's one of the richest men in the world. Is it true?"

"Ask him, Mrs. Bell," Crumonde answered without turning. In the distance, he could hear the shouts of the beaters and the yelps of their dogs. He raised his Purdy gun to the ready position.

Meanwhile in the next butte, Diana Raven spoke in a soft, hesitant voice. "May I ask you something, Nubar?"

"Of course," Gulbenkian answered, swiveling around on his shooting stick. He observed that Diana looked her age—

fifty. Gulbenkian could remember her when she was eighteen, and it made him feel his own age—and sad. She had gone through three husbands before she was thirty, all of whom had married her for her money. Now she was the wife of Sir Anthony Raven, the most ambitious of them all.

"It's about Tony," she began, taking advantage of her first opportunity to speak to Gulbenkian alone. "He's been traveling to the four corners of the earth—and seems utterly exhausted." She knew Gulbenkian would interpret this to mean that her husband was not making love to her, which was true.

Gulbenkian paused a moment to press his monocle under his right eyebrow. He imagined it completed his image by magnifying his otherwise mild brown pupil into the demonic eye of a predator hawk. He knew it also broke the bland symmetry of his face. He never wanted to think of himself as the "moonfaced Armenian" his father had called him when he was a boy. Every morning, therefore, he tweezed his eyebrows into wild, wooly arches, and shaped his waxed beard into a daggerlike V to hide his weak chin. Parting his lips slightly, he now affected his most satyric smile. "Tony has a world to run, the world of oil. He thrives on it."

"Nonsense. He came back from Iran last week looking half-dead."

"Iran?" Gulbenkian repeated quizzically. It was the first he had heard of such a trip. Ever since Mossadeq nationalized the oil there a year ago, production had been entirely shut down. What was Sir Anthony doing in Iran? he wondered.

"It's all business, isn't it? Even this shoot is business," Diana said gloomily.

"Business?" Gulbenkian found that repeating the last word of someone's sentence gave him time to collect his thoughts. Certainly, he had not come to this grouse shoot for

13

pleasure. All his life, he had detested shooting birds, and certainly he had no particular love for Scotland; it was too uncomfortable for his taste. He had come solely because Lord Crumonde had insisted, in his imperious way, that he be there and had even sent a private plane to fetch him from London. Crumonde had said only that there was some new "crisis"—and Raven and Bell would also attend. "Be there," Crumonde had croaked, and then hung up the telephone. Though he still had not been told the nature of the emergency, Gulbenkian had no intention of adding to Diana's obvious unease. "Grouse are not the only sport available this weekend, my dear," he said, leering pointedly at Chris Winchester in the next butte.

Diana smiled nervously. She wanted to know why Gulbenkian had brought this twenty-one-year-old, in her very unconventional clothes, to Crumonde's for the weekend. Nubar always liked to describe himself as a collector of old masters and young mistresses, and Diana wondered whether Chris was his latest acquisition. "Have you known her long?"

"Long? First spotted her in St. Tropez last summer. A very talented girl, as it turns out." He could not tell Diana that it was, in fact, her husband who had first seen Chris that summer. They had sailed down to St. Tropez on Raven's yacht, and Gulbenkian found Tony standing on the deck, peering through his field glasses at this long-legged girl sitting in a café across the harbor. Gamines were Raven's weakness, and Gulbenkian had been well instructed by his father to "either kiss the hand of the man you fear, or better yet, find his weakness." So, without saying anything to Raven, he had sent for the girl.

One hundred feet away, Chris stood behind Raven. What was she doing here? she asked herself. It seemed totally mad when she thought back over the events that had led to her

14

being behind this heap of mud. Only a few weeks earlier, she had been sitting by herself at a table in a peaceful fishing village in the south of France, nibbling at a croissant and enjoying the Mediterranean sun. A handsome sailor with the eyes of a schoolboy had sat down beside her, and pointing out the largest yacht in the harbor, invited her aboard. Why not? she shrugged, and followed him up the mahogany gangplank. He had led her to a table for two set with crystal, under a red-and-white striped canopy, and left her sitting there alone. A waiter filled her glass with champagne. A moment later, Gulbenkian appeared and introduced himself, explaining that the owner of the yacht, Sir Anthony Raven, would like to dine with her. She was too intrigued to do anything but accept; she had always believed in seeing what life had to offer.

She remembered now that Raven had seemed startled to see her sitting there. Throughout dinner, he glared at her with his fierce eyes, but hardly spoke. Then the sailor reappeared and escorted her to shore. That was the last time she had seen either Gulbenkian or Raven until Gulbenkian had called and persuaded her to come to this grouse shoot.

Raven stood perfectly still before her in the blind. Chris couldn't get over how large his head was—it seemed to dominate his entire body. From his face, with its strongly chiseled features, she guessed Raven was around forty. Even though his tweeds were obviously cut from expensive cloth, he seemed oddly disheveled. She thought it might have something to do with his slouched shoulders, or his short legs—or even just his rumpled tie. Crumonde had mumbled something earlier about Raven's having just returned from Iran.

"So you were in Iran," she said, determined to break the silence. "It must have been fascinating."

He turned slowly, looking her over from head to foot. She

15

wore jeans, tightly stretched across her narrow frame, a shaggy sweater, and rainbow-colored socks. Inappropriate for a shoot, he thought, but appealing.

"Did you see any of the ruins of the Persian Empire?" she persisted.

"I saw a country that is a ruin—and may soon be dead," he answered coldly, looking squarely at her until her eyes avoided his gaze. Then he turned back toward the moor.

Lady Crumonde, meanwhile, regarded Frank Bell with some amusement as he gripped his gun. Bell was a tall, muscular man, with closely cropped gray hair and baby-blue eyes. "Not much character," she thought, "but very handsome." She thought her husband had chosen an odd assortment of guests: Bell, who had come all the way from New York; Gulbenkian, an Armenian millionaire who obviously hated bird shoots—not to mention her husband; and Raven, a man of complete mystery to her. Lady Crumonde wondered how much information about her husband's business activities she might be able to pry from Bell. From long experience, she knew that men were more likely to talk when they felt confident. And nowhere, she silently observed, did a man feel more in his element than at a grouse shoot, holding his shotgun in both hands, with the sure knowledge that he would bring down some birds in flight. Just as she was about to speak, Bell whispered to her, with an air of excitement, "Any minute now." The beaters' shouts could be heard just over the rise in the moor. Then the line of raggedly dressed beaters advanced up the moor. Carrying white flags, which fluttered in the wind, the men shouted at the children from the village, who ran ahead of them, poking the bushes with sticks to flush out any concealed birds.

The grouse ran in short spurts, trying to hide in the purple heather, only to be driven out again by the beaters.

They had nowhere to go but forward, where they were blocked by the mounds of earth. As the wall of beaters closed in on them, the grouse raced toward the slopes of earth and tried to fly over them.

Crumonde fired first, winging a bird as it took flight. A second quick shot brought down another bird.

Lou-Anne Bell was too excited by the volley of shots to mark the points at which the birds fell.

Gulbenkian wanted to hold his hands over his ears as the din grew louder, but restrained himself. The waving flags and booming guns brought back for him memories of another massacre. When he was two years old, the Turks had slaughtered thirty thousand of his fellow Armenians in Istanbul, first herding them with shotguns against the rough stone walls of the city and then shooting and clubbing them to death. His family was one of the few that escaped.

As a pair of grouse flew over his butte, Raven slowly wheeled around until he was directly facing Chris. His golden eyes widened as the birds gained altitude. Then he methodically squeezed off two blasts, and both birds tumbled from the sky. Chris did not move. She knew that the explosions had not fully relieved the tension that was pent up in this man.

"Got you," Bell whispered to himself as he hit his third bird. Thirty years of shooting quail in Texas had sharpened his eye.

It was over in less than five minutes. A few birds escaped over the flank, and over Gulbenkian's butte—the rest were dead. In all, the four guns had brought down nine grouse. The dogs quickly retrieved the kill.

Crumonde approached Gulbenkian's butte with angry strides. "Why the hell didn't you shoot?" he shouted.

Thinking that the tiny arc of jagged teeth in Crumonde's enormous mouth resembled the spikes of an exotic flower,

17

Gulbenkian answered distractedly, "Shoot? Sorry, I was waiting for a more sporting shot."

Crumonde walked off shaking his head. As the son of a Scottish bookkeeper, he could not tolerate waste—not even a few grouse.

"Oh, dear, it's starting to drizzle," Lady Crumonde said to Bell. "Pity you won't get in another drive this afternoon. You've come all the way from Texas for this . . ."

"New York," he corrected. Though born in Houston, he had been working in the New York offices of Standard Oil for nine years now, as head of International Marketing.

The group walked together toward a jeep-drawn wagon as the moor began to turn muddy. A flash of lightning cut across the dark sky. The gamekeepers had already hung the dead grouse by their necks on the wagon's sideboards.

"Let's go," Crumonde barked, as he clumsily hoisted himself up on the back of the wagon. Then he lowered the tailgate, which served as a ladder.

The shotguns were neatly stacked in a hand-hewn rack in the front of the wagon, and everyone scrambled aboard and huddled on the narrow wooden benches. Two smelly dogs also jumped on.

The jeep, which the gamekeepers piled into, lurched forward, dragging the wagon behind it. The beaters waved enthusiastically as the shooters left. Their day was over.

Before they had proceeded a mile, the drizzle turned into a drenching rain. Lady Crumonde handed out blankets to the women, but they did little good.

While Lou-Anne sat shivering, faintly resembling a seal in her soaked sable, Frank Bell was telling Diana Raven about quail shooting in Texas. "You'll never get wet there. We just sit inside our little streamlined lots with trailer whiskey and women and use cowboys to get the birds right up to the front door."

18

Ridiculous Americans, Crumonde thought, turning his head away. Looking at Gulbenkian, his eyes focused with displeasure on the blue orchid in his lapel. "Don't you think it's a bit strange to wear an orchid to a grouse shoot?"

"Not for an oriental like me," Gulbenkian replied. He enjoyed rubbing in his oriental heritage. After all, the oil combine that Crumonde was part of owed its success in no small measure to the fact that the Gulbenkians were oriental—and could deal with other orientals.

"Aren't blue orchids very rare, Mr. Gulbenkian?" Lady Crumonde intervened, trying to divert the conversation. The last thing she knew her husband wanted to hear about was orientals. "I don't think I've ever seen a blue orchid before."

"This single flower cost me ten thousand pounds, Lady Crumonde."

"Impossible." Crumonde grumbled.

"You see, blue orchids can be raised only in one area of Tibet, where the altitude and oxygen level are conducive to their growth. I have to organize a private yak caravan to get them to an airport in India."

Gulbenkian had invented the story just to annoy the frugal Crumonde. In actual fact, he had gotten the orchid, like all the rest of his orchids, from Charlesworth and Company in London—and it had cost only one pound. He then had it dyed with blue ink to match his tweed.

Crumonde looked at him goggle-eyed with dismay, then turned back to Bell, who was still talking about quail.

"I'd say it's from the Odontoglossum tribe of orchids, probably dyed," Raven whispered to Gulbenkian.

The Armenian smiled affirmatively. He never ceased to be impressed at Raven's superior knowledge. Always know who you're dealing with, even if it's the devil, his father had impressed on him. Yet Gulbenkian knew virtually nothing about Raven's background—not even his parentage. Raven

19

reputedly had a brilliant war record—headed some super-secret division of British intelligence. And he had made all the right connections, including Diana, after the war. It was Diana's father, Lord Tutman, who had brought him into the oil combine.

Everyone was soaked by the time they reached Lord Crumonde's lodge. A half-dozen servants scurried out, holding umbrellas for them.

The immense lodge was built on the side of a steep hill, overlooking Loch Eddy. A fireplace, large enough for logs to burn vertically, dominated the living room. Above the stone mantelpiece were the heads of stags that Crumonde had shot. On the other walls were oil paintings of Crumonde's bearded ancestors. They all had the same craggy nose with splayed nostrils.

A weathered old servant then passed around mugs of mulled wine, smelling heavily of burnt cloves, which had been prepared in anticipation of the arrival of the hunters.

The women, meanwhile, had been shown to their rooms upstairs. Chris shook her head in disbelief when she saw that her suitcase had been unpacked, her clothing ironed and neatly hung in the closet. It's all magic, she thought. Taking out another pair of freshly laundered jeans, she prepared for lunch.

An hour later, they were all sitting around a massive oak table in the dining room, eating gulls' eggs, game pie, and a crumbling Stilton, and drinking a rich Petrus. Crumonde, having already rehashed every shot of the morning, raised his goblet high and roared a toast. "To all the brave guns that shot this morning!"

"Ah, tradition," Gulbenkian added mockingly, and drained his goblet.

Only Chris did not join in the toast. "Seems like a lot of

effort for a few scrawny birds," she said to Gulbenkian, not meaning to be overheard.

"Scrawny birds, did you say?" Crumonde growled at her.

"You don't understand, Chris," Gulbenkian cut in, in an attempt to deflect Crumonde's wrath. "The sacrifice of game is part of our ritual...."

"Ritual?" Crumonde interrupted, shifting his attention to Gulbenkian.

"The ritual of negotiations. I don't think you could make a proper deal in the oil business without shooting something...."

"Rubbish!" Crumonde barked.

"The first mission my father sent me on when he put me in the oil business was to sit in on the negotiations with Rockefeller's Standard Oil companies in America. That was in 1926 ... before you were even born, Chris." Gulbenkian stopped for a moment and looked at Chris, suddenly feeling very old. When he went on that trip, he had just been graduated from Cambridge University with what they called a "gentleman's degree." His father had arranged for him to work for Sir Henry Deterding, a tough and unyielding Dutchman, who, with Gulbenkian's father's assistance, had turned a few meager oil concessions into the Royal Dutch Shell Company. He became Deterding's personal assistant, and "Deterding's Dauphin" was what they had called him in those days. "Do you know where I wound up on that assignment?"

"Noriah, I bet," Bell said, smiling. He knew that Walter Teagle, Rockefeller's hand-picked successor, always took his business guests shooting at Noriah Plantation in Georgia. It gave him, he had once confided in Bell, "an edge," as he had put it.

"Exactly." Gulbenkian snapped his fingers together as if

21

Bell had helped him to remember. "Yes, Noriah, a thousand acres of rattlesnakes. Never saw anything like it. We sat in the back of mule-drawn carts while Teagle's Negro servants ran through the marsh grass—it was shoulder high—flushing out wild turkey. Teagle claimed Negroes were immune to rattlesnake bites. We spent three days in the sun shooting birds before Teagle would talk."

"Maybe there wasn't anything to talk about in those days—except birds." Bell laughed.

"There were other issues," Gulbenkian answered, with a cryptic smile. Thinking back over the years, Gulbenkian recalled that Deterding had proposed the great oil companies of the world join together, ostensibly to conserve the resources of South America. Specifically, he suggested that Royal Dutch Shell and Standard Oil enter into a secret agreement to limit the production of oil in Venezuela, in which both companies had an interest. Although called a conservation plan, Gulbenkian had known even then that "conservation" was just a euphemism for cutting back oil production.

"And other shoots?" Chris asked. She found his stories a welcome relief from Crumonde's boring toasts.

"I went directly from America to Kuwait. My father wanted me to personally deliver the present of a Silver Ghost Rolls-Royce to Sheik Abdullah. I was also to have a small talk with him about business."

Actually, Gulbenkian's father had instructed him to offer to fill the entire trunk of the Rolls with gold sovereigns, if the Sheik would sign away the rights to his country's oil. Even then, his father had decided it would be better to keep Kuwaiti oil off the world market until the price had risen sufficiently.

Gulping down the remainder of wine in his goblet,

Gulbenkian continued, "No sooner did I show him how to start the car, than he drove me out to the desert to shoot gazelle. He used a falcon to peck out the eyes of the gazelle, and then, when it was running in blind circles, he shot it from the open back seat of the Rolls. I told him it could do forty miles an hour right across the desert, and he turned to me and said, as if it were the solution to all his country's problems, 'Now we can get close enough to shoot the gazelles without first blinding them.'"

"So you accomplished your business?" Raven interjected. Under the table, he reached over and put his hand on Chris's leg.

"Of course." Gulbenkian smiled with an arched brow. For nearly a quarter of a century after that gazelle hunt, the Gulbenkians had managed, through payments in gold to Sheik Abdullah, to keep Kuwait's oil from coming onto the world market—and competing with their own.

"How bizarre, hunting from a Rolls," Diana Raven chimed in haughtily.

"Bizarre? Perhaps, Diana, but we also have had some curious little sacrifices right up here in Scotland," Gulbenkian said, slowly stroking his beard. "Certainly you remember Achnacarry Castle? It was in . . ."

"Nineteen twenty-eight." Diana filled in the gap. "I was only a child then, Nubar, but I'll never forget all the ridiculous guards that stood around all day. And the American millionaires. All very exciting."

Diana recalled that the castle had been sealed off from the public by those round-the-clock guards for a fortnight. Each day, limousines arrived with new guests. And each night, while the children played, the men locked themselves away in the library. Her father wouldn't tell her the names of the other guests.

23

"Two weeks of grouse shooting and trout fishing, as I understand it. Hardly worth bringing up twenty-four years later, Nubar," Raven said pointedly.

"Ah, but what a group of sportsmen," Gulbenkian persisted. "My boss, Henry Deterding, was the host for that gathering. Then there was—let me see, Walter Teagle of Standard Oil, John Cadman of Anglo-Iranian Oil, William Mellon of Gulf Oil, Bob Stewart of Standard of Indiana, and, of course, your father, Diana. We shot over two hundred grouse that September.... And we accomplished a few other minor matters."

"The hell with Achnacarry. Let's drink to our splendid hosts, Lord and Lady Crumonde," Bell cut in. As far as he could see, Nuby, as Bell called him, had had too much to drink. With all the antitrust investigations going on in the United States, this was no time to bring up Achnacarry, Bell decided.

"Hear, hear," Raven added. Everyone rose together, clanged their goblets, drank, and then sat back down in their chairs.

"But what did happen at Achnacarry?" Chris asked. She didn't like being deprived of the ending of a story.

Crumonde glowered at her as if her question were indiscreet. "Nothing at all," he snorted.

"I remember Lord Cadman did magic tricks for us all. He was very exciting," Diana added.

"Yes, nothing much happened," Gulbenkian said, turning to Chris. "Except some shooting ... and a little sleight of hand." The main trick, he thought to himself, had been pooling the resources of the three great oil companies of the world—Royal Dutch Shell, Anglo-Iranian, and Standard Oil—into one all-powerful cartel. Gulbenkian knew he could never discuss this aspect of Achnacarry in public—not even when he was drunk.

"Would anyone like to refresh themselves?" Lady Crumonde asked, as she stood up. It was meant as a cue rather than a question. She sensed it was time to leave the men to talk business. One by one, the women followed her out of the dining room.

Raven waited while cigars were passed out and lit, and brandy snifters filled. He didn't want any of the servants to overhear what was going to be said. "Sorry to bring up business," he began. "But we had some disturbing news from America on Friday. Thought it best we get together to hear what Frank has to say." He nodded to Bell.

"Through means I won't burden you gentlemen with, our Washington liaison has learned that Mossadeq is trying an end run," Bell began.

"End run?" Gulbenkian asked quizzically. A football analogy hardly seemed appropriate for the Premier of Iran.

"He's made a secret offer to the State Department to sell twenty million tons of Iranian oil to independent American oil companies. . . ."

"Iranian oil, Bell? It's *our* oil. That bloody old thief stole it from us . . . !" Crumonde roared out.

"Legally, of course, it is still our oil," Bell continued, trying to placate Crumonde. "But Mossadeq has persuaded the goddamned State Department—and Dean Acheson in particular—that his whole country will go Communist unless they can sell some oil."

"Damn that bloody country! They deserve what they get. Let them try to eat the bloody oil they can't sell. Let those beggars in the desert see what happens if they steal our oil!" From the beginning, Crumonde had taken a hard-line, rule-or-ruin position with his colleagues in the oil business, and he didn't intend to yield now. It was he who had insisted on pulling all the British technicians out of Iran earlier that year after Mossadeq nationalized Anglo-Iranian's oil concession. It was he who had ordered the giant refinery at Abadan closed when Mossadeq refused to relent. And it was he who had personally persuaded Sir Anthony Eden to send British fighters to enforce a blockade against Iran when Mossadeq threatened to sell unrefined oil to the Italians.

"If we give in to Mossadeq, if we let him sell a drop of our oil, every two-bit Middle Eastern sheik will see that he can profit from seizing our concessions," he had told Eden, thumping the Foreign Minister's desk to drum in every word of his message.

"Acheson is not addressing himself to the morality of the situation," Bell said quietly but firmly. "He is arguing that if Iran collapses into bankruptcy, the local Communists there will step in and pick up the pieces."

"Nonsense," Crumonde said. "You were just there, Raven. What do you make of the situation?"

"Our embargo is certainly effective. Abadan is locked up tighter than a drum," Raven began his report. He had made sure that when the 1,800 British technicians were pulled out, they took with them the gauges, servo-mechanisms, and other critical parts without which the refinery could not be operated. And, without the refinery processing the poisonous fumes out of the crude oil and distilling it into usable fuels, the oil fields all over Iran had to be closed down.

"And Mossadeq?" Gulbenkian asked.

"He still runs around in his purple pajamas, weeping to reporters about how much the oil companies are robbing his country." Raven had met Mossadeq only once, a year earlier. At that time, he had reluctantly given him Crumonde's ultimatum: Either admit that the nationalization was illegal, or there will be no oil revenues whatsoever. Raven remembered that Mossadeq had looked at him sadly for a moment, with tears in his aged eyes as he shook his head and said, "It is, and always will be, Iran's oil."

"How much longer can he last?" Bell asked. The American companies that he represented in the cartel were becoming increasingly concerned that Crumonde's intransigence might force the United States Government's hand.

"Iran derived ninety percent of its foreign exchange from oil," Raven quickly calculated. "Given its present reserves, it will be bankrupt in ten months—August, 1953."

"That is, if the United States Government doesn't intervene," Bell added.

"It would be ... unrealistic"—Raven chose the word carefully—"for the American government to try to buy twenty million tons of oil from Iran. Where would it find available tankers?" Raven reckoned that the cartel already controlled ninety percent of the ocean-going tankers on long-term charters. With the help of the Gulbenkian interest, they could tie up another five percent of the ships. Then he could persuade Onassis and the other Greek shipowners that it would be a risky business for them to ship oil from Iran. That would leave only a few old tankers available to the American government.

"I agree we can tie up tankers. But the American government is not going to let the Communists take over Iran," Bell said firmly. Bell had come to Scotland with instructions from his American principals to persuade Crumonde to negotiate some deal with Mossadeq.

"That's why I called this meeting," Raven said. As Chairman of the Coordinating Committee, it was his job to prevent rifts from developing between the American and British members of the cartel. "Obviously, we have succeeded in pushing Mossadeq to the brink. Now ... we need an alternative to Mossadeq—an Iranian government that will allow us to do business there, on our terms."

"But Mossadeq controls the Iranian Parliament. They are

not going to kick him out," Gulbenkian said, shaking his head. He had known Mossadeq for twenty years and fully appreciated the Premier's skill as a politician.

"I'm not talking about an election," Raven answered.

"Well, what are you talking about?" Crumonde had no patience for beating around the bush.

"A coup d'etat," Raven replied.

Chapter II

HARVARD

"Why do we study coup d'etats in a course on politics?" asked Jacob Jasmine, Assistant Professor of Government at Harvard. Jasmine slowly surveyed the packed lecture hall, letting the students stew for a moment in their own silence. The five-hundred-odd seats in Lowell Lecture Hall were full. A few students were even squatting Indian-style in the aisles. Without question, his course on "The Pathology of Politics" was the most popular in the Government Department. Not even the great Galbraith in the Economics Department nor the celebrated Schlesinger in the History Department had as many students in their lectures that year.

"No takers?" Jasmine asked, breaking the silence. His shiny brown hair, which flopped over his brow like a schoolboy's, made him look more relaxed than he was.

"Then let me answer my own question." After pausing a moment, he began. "The coup in its purest form is an act of statecraft. Its objective is not overthrowing the mythic political system nor paper constitutions, but the instruments of power that control the state. Perhaps it is not in your standard textbooks, but the coup cuts to the heart of the study of politics."

Like an orchestra conductor, Jasmine punctuated each point he made with both hands slicing the air. Finishing this brief introduction, he stepped back from the lectern. He tended to slouch slightly when he relaxed. Being nearly six feet four inches tall, he was somewhat self-conscious about his height. The undergraduates seemed quite impressed with his lecture. This was only his third year at Harvard, and already his course had received a rave review in the "Confidential Guide to Classes" published by the *Harvard Crimson*. It described Government 233a as "the hottest thing going on in an otherwise dead Government Department." And it was especially kind to him, noting that "Professor Jasmine avoids the usual humdrum about legalities, constitutions, etc. Instead, he applies his own Machiavellian cunning to political power." It concluded its recommendation with "New, original, and requires very little outside reading." Actually, the review had proved something of an embarrassment. His colleagues in the Government Department were teaching courses about the very sort of constitutions and formalities his course derided. The review added fuel to an already burning fire. Jasmine knew from remarks made at faculty meetings that his colleagues considered his presentation overly dramatic and overly conspiratorial. On the other hand, he was undeniably drawing more students than any other lecturer—and they would have to take that fact into account when he came up for tenure in the spring.

While the class watched, Jasmine quickly drew a maze of circles, squares, arrows, and interconnecting lines on the blackboard behind him. "Think for a moment of government as a labyrinth," he resumed. "Painted on the outside walls of this labyrinth are figureheads—a president, Congress. To find the power, it is necessary to enter into the maze itself. Inside it are bureaus of faceless men that keep the tax records, intelligence reports, and personnel dossiers." He paused to allow the students to catch up with him in their note taking.

A hand shot up in the front row. Jasmine instantly recognized it as belonging to Brixton Steer. Even down to the bow tie, young Brixton looked like an exact replica of his elegant father, Ambassador Steer. Since Brixton was also his tutee, Jasmine knew how conscientious he could be. "A question, Mr. Steer?"

"If I understand you correctly, Professor," Steer began overdeferentially, "you suggested that elected officials are merely fronts for hidden power elites."

"Yes, in this particular model of the modern bureaucratic state," Jasmine qualified.

"Then I don't quite understand why coup d'etats often aim at overthrowing these figureheads?" Steer sat down, knowing his question would be answered.

"Good point, Mr. Steer," Jasmine said, nodding as if he were taking in its fullest implications. He welcomed questions because they broke the tedium of the lecture, and allowed him to refocus the students' attention. "I did not mean to minimize the important function of elected leaders. Even though they do not exercise real power in this model, they still symbolize it in the public's imagination. The first objective of the coup d'etat is to capture the real nerve centers of government. This may be a military communica-

31

tions center, a counterintelligence agency, the censorship authority, or whatever. Once the coup controls the inner machinery that collects and disburses information, it controls the government. If the coup-makers want to publicly identify this change in power, this requires some sort of symbolic coup d'etat—which is what we read about in the newspapers. It involves overthrowing and possibly arresting the elected leaders. Such a symbolic coup should not be confused with the real coup which preceded it."

Jasmine could see that he was losing the interest of the class. The signs were unmistakable: papers could be heard rustling, eyes began wandering around the amphitheater, and shoes scraped together. He could almost feel the students becoming fidgety. He had been too analytical in describing the coup d'etat, he thought. What students at Harvard demanded was not disembodied concepts but interesting anecdotes—especially anecdotes they could repeat in their houses and clubs—or inside information they could use later to impress their friends.

"Consider, for example, what really happened in Venezuela in 1948." As he began his anecdote, he could see students perking up their ears. It reminded him of police dogs responding to a subsonic whistle. "I happened to be in Caracas that year doing research on my thesis. The real coup occurred in October, when the counterelite seized control of such power centers as the liaison with the U.S. Military Mission in Caracas, which then operated all the military airports in Venezuela; the Central Telephone-Telegraph Exchange, which controlled communications between the capital and the provinces; the antisubversive unit of the National Gendarmerie, which held dossiers on key politicians; and the State Security Agency in the Ministry of Interior, which could neutralize any progovernment military unit by issuing fake marching orders. After they had gained the real power, the coup-makers in turn waited until November fifteenth, 1948, before overthrowing the President and closing down Parliament."

He hesitated for a brief moment, seeing Arabella out of the corner of his eye entering the lecture on her tiptoes. As usual, she was late. He wondered if she were coming to the tutorial scheduled for later that afternoon.

When she reached the third row, a young man in a charcoal suit leaped up and, in a sweeping gesture, offered her his seat. Easing one leg over the other, she dangled her long calf so that her toe just touched the floor. Then she looked up—directly at Jasmine.

Her luminous eyes reminded him of grapes he had once admired in a still life by Rubens. He touched his hand to the back of his neck. It was damp—the first sign of anxiety. "The coup may thus provide us with the only glimpse we will ever get of the actual power structure," he said, attempting to jump back from his Venezuelan anecdote to the main subject of his lecture.

Arabella watched him with fascination. He reminded her of a man on a tightrope, who smiled to impress the audience with his utter confidence while betraying his fear with short, tentative steps. At times, she held her breath, sure that he would fall flat on his face with some point he was making, but he always managed, somehow, to get out of his logical tangles. At Oxford, where Arabella had studied Philosophy for three years, she had never seen a professor quite like Jasmine. Initially, she thought that he was pushing his ideas about "hidden power structures" further than they would go for the sake of being dramatic, but as she listened to lecture after lecture, she realized that he was actually on to something deeply important—a notion that politics went beyond explicitly stated arrangements. To get at that, he had to hack away at a forest of misconceptions—and sometimes, in his enthusiasm to clear away the underbrush, he swung out wildly at some bit of conventional wisdom, and sounded ridiculous to her. At other times, his convoluted logic made her head spin, and feel like she had drunk too much champagne. But even when she couldn't follow his argument, she could appreciate his enthusiasm for his subject. Now, as he wound up his lecture, she felt totally magnetized by him.

He concluded just as the chimes began ringing. They signaled the end of the academic hour. Turning to the blackboard, Jasmine began erasing the maze of symbols. He always tried to avoid watching the students as they filed out. Experience had taught him that even the briefest eye contact might cause students to linger and ask half-articulated questions about the nature of politics. He knew by the time the last chime struck the lecture hall would empty out. Like everyone else, students were creatures of habit.

Jasmine whistled a tune he couldn't quite remember as he walked across the Yard. It was only November, but the New England frost had already defoliated most of the trees on the campus. He tried to protect himself against the cold wind by hunching his shoulders, though he knew it was an illogical gesture. It looked like a very dreary winter.

His office was on the third floor of Littauer Center. It wasn't very large, but he had taken pride in furnishing it with the few possessions he prized. His mother had given him the Armenian dragon carpet on the floor—a lover, whose name he chose to forget, had sent it to her in lieu of himself. He had bought the Spanish colonial desk in Venezuela. Other than a few unpleasant memories, it was all he had to show for his four years of service there in the Coordinator of Information Office. The leather Chesterfield sofa he had bought at an auction in downtown Boston. It was just long enough—seventy-six inches—for him to stretch out on in between tutorials. Over the desk was his latest acquisition—a Belle Epoch etching by Beardsley. He had seen it in a bookstore only three weeks before and splurged all his savings on it.

The rest of the furnishings, including a drab filing cabinet, a swivel chair, and adjustable bookshelves, had been supplied him by the Government Department. The shelves were conspicuously empty of books. As far as he was concerned, few books had been written on politics that deserved to be there.

Before doing anything else, he carefully studied the chessboard on his desk. He had been playing this game for nearly two years by correspondence with an opponent he had never met. Yes, he thought, looking at a postcard he had received that morning, he's attempting to lure me over to the Queen side. He tested his move by shifting a pawn one space, then scribbled his move on a postcard.

A knock on the door interrupted him. Through the translucent glass, Jasmine could see a woman's silhouette. "Come in, please," he called, as he lifted the chessboard out of sight.

"Sorry to break in on you like this," Arabella said, standing in the open doorway. "I was hoping that we could rearrange my tutorial."

"Isn't it scheduled for this afternoon at four P.M.?"

"Yes, but my sister is arriving from England then, and I have to go to the airport ..." She was quite content to let her sentences dangle in midair. Men usually rushed in to complete them favorably for her.

"Do you want to shift it to now?"

"That would be perfect for me." She quickly made her way toward the Chesterfield, leaving the door slightly ajar.

Jasmine leafed through the report on his desk on "Praetorian Politics." He had just prepared it for a colloquium he was going to in New York.

Arabella folded her legs under her skirt and poised her head, sphinxlike, on a bridge she made for it by clasping her hands together. The sun, streaming in the window behind her, revealed the outlines of her lithe body through a loose gauze dress.

He again felt beads of perspiration forming on the back of his neck. He wondered why. He had known Arabella only since September, when she had transferred from Oxford to Harvard. Although she was only nineteen, she applied the rigor of a trained logician to everything said in her presence. A *belle dame sans merci*, he thought, after his first tutorial with her. He wondered whether it was her beauty or lack of mercy that now aroused his anxiety. He could see that Arabella relished challenging whatever points he made. And now he had assigned her a draft of his first book. "Have you had a chance to read the chapter on the labyrinth, Arabella?"

A nod of her head made it clear that she had indeed read it.

"Do you understand why I argue that possessing a blueprint to the labyrinth of government is in itself tantamount to power?"

"The terms of your argument are clear enough. The power to control a government resides in the agencies that control intragovernment communications. If a potential usurper can identify and locate these agencies, his chances of success are increased."

"That's an excellent summary of the thesis." He liked the terse way she stated things, like precise hammerblows on a nailhead.

"It's your basic assumption I question." As she spoke, her eyes remained fixed on him.

"Yes?" He swiveled uncomfortably in his chair, opening himself to her attack.

"You assume that power will be concentrated in a few key centers, but what if it is widely distributed throughout a government?"

"Even if power is dispersed, communications will inevitably be focused in a few command centers."

"Why inevitably?" She spoke without hand gestures. Her body held its positions as tenaciously as her mind.

"Because that is the model that I've chosen to describe: a nation in which communications—especially secret communications—are transmitted through closely held channels." He strode over to point out the relevant section on "Selection of models" in the manuscript she was holding.

"Then it's a tautology," she said, defiantly looking up at him as he bent over the manuscript.

"In social science, we describe empirical situations—"

"The jargon confuses me. . . ." As she slowly shook her head, her long brown hair brushed against his hand.

"It's not jargon! Listen for once!" he shouted at her.

Looking down, she shook her head again, as if she could not comprehend what he was saying. Suddenly, she found him gripping her by both shoulders.

"I'm sorry. I didn't mean to—" He stopped short, not knowing what to say. He had never touched a student before. What had come over him, he wondered.

Arabella moved quickly toward the open door. Jasmine shuddered as he thought of the *Crimson* headline that could result—HARVARD PROFESSOR MOLESTS COED. If she did no more than whisper a complaint to the Dean of Women, it would still probably be the end of his teaching career.

37

Even after the door banged shut, it took him a moment to realize that Arabella was still in the room. Only then did he understand that she had construed his touching her in a totally different way from that he had initially imagined.

"I still say it's a tautology," she whispered softly. Without waiting for a reply, she cupped his face in her hands and pressed her lips against his.

As he felt her body against him, he reckoned that the potential consequences of continuing the embrace probably outweighed the pleasure he might derive from it. She was his student, and Harvard had two months earlier summarily dismissed an Assistant Professor of History for just such an indiscretion. Yet, he knew that it was no use pretending that he could be a rational calculator in this situation. He could feel his excitement growing. He wanted Arabella more than anything else. He had felt a desire for her build inside him each time she challenged him in tutorial. Up until now, it had been merely a secret fantasy that he had managed to repress.

Quickly, Jasmine unbuttoned her dress, and, with a firm tug, pulled it over her head. Raising her hands in mock surrender, she allowed him to finish undressing her. Her skin was smooth and ghostly pale.

Suddenly he heard footsteps shuffling down the corridor. "You can't believe what's happening in Washington," a distant voice was saying. Jasmine recognized it as the voice of Professor Edward Wiley, the antitrust expert, who taught at the law school. "Are you telling me that they are going to drop the cartel case, Wiley?" said Professor W. L. Lock, Chairman of the Government Department. Lock's office was next to Jasmine's.

Jasmine froze as he listened to Wiley and Lock chatting in the hall about some obscure case. They paused for a moment, and then continued into Lock's office.

"They are now claiming that national security considerations in the Middle East transcend the criminal code of justice," Wiley continued in an agitated voice.

"Bosh, it's oil, that's all," Lock replied.

With an effortless motion, Arabella opened Jasmine's zipper. He could no longer concentrate on what was being said in the adjoining office. All he could think about were Arabella's hands. He tried to control his excitement.

Arabella, breathing hard, gave a soft moan of pleasure when he touched her breast. He quickly put his other hand over her mouth to muffle the sound. Professors Wiley and Lock were barely fifteen feet away. They would have to make love in complete silence.

The enforced secrecy only intensified Jasmine's excitement. He had always accepted stealth as a necessary part of life. Even as a child, he had lived in a world of shadows. His mother, Julie James, had refused to tell him even his father's proper name. All he had ever learned of him was that he was some sort of international tycoon, who sent checks regularly. Most of Jasmine's youth was spent traveling through Europe with his mother. She usually identified him as a nephew or cousin. He played along with this deception, changing his identity and cover story to fit hers. Only after she died in a car crash did he begin to establish his own identity—first as a political scientist at UCLA, then as a propagandist in Venezuela. Now, at thirty-three, he was an assistant professor at Harvard, risking everything by seducing a nineteen-year-old student.

As their dreamy ballet continued on the couch, Jasmine could hear Professor Wiley in the next office explaining: ". . . seven companies. They control everything—ships, pipelines, refineries, even the British government. The risks would be enormous in prosecuting that case . . . just enormous . . ."

39

"Enormous," Arabella whispered, echoing the conversation next door.

He silenced her with a kiss this time.

"Of course, you'll have to keep all this secret, Lock. It's all still very hush-hush," Wiley was telling his colleague as they walked out into the corridor, their footsteps slowly trailing away.

"So it's all very hush-hush, is it," Arabella said, jumping up to put on her dress with a burst of energy.

"Arabella, I'm sorry," Jasmine found himself apologizing. He wondered how he could possibly continue being her tutor.

"For what? I thought it was our best tutorial." She gathered up her underwear as she spoke and stuffed it into her bookbag. "Where did you get the name Jasmine?"

"It was my father's favorite flower—*jasmine numandia.* That's all I ever knew about him."

Arabella looked baffled, then smiled and darted out the door. Seconds later, she reappeared to say, "I'm looking forward to our tutorial on Friday."

The door slammed before he could tell her that he had to be in New York on Friday for the colloquium on Praetorian Politics.

CHAPTER III

THE RED LINE

"Did you come all the way to Lisbon just to tell me about Iran?" Calouste Gulbenkian asked. He squinted at his son with one eye, as if he were having trouble recognizing him.

Nubar tried, but couldn't look his father squarely in the eye. He never could. Something about the way his father's thin skin was stretched over his skull reminded him of a death mask he had seen once in a museum. His father was over eighty, and dying, but he still made Nubar feel like a child. Nubar let his eye wander around Suite 42 of the Hotel Aviz. There was a Louis Quatorze settee, two uncomfortable chairs covered in green silk, a small Chinois table in the sitting room, and little else.

"I thought it was important," Nubar said wearily.

"For this, you wasted an air ticket?"

41

"I didn't waste an air ticket, I used one ..." Nubar stopped in midsentence. He felt a shiver deep inside his stomach. His father always made him feel like a wastrel. Could his father—probably the richest man in the world— really care about a one-hundred-pound air ticket? "I'm not sure I made it clear, Father. Raven wants us to use our contacts in Iran against Mossadeq. It could be dangerous to get involved in politics." All his life, Nubar had tried to avoid unnecessary entanglements. His family had more money than it could ever use. He himself had all the amenities he wanted. He could see no point in aiding this plot of Raven's. If it backfired, it could lead to very unpleasant vendettas.

"How many times have I told you, Nubar, oil is politics? It is the nature of our business to get involved—but on our terms." Calouste shook his head as though his son were a poor student.

"But need we cooperate in a coup d'etat? We have important friends in Iran...." He saw the futility of arguing with his father.

"Why should we cooperate?" Calouste repeated after him, looking out the window as if waiting for something. Outside, a tram clanged its bell on the Avenida de Libertas. "Do you remember what happened at Baba Gurgur?"

"Of course. It was our first oil strike in Iraq."

"October fourth, 1927. It sounded just like an approaching locomotive from deep underneath the desert. Then the oil blew the derrick a hundred feet in the air, like a cork on a champagne bottle. And it kept rising until it looked like a giant black cyprus tree in the middle of the desert. Once we got it under control, that single well produced more than a ton of oil a minute. Enough oil to supply one-quarter of Europe. Do you think that was a great event for us?"

"I know what happened, Father." He had heard his

father tell the story a hundred times before—and knew that Calouste had never seen an oil well in his life.

"It was a disaster for us! All that oil! If we could find such a well in the Middle East, so could our competitors. The price of oil would collapse. We would all be ruined. There was only one thing to do when Baba Gurgur came in—cooperate."

"That was twenty-five years ago . . ." Nubar interrupted. Seeing a spark of enthusiasm in his father's eyes, he let the old man continue. Nubar knew what was coming. His father's moment of glory—the Red Line Agreement.

"Yes. I sat all the oil powers down around a table—Teagle of Standard, Deterding of Shell, Cadman of Anglo-Iranian. They watched, and I drew a red line around part of the Middle East. I suggested that within the area enclosed by the Red Line—Arabia, Syria, and Palestine—none of us would explore for oil on our own. No competition. They signed an agreement, of course. They understood what could be gained by cooperating."

"But they broke the agreement, Father. The Americans crossed the Red Line into Saudi Arabia."

"Ah, no deal lasts forever. Not even Anglo-Iranian Oil's deal in Iran. And when they recognize that it is gone—who will be in a position to take over? Certainly not the Iranians."

Nubar gradually began to see what his father was driving at. The Gulbenkians might have a role in Iran, after all. "Then you think we should encourage Raven's idea of a coup d'etat?"

"Up to a point. Oil friendships are slippery. But we must be in a position to know what our friends are planning to do in Iran." He suddenly turned his head toward the door.

A young girl, no more than fifteen, stepped into the room. "Oh. Hello, I'm Nicole."

43

Gulbenkian clicked his heels together, and bowed slightly with his head, in mock salute. He had never seen Nicole in person before, but he recognized her instantly. He had picked her photograph out of an album, shown to him by a Madame Claude's in Paris. It was a service he had performed for his father for almost thirty years now—the only field in which his father fully acknowledged his judgment. He looked at Calouste's bald head, and smiled to himself. His father would have given anything for a remedy to stop his hair from falling out. He had been obsessed with it for half a century. When all of the hair specialists imported from the four corners of the earth—even a Korean shaman—had failed to arrest his receding hairline, he resorted to a more traditional oriental remedy—young girls. As he became progressively balder, he insisted on progressively younger girls. Nicole had been thirteen when Nubar found her.

"It's time for my massage, Nicole," Calouste Gulbenkian said, propping himself up by pushing down with both hands on his cane. "We'll talk more about Raven at dinner, Nubar." With Nicole's thin arm for added support, he walked down the corridor to the bedroom.

Nubar watched the bedroom door close. He could hear the bed arch, and Nicole's laugh. He wondered what kind of a massage this waif of a girl gave his eighty-four-year-old father. Just then, Korkik brought him a cup of coffee, interrupting his thoughts.

Korkik had been his father's coffee waiter for as long as Nubar could remember. In Istanbul, Korkik was so punctual in bringing coffee every twenty minutes that his father used to brag he had no need of a watch. When they fled the Turkish massacres in 1900 on Nubar's grandfather's yacht, Calouste took Korkik along, first to Egypt, then to London, then Paris, now Lisbon.

On the yacht, it had been Korkik who first saw Mantachoff, standing on a burning pier, waving to them. Calouste Gulbenkian instantly recognized the seven-foot-tall Armenian. He had met him years earlier in Baku, where Mantachoff owned the biggest oil field in Russia. Mantachoff was then so rich that he gave away Circassian women as door prizes at his weekly bacchanals. Calouste not only waved him aboard, but gave him his wife's cabin as well. He realized even then that Mantachoff's oil could be extremely valuable to those who were trying to break Rockefeller's stranglehold on the European kerosene markets. By the time their ship reached Egypt, he had become Mantachoff's private secretary and general factotum.

Once in Egypt, Calouste Gulbenkian wasted no time in getting in touch with Nubar Pasha, the relative after whom his son was named. Nubar Pasha represented the Rothschild banking family in Egypt. The rest was easy. If a man like Calouste Gulbenkian had not existed, the Rothschilds would have had to invent him. They needed an agent who knew how to deal with the machinations of the Ottoman Turks, who at that time controlled almost all of the Middle East. As an Armenian, Gulbenkian understood baksheesh—bribery—in a way no Westerner could.

He knew the precise position of every court official in the price chain, from the bottom to the top of the hierarchy, and paid informants to apprise him of the exact state of mind of each key official in the Sultan's court. He would find out when someone had had a satisfactory time with a woman, or when, through some business reverse, someone was more amenable to accepting a bribe. He would even secretly consult the court astrologer, who, for a price, would supply him with the charts he had drawn up for each official, so that Calouste could offer them a bribe on the very day that they were expecting good fortune. When the right moment finally came, he would present the offer in a way that would not involve a loss of face for the official. For this purpose, he gave them Korans encrusted with diamonds and emeralds—since they could gracefully accept the word of Allah. By the time the Sultan was driven from power in World War I, Nubar's father had put together the Iraq Petroleum Company from the Turkish concessions, and retained for himself five percent of all the revenues the concessions produced.

Now, there was silence in the bedroom. Nubar got up and began pacing back and forth the length of the hotel room; he was beginning to feel like a caged animal. How could his father, with all his immense wealth, live in such a small, nondescript hotel suite, Nubar wondered. But Calouste had always preferred hotels. He gave his house on Rue de Grenelle in Paris to Henri Berenger, the Finance Minister of France, for services rendered in arranging for the Gulbenkians to share the Mosul oil fields, and then moved into the Ritz. He built several other houses, but never lived in them. It was as if he were waiting to return to his ancestral home in Armenia.

Korkik brought Nubar nine more cups of coffee during the more than three hours that he waited. Then he saw his father hobble slowly toward him, using his cane as if it were a third leg. He was relieved to see that Nicole was not with him.

"I'm still on my mineral-water diet," his father said, sitting at a small table in the corner of the room, "but you order whatever you like."

"I have to catch a plane back to London tonight. I'm having dinner there. Sorry ..." Nubar's relations with his father had always been difficult. Here he was, a fifty-six-year-old millionaire, who would soon inherit a share equal to five percent of all the oil in Iraq, and his father still treated him as though he were a young clerk, just learning the business. Each time his father scowled at him, he could feel his insides tremble. No, he wouldn't stay for dinner.

"We should talk about Raven," his father began very slowly. His hand trembled as he filled a glass with mineral water. It was all he would consume when he was on his regimen. "He is a man, I think, who deserves your respect—and fear."

"Presumably Raven works for us on the Coordinating Committee," Nubar said aloud. But, he thought to himself, Raven is more than a mere technician. He had, after all, managed to maneuver his way practically to the top of Royal Dutch Shell in five short years. And then he had gotten himself selected to head the committee. He was a master at either manipulating or destroying all who stood in his way. And the Gulbenkians, with their five percent interest, might soon find themselves a target of the cartel, rather than a partner. As usual, his father was right. Raven, as much as Nubar admired him, was a threat.

"Have you found his weakness yet, Nubar?" It was a question Calouste always asked.

"Perhaps." He smiled, thinking that Raven shared the same weakness as his father: young women. It struck him as odd, in both cases, that men so powerful and clever should consider women the only meaningful test of themselves. On the grouse shoot, he had seen that Raven was willing to devote himself to the task of winning Chris Winchester. Knowing Chris, he suspected that Raven's driving lust would only succeed in frightening her away. A perfect mismatch, he thought. He considered telling his father how he had arranged it, but decided it would only increase the old man's suspicions of him.

"Then you must exploit it—but slowly and carefully. Raven mustn't guess he is being cultivated."

"Cultivated?" Nubar asked with a puzzled look. Did his

father think that a man like Raven could be cultivated—like an orchid, where all the conditions are perfectly controlled to produce the exact coloring and texture desired?

"We are rich, Nubar—but only so long as we hold on to our five percent interest. And there are armies of lawyers and intriguers ready to take it away from us. Our only defense is—foreknowledge. Use your connections to find out exactly what Raven is planning."

"Raven wants me to arrange for him to meet the Shah."

"I see. But the Shah is nothing more than a figurehead in Iran—no power at all."

"Perhaps Raven is planning on changing that . . ."

"Interesting." Calouste poured himself another glass of mineral water, and frowned as he swallowed. "Why not put him in contact with your friend Darius?"

"Darius?" Nubar had known Darius Ali since Cambridge, and still gambled with him at least once a year at Monte Carlo. Darius came from one of the twenty families that owned the only arable land in Iran. He had been the Teheran representative of Anglo-Iranian Oil until Mossadeq nationalized it. Now, he spent most of his time playing tennis and skiing with the Shah.

"Yes. . . . He has done us favors in the past . . . and he has gambling debts." Calouste always noted a man's vulnerable points. "He'll be the perfect go-between."

Gulbenkian excused himself, and, backing away, kissed his father's hand as he had when he was a boy. At fifty-six, he still feared it.

CHAPTER IV

JOIN THE CLUB

"Dr. Jasmine, Professor Tracy is waiting for you in the library. Please follow me." The white-haired porter whispered just loud enough for Jasmine to hear him. The Brook was a club that prided itself on its exclusive quiet. Its heavy stone walls and shrouded windows were meant to keep out all the street noise of midtown Manhattan.

Jasmine walked a few paces behind the porter up a carpeted staircase, then down a mahogany-paneled corridor. On the walls were oil portraits of the Vanderbilts, Morgans, Wideners, Roosevelts, and other founding members of the Brook. Jasmine felt slightly intimidated by the gauntlet of domineering faces. The library, with its floor-to-ceiling rows of dusty books, was a welcome relief.

Bronson Tracy was standing on a small fenced-in plat-

49

form on top of a ladder, absorbed in his search for a missing volume. He turned around abruptly as he sensed a visitor, and gestured with a hand motion that he would be right down.

Jasmine noticed that even the rungs of the library ladder were padded with carpeting as Tracy climbed down it with long strides. From his craggy face, he guessed that Tracy was in his midforties. Though he was quite tall, Tracy did not seem conscious of his height.

"Sorry to drag you here, Jake," Tracy said in a cultivated accent that distinguished him as a Boston brahmin. "Just wanted to finish some work before dinner, and with the traffic, I didn't know what time you'd get here."

"It's quite an impressive library." Jasmine found himself whispering, though there was no one else in the room. "Do you spend much time here?"

"The Brook is my working habitat in New York. So quiet you can hear a pin drop. You should think of joining, Jake."

"I don't get to New York that often," Jasmine demurred. He was not a joiner, and anyway he doubted that he would be accepted. He had only met Tracy a month before, at the colloquium on "Political Succession in the Age of Bureaucracy" at Pierson College at Yale. Tracy was the only political scientist there that seemed to understand the distinction he tried to make between the traditional army putsch and the modern coup d'etat. Jasmine was quite surprised by his quick grasp of a problem that he himself had been laboring over for months. Despite his trendy appearance and impeccable credentials as a traditional political scientist, Tracy seemed to appreciate his ideas on the mechanics of power better than most of the postwar generation political scientists. He must have impressed Tracy as well, since Tracy had invited him to attend his present seminar on "Praetorian Politics in the Nuclear Age," which was being sponsored by the Council on Foreign Relations.

"Understand you spent some time in Venezuela working for Rockefeller," Tracy murmured as he lit his pipe.

"In a manner of speaking. I was sent to Venezuela at the beginning of the war to do political analysis for the Office of Information. Rockefeller was Coordinator of Information, but I didn't have much time to see him ..."

"Spent the whole war there?" Tracy was obviously adept at eliciting information.

"From 1942 through 1947."

"My understanding is that Rockefeller was doing a bit of psych warfare—or whatever they call it."

"He called it that. All I was involved in was writing news releases that we fed to the wire services."

"Aren't you being a bit modest, Jake? I understand you received a personal commendation from Rockefeller?"

"Well, the stories were, of course, designed to provoke a reaction against the Nazis in South America ..." Jasmine hesitated, wondering how Tracy knew so much about his wartime service record. He and his small staff in Caracas had actually written or edited more than 90 percent of the "hard" news in South America, and had carefully designed it to manipulate the actions of every country on that continent. The ease with which this sort of "disinformation" could be put onto the news wires, unchecked and uncon- firmed, had given him many of his ideas on the vulnerability of government to well-organized conspiracies.

"Yes, of course," Tracy said, cutting short his inquiry. "Let's have something to eat."

The oval dining room, like the club itself, was small and intimate. Rather than individual tables, there was a common table. Tracy quietly introduced Jasmine to the other members at the table. Their names all sounded like endowed buildings at Harvard.

A waiter wheeled over a cart with a side of roast beef on it. Tracy nodded, and the waiter cut off an end piece for him. "Do you like your beef rare, or well done, Jake?" Tracy asked.

Jasmine pointed to the rare side of the beef. The waiter smiled indulgently, as though Jasmine had made an extraordinary request, and cut him a blood-red piece. He garnished it with a small baked potato. Decanters of red wine were already on the table. Jasmine noticed that although the members of the Brook sat around the same table, they made a point of not talking to, or even looking at, each other. They might as well be seated at separate tables, he thought.

"I've been involved in something that I thought might be of interest to you, Jake," Tracy began.

"At Yale?" Jasmine asked. He had heard that Tracy was being considered as the next master of Pierson College there.

"No, in Washington. I've taken a temporary leave from Yale to work out a problem for the State Department."

"What kind of problem?"

"The State Department is concerned that its diplomats are not prepared for the sort of crisis that might occur these days. We're attempting to design a few simulated crises. It's a sort of board game for diplomats."

"Board game?" Jasmine had always been intrigued by games. The idea of the State Department using them to simulate the real world piqued his interest.

"Well, it's not exactly like Monopoly," Tracy explained, slowly pouring a glass of wine for Jasmine. "It's called the Game of Nations. The diplomats who play the game are each assigned some special role—they might be a king, intelligence chief, or what-have-you—and they have to respond to a hypothetical crisis that we design for them. It's all adjudicated by a UNIVAC computer."

"Sounds almost useful ..." Jasmine began, when Tracy interrupted: "Does your teaching contract at Harvard allow you to consult?"

"Yes—as long as it's only part-time."

"You might try your hand at designing a scenario for us."

"What kind of crisis would you want?" Jasmine smiled.

Tracy nodded good-bye to one of the men who was sitting across the table from him. Then he turned back to Jasmine. "You teach a course on coup d'etats, don't you?"

"It's really on political pathology, but it includes analyzing coups." Jasmine looked around. The dining room was empty, except for himself and Tracy.

"What about designing a coup? I would, of course, give you the basic parameters. You could work it out in, say, thirty-six moves? The game is based on thirty-six moves."

"Are you serious?" Jasmine asked, then decided from the look on Tracy's face that he was, in fact, making a deadly serious offer.

"Of course." Tracy looked at his watch with some concern. "I had no idea of the time. I hope you don't mind if I rush off." It occurred to Jasmine that Tracy had avoided saying where he was going.

After leaving the Brook, Jasmine walked from Fifty-fourth Street up Madison Avenue to Eighty-sixth, peering into the galleries along the way. He looked at paintings, sculptures, furnishings, carpets, and advertisements, as well as at other window shoppers. It was all part of the same visual feast for him.

He stayed that night at the Croyden Hotel. In the morning he had to wait fifteen minutes for the receipt for his breakfast, which he needed in order to get reimbursed by the Council on Foreign Relations. Then he rushed to LaGuardia Airport.

During the bumpy flight back to Cambridge, Jasmine thought about his odd conversation with Bronson Tracy. Designing scenarios for some State Department game sounded like a fairly juvenile idea. But Tracy had offered him a consulting fee of one hundred dollars a day and travel expenses to Washington. This would help him finance the additional research he needed for his book. Organizing these hypothetical scenarios, no matter how nonsensical, would also give him a chance to work out some of the theories he had been developing on coup d'etats. The most important consideration was, however, Tracy. Jasmine knew that Tracy was well connected at Yale, and could be very helpful in finding him another job if Harvard failed to promote him. Yes, he would do it, he decided, as the wheels touched down on the runway at Logan Airport.

When he got back to his office, he found two notes slipped under his door. The first was from Brixton Steer: "Dear Professor Jasmine, Would it be possible to write a paper for you in lieu of taking the Midterm exam on December 16? To be perfectly frank, I haven't seen my father for nearly a year, and was hoping to go to Teheran for Xmas (which would mean leaving Cambridge December 15). If this would be permissible, I would like to write a paper on the 'Politics of Usurpation in the Middle East,' and do research on it over the Xmas recess. Yours truly . . ."

Jasmine smiled to himself. Steer knew how to get a little leverage out of being the Ambassador to Iran's son. "Excused from exam. Look forward to reading your paper—J.J." Jasmine scribbled on the bottom of the note.

The second note was from Arabella. "Sorry *you* missed our tutorial. In case you want to give me a make-up assignment,

I'm willing to do whatever you suggest (Pathological Politics, indeed). I'm staying with my sister while she's in America. She's borrowed a house (once you meet her, you'll understand how). The address is 11 Sparks Street. Phone JK-5-4569. Love, Arabella."

Jasmine followed each twist and turn in Arabella's uninhibited scrawl, trying to figure out exactly what she meant to say. It was clearly very suggestive—but of what? Did she merely want to continue playing around during tutorials? Or was she suggesting a more involved affair? It made very little sense for him to continue seeing her on any basis, he decided. Of course, he was attracted—even her note aroused him—but at this point in his career he couldn't risk getting thrown out of Harvard. He would explain it all to her in their next tutorial. With a shrug, he crumpled up the note and threw it in the trash can.

CHAPTER V

APPOINTMENT IN MILAN

Raven looked at his watch with some impatience. Nearly twenty minutes had passed since Enrico Mattei had excused himself from the meeting for *"uno momento."* What did this haughty Italian think would be accomplished by keeping him waiting? Raven wondered.

As always, Raven had made a careful study of his quarry. He had found that Mattei's success in building ENI, the Italian National Oil Company, into a force to be reckoned with proceeded from a combination of bluff and ambition—nothing more. Mattei began in 1947. At that time, he was a thirty-nine-year-old bureaucrat with a few good connections in the Christian Democratic Party. Suave and good looking, he had gotten himself appointed head of ENI, then a small, government-owned gas company in the Po Valley. Then

Mattei used his bluff to convince journalists that ENI was sitting on top of enormous gas reserves, and to cow other bureaucrats into lending ENI state funds to develop these putative resources. With the government funds, he constructed refineries, chemical plants, fertilizer companies, pipelines, gas stations—even hotels. The only problem was that ENI had, in fact, no energy to run this growing complex. As ENI became more and more financially overextended, Mattei upped the bluff. He demanded that the Italian government grant ENI the funds to seek its energy abroad. The politicians had little choice. They couldn't let Mattei's little empire collapse into bankruptcy, so they allowed him to raise the money with government-backed bonds. Still ENI found no oil—only a hundred dry holes.

The moment Mattei saw that the cartel was in trouble with Mossadeq in Iran, he flew to Teheran. Being supremely ambitious, he saw the problem as his golden opportunity. He told Mossadeq that ENI would take all the oil that was formerly purchased by the cartel, refine it in Sicily, and then sell it throughout Europe.

All this had been duly reported to Raven by Anglo-Iranian agents in Teheran. Now, in Milan, Raven was trying to reason with Mattei. First, he pointed out that ENI did not own any ocean-going tankers. "How would you ship a million barrels of Iranian oil a year?" Raven asked.

"We'll charter the ships we need—and if we can't charter enough tankers, we'll build them," Mattei answered.

Next, Raven had argued that the oil in Iran legally belonged to the Anglo-Iranian Oil Company, not Iran, and Mattei would be buying stolen property if he bought the oil that Mossadeq had illegally nationalized.

"Will you sue Italy?" Mattei had scoffed, blushing as he tended to do when he felt prodded or pressed.

At that point in the meeting, a buzzer sounded and

Mattei, with a surprised look on his round face, picked up the red phone on his desk, listened a moment, and then rushed out of the office.

Raven had a fairly good idea what the call was about. Earlier that morning he had sent out telegrams to the seven companies participating in the cartel—Standard Oil, Mobil, Shell, Gulf, Texaco, Anglo-Iranian, and Socal. Under no circumstances were any of these companies, or their subsidiaries, to deliver oil to Italy, until they received clearance from Raven's Coordinating Committee in London. Tankers headed for Italian ports were to turn around immediately and maintain radio silence. Likewise, pipelines in Germany, Austria, and Yugoslavia were to cut off both oil and gas to Italy under the pretext of urgent repairs.

Mattei returned to the room looking grim. His black hair was slightly ruffled. "Sorry to keep you waiting, Sir Anthony . . . but there has been an unfortunate avalanche in the Austrian Alps."

"No one hurt, I hope." Raven smiled politely.

"No, but it buried a pumping station and seems to have shut down the pipeline."

"Bad luck."

"Yes. There also seems to be a storm in the eastern Mediterranean . . ."

"Which could interfere with shipping, if it doesn't blow over," Raven said, sitting back. "Not much you can do about *force majeur*, Dottori Mattei. Unfortunately, you can't sue nature."

Mattei's eyes narrowed, focusing on Raven. He was beginning to realize that the "avalanche" and the "storm" might be manmade. "I hope that the oil companies are not foolish enough to try and blackmail Italy . . ."

"You shouldn't read too much into a storm at sea. Of course, it might continue for a week or so. Then the chemical plants would run out of feed stock and have to shut down. There would be no fertilizer for the crops. No fuel. Everyone would begin asking what happened to ENI's vast store of gas oil . . ." Raven's head remained immobile as he sketched out what would happen to Italy—and Mattei—if oil shipments were not resumed immediately.

"Are you threatening me, Sir Anthony?"

"No need to threaten. No man in your position would risk seeing the entire Italian economy grind to a halt because of a lack of oil." Raven stood up and turned to leave the room. His point was now made and he saw no reason to continue the conversation. He had a luncheon appointment with Emilio Furiosa at the Galleria at one o'clock. Furiosa was a power in Milan's Christian Democratic Party—and also a man who had been secretly financed by the oil cartel for a decade. Raven knew that after lunch Furiosa would call Mattei. He would also arrange for Montacattini Chemical and Fiat to begin pressuring ENI for gas deliveries. Raven knew that Mattei was not a man who could stand up under such pressures. His power rested solely on his reputation as a producer of energy supplies. If this buckled, Mattei was through as a political force in Italy—and Mattei understood his public relations even better than he did his economics. Mattei, Raven knew, could not afford to have his bluff called over Iran.

At 5 P.M. that afternoon, Mattei called a brief press conference in his offices at ENI. He announced that Premier Mossadeq of Iran and he had reached an "agreement in principle." Italy would buy Iranian oil.

A few reporters rushed toward the telephones that ENI had conveniently provided, but Mattei held up his hand to signal a halt, and went on to explain that Italy would not take delivery of any Iranian oil until after the International Court in the Hague had ruled on the legality of Iran's nationalization of foreign oil concessions, a decision that could take a year—or more.

It took a moment for the reporters to take in the implications of what Mattei was saying. He had, in effect, reversed himself. Italy would not be buying Iranian oil in the near future.

An hour later, the captain of the S.S. *Drake,* a sixty thousand-ton tanker anchored off the Tunisian coast, received a telegram from the Coordinating Committee in London. He was to weigh anchor immediately and head for Naples, where he was to deliver his cargo of oil. He had never understood why he had been ordered to anchor off Tunisia in the first place.

Chapter VI

THANKSGIVING

Jasmine drove slowly past the house at 11 Sparks Street. It was not quite one o'clock, and he didn't want to arrive early for Thanksgiving lunch. He was already beginning to regret that he had accepted the invitation. He had meant to break things off cleanly with Arabella in their last tutorial on Tuesday. But when she touched him, her hands betrayed her own nervousness and he found he couldn't talk. Instead, they had made love.

Turning on the car radio, he listened to the news as he drove around the block for the third or fourth time. In a Thanksgiving Day speech, John Foster Dulles, the newly designated Secretary of State, was issuing a stern warning: "In this war for the minds of men, every nation must choose between democracy and communism. Neutrality is no choice ..." Jasmine shook his head at the illogic of the speech, then switched off the radio. In politics, he distrusted moralists and zealots equally. Dulles represented both.

When he finally parked the car, it was ten minutes after the hour. Arabella flung open the door just as he was about to ring the bell. She wore a gravy-stained apron over her loose-fitting dress.

"Watch your head," she warned as she beckoned him in. "This house was meant for a man half your height."

Looking around, it seemed to him as if the house had indeed been designed for a midget. Everything about it, even the furniture, was diminutive, though in perfect scale.

As he followed Arabella up the twisting stairs, Jasmine noticed that all the walls had been stuccoed white and that the well-worn beams had been artfully restored. A mass of green ferns hung from the top of the stairwell, looking like some topsy-turvy tree. Through a brick arch, he could see three rattan chairs set around a small marble table. It seemed that there were only going to be three for luncheon.

"Jake, this is my sister Tina."

Tina smiled mischievously, as if she already knew Jasmine. She was a tall, thin girl, with cheeks that puffed out when she smiled, and long black hair that hung to her waist. She was wearing a pale blue sweater, tight jeans that didn't quite meet the sweater, and multicolored socks—but no shoes or belt.

"Nice meeting you, Tina. How long will you be in Cambridge?" Jasmine asked, unable to take his eyes off her. Arabella had told him a little about Tina, but had said nothing to prepare him for her stunning beauty.

"As long as it takes to organize this exhibition at the Fogg ..."

"Tina is now presumed to be Britain's leading authority on pre-Raphaelite art," Arabella cut in.

"So I understand," Jasmine said, slipping off his coat and tossing it over the stair railing. Arabella had already told him how Tina had achieved this status at the age of only twenty-two. Tina had had no training in art history. When she was fifteen, she had attended an exhibition of pre-Raphaelite paintings at the Tate in London. Shaking her head at a painting of a young girl attributed to Rossetti, Tina had insisted that it was a fake. She explained to a befuddled curator that the color hues in that painting were not consistent with those in the other paintings in the exhibition. He had laughed at her impudence, and told her that the painting had been authenticated by experts at Oxford, and that the Tate had recently paid fifty thousand pounds for the portrait. Three months later, however, the painting turned out to be a fraud. Then a story in the *Times* told how Tina had correctly identified it as such. From that point on, art collectors began consulting her about paintings they intended to purchase. Arabella, with an amazing ability to be objective about her sister, had explained to Jasmine that there were two prevailing theories about Tina's success. The first held that she had an ocular genius in art analogous to perfect pitch in the perception of music. The second held that she was a brilliant fraud who had parlayed a lucky guess into a lucrative business. From the way Arabella told the story, it was clear to Jasmine that she herself subscribed to the latter theory.

"Arabella exaggerates, of course. I'm still just learning about art." Tina's eyes flicked quickly from Jasmine to Arabella, then back again to Jasmine.

"I'm quite impressed with this house," Jasmine said to fill the awkward silence that followed Tina's statement.

"Tell him how you got it, Tina," Arabella said, enjoying the chance to put her sister on the spot.

"It's really an absurd story. The house is owned by a

rather eccentric Japanese art historian. He needed someone to look after his cat while he's in the Far East." She paused. Like her sister, she didn't bother completing obvious explanations.

"So you're cat sitting?"

"Except the bloody cat's run away," Arabella interjected.

"What happens if you don't find the cat?" Jasmine asked, still looking at Tina.

"I will just have to go to a pet store, order another Siamese of approximately the same dimensions and coloring, call it by the same name, and pray to God the landlord doesn't notice the difference." Tina's eyes glistened as she spoke.

Arabella laughed uproariously. The idea of substituting cats struck her as an immensely perverse joke. Taking Jasmine's hand, she tugged him toward the kitchen. "Let's eat. I'm famished."

The tiled kitchen wasn't much bigger than a large closet, yet it seemed to contain every conceivable device for cooking. Tina, who had followed them into the kitchen, knelt down to remove the capon from the oven. As she did so, her sweater pulled slightly, exposing her lower back. Jasmine couldn't help noticing the graceful symmetry of her muscles as she lifted the bird. She gave him a quick look over her left shoulder, as if she sensed that he was staring at her. The bird was quickly transferred to a serving platter, which Jasmine carried to the table. Arabella followed with a decanter of white wine.

The meal was much more tense than he had expected. He was seated between the two sisters, and whenever he would turn to listen to Tina, Arabella found some way of competing for his attention. Trying to find some neutral ground, he asked Tina, "How do you select which paintings will go into the exhibition?"

"I just pick those that mean the most to me in terms of their internal tonal integrity."

"Which means?" Arabella interrupted caustically, her right eyebrow raised.

"Nothing I can explain. It's like trying to define the morning light," Tina answered with some annoyance.

"Ah, we're back to your intuitive sense of color." Arabella made "intuitive" sound derisive by her tone of voice. As far as she was concerned, intuitive was the opposite of logical.

Tina just smiled at her younger sister, without attempting any further explanations.

"Where will you have to go to find these paintings?" Jasmine asked politely, trying to change the subject.

"I have to go to the Metropolitan in New York this week and see what is available ..." Tina paused, sensing Jasmine's interest in her travel plans. "I should be able to find whatever else we need at the Fine Arts Museum in Los Angeles—and of course the Mellon Collection in Washington."

He poured himself another glass of wine, trying to conceal the excitement he felt suddenly at the possibility of seeing Tina alone. He was still looking at her when he felt Arabella's foot under the table. He tried hard to ignore it as it traced a provocative line up his calf.

Tina could see that something was going on. She turned to her sister, who had an overly innocent smile on her lips; then back to Jasmine, who was sitting rigidly upright with his palms pressed tightly on the table surface.

"I think it's time I did my exercises," Tina said. She could see the dampness on the back of Jasmine's neck as she brushed past him.

When Tina disappeared through the arch, Jasmine started to get up out of the rattan chair, but felt Arabella's hands pressing him back. He gave up and sank back. Arabella stood over him like a genie he had inadvertently summoned out of her bottle. She placed a cool palm over his eyes, blocking out the rest of the room. For a moment, he feared that Tina might reappear in the room without his being able to see her. Then, to his relief, he heard a scale being played on the piano in the living room. For the first time, he realized what Tina had meant by "exercises."

"Just think of yourself as Gulliver captured by the Lilliputians," Arabella whispered in his ear. She slipped her hand inside his shirt, tapping her fingernails into his chest. The pinpricks of pressure slowly advanced toward his waist. He remembered seeing a movie, when he was a child, of an army of Lilliputians binding the giant Gulliver. But how had Arabella touched his childhood dream, he wondered. Then he remembered that he himself had used the image in a lecture on bureaucratic power. While Tina played the same theme over and over again on the piano, Arabella toyed with him. Finally, he had been teased enough. He felt a sudden flush of anger—directed mainly at himself. Jasmine, the Jejune. Why had he let things get so out of hand? Tightly grasping both of her hands, he lifted them off himself. "This won't do, Arabella, for either of us."

For a moment, she looked blankly at him without betraying any feeling or reaction. Then she whispered, "Be careful of Tina, Jake. She's more dangerous than she looks."

"You're being ridiculous, Arabella," Jasmine said, hearing the anger in his voice.

"Of course, she doesn't mean any harm," Arabella continued. "She just never quite realizes the reactions she provokes in men, with her coy little smiles and glances. She's like a puppy who loves to play, then runs away, not even aware how she's changed things."

"Arabella, you're exaggerating for effect . . . trying to make your sister into some sort of femme fatale."

"Perhaps I am." Arabella could see that there was no point in continuing the discussion. She could tell Jasmine was more vulnerable than she had thought to the fantasies that Tina inspired. Pressing her lips against his ear, she murmured, "Fool."

Jasmine pulled away from her, tucking in his shirt. "I have to get back to work now."

"But it's Thanksgiving—no school tomorrow."

"I have something I have to finish for the State Department."

"The State Department?" she asked curiously.

"Yes. A little consulting on the side. In fact, I'm off to Washington on Saturday. Say good-bye to Tina for me."

He rushed out without taking his coat. As he reached the bottom step, he heard the piano stop.

Chapter VII

THE SHAH'S RETREAT

Nubar Gulbenkian plodded toward the chalet against a cold Alpine wind. He was not accustomed to the altitude of St. Moritz and was already out of breath. Nor was he used to the subfreezing temperature. His beard felt like a jagged icicle, and he feared his other extremities would soon freeze. Why did he abhor extremes, he wondered—extreme weather, extreme behavior, extremes in style? All were intolerable to him, they lacked finesse. Gulbenkian's preoccupation with inner refinement was interrupted by the sight of a figure on skis heading his way. The skier stopped dead in front of him with a beautifully executed parallel christie. The moment the skier raised his black goggles, Gulbenkian recognized him and bowed his head in courtesy. It was the Shah of Iran.

He looked a good deal older than he did in official photographs. In fact, he was only thirty-two, but his hair was gray at the temples, his brow was cut by deep wrinkles, and his eyes seemed sad. About six feet tall, he looked extremely handsome in his raw silk parka. He stood ramrod straight as he greeted Nubar by his formal name—Nubar Sarkis Gulbenkian, son of Calouste—and pointed him back toward the path to the chalet. Plunging his poles into the snow, the Shah continued his downhill course. Two bodyguards shadowed him as he zigzagged down the slope. Despite his obvious skill as a skier, he seemed nervous. But why shouldn't he be nervous, Gulbenkian thought, as he trudged up the path. There had been three recent attempts to assassinate him, and his throne in Iran was becoming increasingly shaky. The dynasty was only twenty-seven years old. The Shah's father, Reza Khan, had begun his rise to power as an uneducated soldier in a Russian-trained Cossack regiment. He was, however, a man of great strength and daring, and when a virtual civil war broke out among the Russian officers of the regiment during the time of the Bolshevik Revolution, he took advantage of the confusion to seize control of the Cossacks. With the only disciplined military force in Iran under his command, he went on in 1921 to engineer a coup d'etat against the reigning Qajar dynasty. As a military dictator, he was not a man to tolerate distractions. He had his enemies in the army hanged by their heels, and whenever he slept in a village he had all the dogs in the area killed lest he be wakened by the barking of one. In 1926, he had himself proclaimed "Shah Reza Pahlaver." He took his new surname from the ancient Persian word for language. He was crowned "King of Kings" on the Peacock Throne—an emerald-encrusted trophy that the Persians had stolen from India centuries earlier.

It was Iran's only asset at the time except for oil.

Gulbenkian had heard from his father how Shah Reza had turned his attention to the rich oil fields in the south of Iran. They were then leased to the Anglo-Iranian Oil Company, and provided the oil that floated Britain to victory in the First World War. Anglo-Iranian was paying only a million pounds a year rent for these fields, and the Shah thought he could negotiate a higher price by threatening to nationalize them. The company cut the payments to three hundred thousand pounds, and the Shah, threatened with imminent bankruptcy, gave in and granted the company a new sixty-year lease. That was in 1933. A few years later, the Shah tried to escape from his dependency on the British by inviting the Germans to build a railroad. He loved to ride on trains. The British responded in August of 1941 by dropping paratroopers into the southern provinces of Iran. They had made a secret deal with the Soviet Union, which invaded the northern provinces at the same time, to partition Iran for the duration of the war. That had been the end of Reza Shah. He abdicated in favor of his twenty-two-year-old son Mohammed, and then went in exile to Africa, where he died three years later. The new Shah had no choice but to reign as a British puppet while the occupation continued. In 1946, when the British and Soviet troops finally left, a group of feudal landlords used the Iranian parliament to gain personal power for themselves, and retained the Shah only as a convenient figurehead. Then the forces of nationalism had brought Dr. Mossadeq to power. It was now doubtful that the Shah would remain—even as a token ruler.

Gulbenkian pulled himself up the wooden steps of the chalet, using the rope handrail for support. His handcrafted leather boots were heavy with snow and felt cold and

70

clammy on his feet. He wondered who would be inside in the middle of such a brilliant skiing day, and was relieved to see his old friend Darius Ali. Darius had the proportions of a bear, but an extraordinarily gentle face. He practically lifted Gulbenkian off the steps with his hug.

Inside, Gulbenkian shuffled across the Isfahan hunt carpet to the stone fireplace, shaking the snow out of his hair as he moved. He sat on the fender of the fireplace, which was covered in needlepoint. Leaning the weight of his torso on his right arm, he stiffly extended first one leg, then the other, to a servant who, with a dazzling zigzag motion, unlaced and pulled off his boots. A magnificent tapestry of stylized lions chasing a deer filled the wall opposite him.

Darius brought him some mulled wine and asked, "What happened to the mysterious guest you were bringing for lunch?"

"Raven decided to charter a helicopter from Milan. Perhaps the weather held him up." Gulbenkian drew a leather case from a pocket deep inside his gray wool jacket and handed Darius one of his custom-blended cigars from it. He put one in his own mouth, and a servant promptly lit them both.

"And who exactly is this man?"

"Anthony Raven? Surely you must have heard of him. He is the director of our Petroleum Export Association."

"Ah, I see, he is with the cartel." Darius gritted his teeth as he said "cartel." It had always given him some pain to think of this group of oil companies controlling Iran's economy.

Gulbenkian explained, "I first ran across Raven in 1943 when I did a few favors for British Intelligence in France. Raven was then working for counterintelligence . . ."

"Wasn't he the head of it?" Darius interrupted.

"Possibly. When I met him again after the war, he was with Shell Oil." Nubar knew that Darius, who was one of the Shah's most informed economic advisors, would be well briefed on Raven's career in the oil combine.

"Is he interested in anything aside from oil?" Darius looked squarely at Gulbenkian.

"Only in power. He derives an unhealthy enjoyment out of persuading people to do things they prefer not to do."

"Is he very successful at it?"

"From what I've seen, he has an absolutely uncanny ability for finding whatever lever he needs to move a person. For example . . ." Gulbenkian hesitated. Considerations of business had dictated that he arrange this meeting between Raven and Darius. Considerations of friendship now required that he forewarn Darius of Raven's tactics. At least then they would be on equal footing.

"For example . . . ?" Darius repeated.

"This might amuse you. Recently Raven was in hot pursuit of an exquisite young girl in London. At first she would have nothing to do with him. She even made the mistake of laughing openly at him at a dinner party. His friends were amused, but he was not dissuaded. Before he saw her again, he did some careful research on her at the Courtauld Institute of Fine Art, where she was a student. He found that she was fascinated with the early paintings of Gabriel Rossetti—and with one in particular called 'The White Damsel,' or something that sounds like that, in which Rossetti had used his own sister as the model. Raven actually bought the painting. He put it over his fireplace and invited her to his apartment, ostensibly for a cocktail party. She was still there, staring at the painting, when the last guest left. He put his arm around her and offered it to her. He claims she went dead white."

"Did he wind up acquiring her?"

"He's apparently in the process."

Darius stood up and shrugged his powerful shoulders in a gesture of indifference. "Are you trying to tell me that Raven has a weakness for young women, or that he gets what he goes after?"

"Both." Gulbenkian reclined on the fender, leaving one slippered foot dangling in the air.

"And what does he want from me? I hope he is not coming all this way in the hope of finding a young girl."

"He tells me he wants to help the Shah."

Gulbenkian wondered what was keeping Raven. He had never known him to be late before.

Darius walked over to the window and stared at the mountains in the distance. "There was a time when I assumed that all the things that happened in the Middle East—assassinations, revolutions, tribal wars, coups d'etat, and so on—were unconnected events."

"And now?" Gulbenkian asked.

"Now I know that no matter how random events seem, they are pulled into position by a single force—oil. . . ." His voice trailed off, then he raised his hand and pointed outside. "Your friend Raven has just arrived."

Raven burst through the door, beaming and exhilarated, bringing with him a pocket of cold air from outside. Apart from a slight reddening of his ears, he seemed oddly untouched by the storm outside. He transformed himself from a traveler to a guest with great dispatch. Before Gulbenkian had even finished the introductions, Raven had thrust his parka into the outstretched arms of one servant and taken a goblet of wine from another. Quickly, he shed his zippered boots and stepped into a pair of felt slippers— all the while apologizing for arriving late. He always made himself instantly at home wherever he was. His air seemed easy, his brown suit still crumpled from long hours of travel, his hair unruly, and his tie—made of alligator skin—skewed slightly to the left. Gulbenkian could see that Raven remained somehow unaware of his own appearance, but at the same time, he was keenly alert to all that was going on around him.

Extending his hand to Darius, he said warmly, "Dr. Ali, I've so looked forward to meeting you." Raven made it a point, Gulbenkian recalled, to always call orientals by an honorary title, though it was actually appropriate for Darius, who had earned his doctorate in economics at Harvard.

"I've heard a great deal about you, Sir Anthony," Darius answered, leading his guests to a small wood-paneled dining room. As the three of them sat down, a waiter placed a bowl of pearly caviar on the table and uncorked a bottle of champagne. Darius performed the ritual of preparing caviar sandwiches on black bread for his hungry guests. "I hope you don't mind eating black-market caviar," he said smilingly as he passed a sandwich to Raven. "Unfortunately, we granted the Russians the concession to market Iranian caviar. It's rather sad what has happened to Iran: the British claim our oil, the Russians our caviar." He passed another sandwich to Gulbenkian.

"A temporary situation," Raven said, without looking up from his caviar. Running his tongue over his teeth, he savored the individuality of each tiny egg's oily contents as he crushed them. "The future will be much brighter for Iran."

"I understand that you are interested in our future."

"Let me be perfectly frank with you, Dr. Ali." Raven's amber eyes softened with affected sincerity. "I am primarily interested in helping the oil combine I represent, not Iran—but in the case of the Shah, I think we have a coincidence of interest."

Gulbenkian marveled at the speed with which the conversation turned from caviar to politics. This was sport he could enjoy watching. His eyes roamed back and forth between the two men as if he were watching moves in a chess tournament.

"I am not sure I un- understand you," Darius said, spreading his palms in a gesture that invited Raven to continue.

"We all know that Mossadeq's time is limited. According to our calculations he does not have the money to last another nine months. He won't survive past August, and someone will have to take his place in Iran. It will either be the local Communists with Soviet backing, or the Shah. We want to make sure it is the latter. But I think you understand, Dr. Ali."

"Unless I am mistaken, you think Mossadeq won't be able to sell any substantial quantities of oil in the world market. Right?" Darius adjusted his posture until his large frame squarely confronted Raven's.

"Up until now, our boycott has been quite successful. Not a single tanker has gotten through to Iran."

"Yes, but I understand that Mossadeq is on the verge of concluding a deal with Enrico Mattei, who wants to buy the oil for the Italian market. Won't that disturb your timetable for Mossadeq's collapse, Sir Anthony?"

Raven gave a short laugh, then the contours of his mouth abruptly became serious. "It would, of course," he responded, "if the deal actually went through. But I can assure you that it won't. Mattei is essentially a political operator, not an oil man. ENI has no oil of its own. We could cut off Italy's imports any time we wanted to."

"But Mossadeq is counting on Mattei."

"I've just come from Milan. I can guarantee that the negotiations between Mattei and Mossadeq will not be resumed. Mattei will gracefully withdraw, leaving Mossadeq with no customers for his oil."

Darius rocked his head slowly back and forth as he digested this new information. At last he said, "Except perhaps the United States."

"It was—perhaps—a hope before the election last Tuesday—who knows what Adlai Stevenson might have done if he were elected?—but with Eisenhower as president, there is no chance that Mossadeq will receive any last-minute aid."

"You're certain of that, Sir Anthony?"

"Absolutely," Raven said, smiling triumphantly. "Eisenhower is going to turn the problems of the Middle East over to the Dulles brothers. Allen, who will be appointed Director of Central Intelligence, assures me that they will never assist Mossadeq—or any other leader in the Middle East who nationalizes oil concessions."

"Just for the sake of argument, let's assume you're right and the Mossadeq government collapses. How can you be sure it will be the Shah and not the Communists who pick up the pieces?"

Gulbenkian nodded. He had been just about to ask the same question.

"There is only one way to be sure." Raven paused for effect. "The Shah must seize power before Mossadeq actually collapses. That is what we propose to help you arrange."

The three men were silent while two waiters carried a tray of veau en papillotes into the room and placed it in front of Darius. Then they brought fresh glasses for each man. The wine, Gulbenkian noticed, was Batard Montrachet, which went perfectly with the veal. Gulbenkian looked on as Darius carefully unwrapped the veal from the paper parcels. He knew how important food was to oriental transactions. He remembered his father explaining to him that the Sultan in Turkey insisted on serving sweet, syrupy pastries such as baklava, because they would perfectly conceal the taste of any poison, and therefore those who did business with him knew that they were always at his mercy. And now, he mused, the fate of Iran was waiting in abeyance for veal to be unwrapped and served.

When Darius had finished serving the portions of veal, he answered Raven. "What you are proposing sounds to me like another British intervention in Iran, Sir Anthony. How will you manage it this time? Will British paratroopers land in Teheran and assassinate Mossadeq? Or will British agents lead a tribal revolt in the desert?"

Raven arched his scraggy eyebrow at Darius' sarcasm. "Do the details of the transaction really matter? Who will care or know how his Imperial Majesty regained his rightful position?"

"The Shah will know," Darius said, dropping his voice to an even lower pitch. "I don't mean to sound pompous, or ungrateful for your interest, but he would never allow the British to intervene in Iran again, even on his own behalf..."

"Does His Majesty really feel that strongly?" Gulbenkian interrupted. He knew the answer to his question, but wanted Raven to hear it.

"Do you think he could ever forget that they invaded his country when he was Crown Prince, sent his father off under armed guard to die in exile, and then humiliated him for five years by making him issue royal decrees protecting the privileges of British subjects in Iran? He would rather be deposed as Shah than accept help from the British. I am sorry..."

"I fully understand your position, Dr. Ali. The British, of course, will have no role in this." Raven deftly altered the tense from the conditional to the more positive future.

77

"No role? But how will this transaction come about?" Darius reached forward, palms outstretched.

"Would His Majesty object to American assistance?" Raven asked, knowing that he had played his trump card at precisely the right moment.

Darius stood up and looked at his pocket watch. "It's getting late. I will see about our dessert." He bowed his head slightly and left the room.

It was only 2 P.M. Gulbenkian hoped Raven had not insulted his friend with his abrupt proposition. He began rehashing the sequence of events in his head. He wondered how the Shah knew who he was, and why Darius had drawn Raven out about his proposal. It would have been better if he had cut him off the first time he brought up Mossadeq. They could have talked about women and paintings, and not made enemies, he thought. Raven looked at him, smug with the thought that his performance had met with some success.

Darius returned five minutes later. He was followed by waiters carrying cerises au kirsch. "I'm sorry to rush you through lunch," he explained, "but His Majesty would like you to stop by his villa for tea at two-thirty. I lost track of the time."

Gulbenkian was stunned. Darius was not a man who lost track of time. He realized that Darius had arranged the meeting with the Shah only after Raven suggested using the Americans to pull off the coup. Yes, he concluded, Raven had obviously telephoned the Shah when he went for dessert. Gulbenkian turned to Raven, who seemed unsurprised by the invitation.

It took them less than five minutes to walk from the chalet to an immense house across the road. They passed six armed guards policing the compound. Promptly at 2:30,

they were ushered into a sitting room of palatial proportions. Almost sixty feet long, it was divided midway by a set
of six steps into an upper and a lower level. The eaves, roof,
and exposed rafters gave it the feeling of a hunting lodge,
which somehow seemed appropriate. The windows were
completely shrouded with heavy velvet drapes, which Gulbenkian assumed were a security precaution. The carpets
and furniture were all museum pieces that the Shah had
flown in from Iran, along with his wife and forty members
of the royal entourage.

On the lower level, about fifty guests in casual after-ski
clothes milled about in small clusters while an almost equal
number of tuxedoed waiters circulated, pouring tea from
ornate samovars and offering pastries from silver dishes.
Four huge Cossack guards in their native Chekessa tunics
stood at attention at the top of the stairs, part of the
formidable barrier that separated the king from his court.

On the upper level, four people sat conspicuously at a
table playing bridge. The Shah, in his white turtleneck
sweater, seemed as tense playing cards as he had a few hours
earlier on skis. He chain smoked gold-tipped cigarettes and
drew in his cheeks in moments of deep concentration. The
dark woman across from him so closely resembled him that
Gulbenkian guessed it was his twin sister, Princess Ashraf.
He had no idea who the opponents of the royal twins might
be. As he drew closer to the stairs, one of the guards gave
him a look that made him think that it might be bad form
to watch the Shah too closely.

Looking away, he saw a young Persian woman with long
black hair, whose hands moved in almost perfect symmetry
as she told a story to three men. For some reason, she
reminded Gulbenkian of a girl he had met recently in
London. Suddenly, he saw that Raven was also staring at

the girl, and he realized who it was she reminded him of. He nudged Raven. "She looks remarkably like your friend Chris, doesn't she?"

"Her hair is almost as long," Raven said, accurately measuring her. "But Chris is in America."

At that moment, Darius broke through a group of people and drew Gulbenkian and Raven aside.

"After you meet His Highness, back slowly away. Be sure not to turn your back on him. He's just in the process of making a grand slam." Darius signaled with his hand, and the Cossacks stepped aside for them. They stood to one side of the bridge table, about seven feet from the card players.

The Shah laid down his hand, claiming the rest of the tricks. All congratulated him on the slam. When he looked up, Darius presented his guests.

"Have you recovered yet from the storm?" the Shah asked Gulbenkian in a deep, melodious voice. His eyes then moved to Raven. "We're showing a film later, an American western. Can you stay, Sir Anthony?"

"Unfortunately, Your Majesty, I have a flight tonight to Washington." Raven seemed perfectly at ease with royalty.

"Yes, I wouldn't want to delay you. I understand you are negotiating a very interesting arrangement there. Good luck, gentlemen." The Shah was dealt a new hand. He studied his cards with approval as Raven backed away. The audience was over.

Gulbenkian watched as Raven moved down the stairs and toward the door, arm in arm with Darius. He knew that Raven had gotten the signal he needed from the Shah and would use it to advantage in Washington. Gulbenkian also realized that he himself was now more than ever involved in a political conspiracy over which he had no control. He shrugged, and made his way toward the Persian girl.

Chapter VIII

GAME OF NATIONS

Jasmine watched in amazement as a large bald man wearing earphones and carrying a four-foot pole crawled around the floor of the Gaming Center. He looked something like an old-time prospector searching for water, poking the pole under various objects in the room. Then he disappeared under the huge round table in the center of the room. When he finally resurfaced, he made another slow reconnaissance around the edges of the room on his hands and knees, waving the pole in front of him. Jasmine was still not sure what was going on. The man had arrived just as he was in the process of restating the rules for the newest variation in the Game of Nations.

Identifying himself only as "McNab, Security Officer," the man had herded all sixteen players into one small corner of the room. McNab explained, while popping chocolate mints into his mouth, that he had to "sweep all the damn operations rooms in the State Department just because one lousy limpet was found in the Secretary of State's dining room." A "limpet," it turned out, was a miniature radio transmitter used by foreign intelligence agents. "Someone stuck it under the table with chewing gum," McNab explained as he plunged under a swivel chair.

Jasmine found the idea of a secret agent eavesdropping in the Gaming Center amusing. How would he interpret all the fictitious scenarios for coup d'etats? Would moves in the game such as "economic destabilization programs," "clandestine arms shipments," and "assassinations" be misconstrued by some foreign intelligence agency as stages in a real American plot? Would they assume that places with such odd names as Zemblia, Transvestania, and North Arcania were code names for existing countries? He could envision it turning into a huge international muddle—John Foster Dulles attempting to explain to his Soviet counterpart that what was overheard at the Gaming Center was nothing more than hypothetical scenarios used as exercises for training budding diplomats in crisis management, and that the sinister-sounding conspirators were only junior academics, working as part-time consultants for the State Department. His thoughts were cut short by McNab, who announced, by making a zero between his thumb and forefinger, that there were no bugs. The Gaming Center was perfectly secure.

The moment McNab departed with his electronic equipment, Bronson Tracy ordered the players to take their respective positions around the table. When Tracy had first mentioned the Gaming Center, Jasmine pictured it as something housing a collection of chess- and checkerboards, or even some sort of Monopoly game. But he had found on his first trip to Washington that the Game of Nations was a highly sophisticated bit of electronic equipment set into a round table that occupied the better part of a large room. The table itself visually resembled a giant, sixteen-hand Chinese Checkers game. Inlaid into it were sixteen triangles, one for each player. Each triangle contained different-colored pegs representing the "resources" allocated to that particular political role. Each player moved by "filing action plans" on his individual telex, which committed his "resources" to different parts of the board. A UNIVAC computer would then, according to the outcome of each move, automatically reallocate the "resources." A video screen would announce what each player had won or lost. Tracy explained the mechanics for the benefit of the new players: "For this particular round, a thirty-six-step scenario will be used to simulate an attempted coup in a fictitious nation." He seemed to Jasmine to get progressively more excited as he described the details.

"Professor Jasmine will give the briefing for the Ajax round. I am sorry about the interruption," Tracy said, motioning for Jasmine to take over the presentation. Jasmine suddenly felt slightly unprepared. Tracy had given him only three weeks to design the Ajax round, and had insisted that the scenario be ready for this December first session.

"There are a number of special rules in the Ajax round," Jasmine began, as the players leafed through their mimeographed briefing books. "First of all, note that the port of Achillea is highly flammable, and any military action there will destroy it and end the game with a loss for all players."

"What's the reason for that rule, Jake?" Wilmot Abraham asked. An overweight and overserious political scientist from the University of Michigan, he annoyed Jasmine with his pedantic queries. What difference does it make why Tracy wanted some special rule, Jasmine thought.

"If you look at page one-thirteen of your briefing book, Dr. Abraham, you will see that Ajax is the world's leading exporter of chromium, which is vital to the production of steel in the Free World. Achillea is the only deep-water port. If it is destroyed, there will be no means of shipping the chromium. Ajax will go bankrupt and everyone loses," Jasmine explained impatiently.

"The point is that no strategy will be considered successful in this round if it results in military action in Achillea," Tracy added.

"The second special rule is that any intervention by the chromium cartel on behalf of the King of Ajax must go undetected. If it is traceable back to the cartel, the King loses automatically," Jasmine continued explaining the rules. The participants nodded in agreement.

The moment Jasmine finished, Tracy gave a short chop with his hand, and the lights in the room dimmed. On a large screen overlooking the table, the first move flashed in computer type: #1. CHROMIUM CARTEL ANNOUNCES SUSPENSION OF ALL FURTHER PAYMENTS TO THE GOVERNMENT OF AJAX. As the syncopated clock clicked out the time remaining to complete the move, the players scrambled for their phones. Wilmot Abraham, whose placard identified him as KING, AJAX, instantly called Myles Smithline, a bright-faced State Department employee who sat behind the ominous placard CHIEF OF STATE SECURITY, KREMLIN. Other players dialed 001 on their telephones, which connected them with the data bank from which they could obtain technical information about the situation in Ajax. After five minutes had elapsed, a red light blinked, requiring all players to type their "action plan" into the computer. This was Jasmine's favorite part: the whirling of lights and the automatic changing of positions on the Chinese Checkers board.

By the time the screen flashed the sixth move, KING

SENDS ORDER DISMISSING MINISTER, a small group
of men had entered the room from a door behind the
players. One bullheaded man who walked with a limp
looked somewhat familiar to Jasmine. He looked like some
oil painting Jasmine had seen at the Brook Club. Tracy
tried to relieve the tension that had mounted by announc-
ing, "We have some observers tonight. Please proceed without paying any attention to them." By the time the screen
flashed the twelfth move, KING FLEES AJAX BY PLANE,
all the observers had left except the bullheaded man, who
stood directly behind Jasmine and watched the printout of
the telephone traffic between the players. He seemed discon-
tented with it, and stayed on for another three moves.
Jasmine noticed that before he left he called Tracy aside
and counted off four different matters on his fingers. It was
past midnight by the time the last move was made. Jasmine
was exhausted; he had been up the night before completing
the scenario and thinking of Tina. As the room brightened
and Tracy thanked the players, Jasmine slipped on his
jacket and headed for the door. He didn't want to be
trapped into any postmortem analysis of the game by any of
his colleagues. He was already in the hallway when Tracy
called to him.

"Jake, can you wait a minute? I'll drive you back to your
hotel." It was more a command than a request.

It was a freezing December night and it took a moment
for Tracy to warm up the engine of his Mercedes. Jasmine
could tell he was unhappy with the way the Ajax round had
gone. He decided to preempt him. "Sorry if the game was a
little confused tonight. I was a bit rushed . . ."

"It's my fault. I should have given you more time to
prepare it," Tracy replied. "Actually, it was a useful trial
run. We've decided to do another Ajax round. Do you have
time for coffee?"

"Why not?" Jasmine weakly agreed. Although he was

tired, he was also intrigued by Tracy's request. He wondered what had gone wrong with the night's round of Ajax.

Tracy wheeled the car around corners. He obviously knew exactly where he was headed, Jasmine thought. When they passed the White House, Jasmine tried to break the heavy silence by commenting, "Truman must be sorry to leave. . . ." Tracy smiled, but did not reply. From that, Jasmine concluded that he was an Eisenhower Republican. The car turned down Wisconsin Avenue toward Georgetown.

Jasmine tried again to spark a conversation. "Do you think the Russians really planted a bug right under the Secretary of State's nose?"

This time Tracy answered. "Why assume it was the Russians? It could have been Joe McCarthy looking for striped-pants Communists in the State Department. Or it could have been one of our allies. The Secretary had the ambassadors from NATO to lunch the day the bug was discovered in his private dining room." He ticked off the possibilities as he pulled the car into a parking space in front of Clyde's café.

Jasmine had been to Clyde's once before. He remembered the food as tasteless and boring, but liked the fact that it was open past midnight. He was a night person and whenever he spent time in a city, he always acquainted himself with all the postmidnight restaurants.

Jasmine ordered an espresso. When Tracy decided to have eggs Benedict and Courvoisier, Jasmine realized it was going to be a long night.

"The trouble with Ajax tonight was, quite frankly, that there were not enough options to play with," Tracy began when the waiter brought him his Courvoisier. The waiter lingered long enough to overhear part of what he was saying, and he shot Jasmine an odd look.

86

"That was never a problem before when we discussed it," Jasmine said, thinking out loud. "What options were we missing?"

"For example, I think there should be more possibilities than merely exiling the Prime Minister of Ajax."

Jasmine struggled to grasp Tracy's point. "I guess there could be an option of his staying in the country."

Tracy shook his head. "I was thinking of . . . couldn't there be an assassination option in the scenario?"

"Why not?" Jasmine answered indifferently. "But does it mean completely revising the thirty-sixth move?"

Tracy finished his Courvoisier and ordered another. "Actually, I was thinking that there could be two options on that move. Option A would be exile, Option B would be assassination."

Jasmine looked wearily at his watch. It was 3 A.M. He had been up for thirty-eight hours straight. He remembered reading somewhere that more than forty hours deprivation of sleep could lead to hallucinations. He blinked his eyes, another gesture meant for Tracy. "Sorry, but I seem to be falling asleep. It's been a long day for me." He began propping himself up to leave.

"Sorry, Jake, I didn't notice you needed another espresso," Tracy said, motioning Jasmine back into his chair. *"Garçon, encore du café."* A waiter instantly rushed over with a pot of bitter black coffee and refilled Jasmine's cup.

"Perhaps you want to make a few notes." Tracy handed him a thin gold pen. "Why don't we have Option B take place in the back of an armored car? Yes, that's it. The Prime Minister thinks he is escaping in it, and when he gets in, the guards lock the door from the inside and shoot him. Got it?"

Jasmine scribbled Tracy's idea for Option B on the back page of his briefing book. His eyes were so bleary he could hardly see what he was writing, and he wondered if he might not be imagining this entire assassination option. It seemed absurd to be assassinating a deposed prime minister in a ridiculous game. He handed back the pen and began to stand up.

"By the way." Tracy always used the phrase to change subjects. "I understand we're going to have an opening in the Politics Department at Yale."

Jasmine sat down again. Even at this hour he was interested in hearing about an opening at Yale.

"Do you have a commitment to stay at Harvard?"

"I have a year left in my contract. If they don't offer me tenure, I'm not sure what I'll do."

"An offer from Yale couldn't hurt then, could it?"

Jasmine knew as well as Tracy did that an offer from Yale would force Harvard to make a counteroffer. He also knew that Tracy was well connected in the Yale network, and suddenly he felt buoyed.

"Ibor Lassbloom, an old friend of mine, is arranging a new position in International Politics. Do you know him?"

"I know of his work, of course." Lassbloom was possibly the most influential professor at Yale.

"You should meet him. I've told him about you. You're going to be here on January eighteenth, right?"

"January eighteenth?" Jasmine echoed.

"Yes, that's when we'll replay your Ajax round with Option B." Tracy paused to make sure Jasmine understood him. "Stay over for the nineteenth. I'm having a little dinner party and Lassbloom is coming. Can you make it?"

Jasmine nodded.

"It's black tie, of course. A waltz night."

Tracy signaled for another drink. "By the way," he began again, "the committee was very impressed with the way you handled the game tonight."

Jasmine assumed Tracy was referring to the unidentified group of observers who had watched six moves. "They didn't look impressed.... Who was that man who was breathing down my neck for three moves?"

"Didn't you recognize him? There was a story about him today in the *Post*. He's joining the personal staff of John Foster Dulles. He's quite a character—taught History at Harvard for a while."

"Who?" asked Jasmine, not understanding.

"Kim Adams. The great-great grandson of the President. Quite a fellow A great man. I'll introduce you next time."

Jasmine dimly recalled reading something exciting about Kim Adams, but he couldn't remember exactly what it was. He was quickly approaching his fortieth hour without sleep. "I'd really better get back to my hotel now ..."

"I'll drive you," Tracy said, raising his glass to empty it. "By the way, let me know if you'll be bringing anyone on the nineteenth."

Finally, Jasmine managed to stand up. He feared he had actually reached the hallucinatory threshold. He pictured Tina's long hair flowing around him as he whirled her in a waltz.

It was snowing outside. Jasmine was still dreaming about Tina and didn't realize until he was outside that Tracy wasn't behind him. Turning around, he saw through the door that Bronson had stopped to chat with a red-haired woman and her escort. It was his opportunity to escape. He leaped into a waiting taxi.

CHAPTER IX

GOLD SOVEREIGNS

Raven's plane circled for more than an hour in a snow-storm over Washington before finally receiving permission to land at National Airport. He had long ago cushioned himself against the inconveniences of traveling. The cabin of his corporation's Constellation was fully insulated, with carpeting, soundproof wall panels, and built-in suede furniture. It served as a fairly comfortable office. In fact, Raven hardly looked up from the papers on his desk when the wheels of the aircraft crunched down hard on the snow-frosted runway. He had made such landings many times before, and he knew that he had to finish reading the papers in front of him and destroy them before disembarking. It was highly unlikely that even a customs inspector would read them, but he felt he could not take the chance. They were illegal intercepts of conversations and correspondence between Secretary of State Dean Acheson and his senior advisors on the Middle East.

What he had already gleaned from the file made him very uneasy. R. E. Steer, the American Ambassador to Iran, was urging American assistance to Mossadeq. A barrage of cleverly argued telegrams from the Embassy in Teheran warned of imminent disaster if Iran were allowed to go bankrupt. The file further showed that Acheson had decided to ignore a warning cabled by Sir Anthony Eden on November 4, 1952, which said: THE UNITED STATES GOVERN-MENT WOULD BE FAR BETTER OCCUPIED LOOKING FOR ALTERNA-TIVES TO MOSSADEQ THAN TRYING TO BUY HIM OFF. Raven smiled with satisfaction. He had a hand in drafting that message from the Foreign Minister, and even though it failed to sway Acheson, he took pride in seeing his work used by Eden. He read, then reread, the next intercepted conversation with a flush of undisguised horror. On November seventh, the day after the Democrats lost the election, Acheson told his colleagues, "I asked President Truman, if it proved necessary to save Iran, whether he would be willing to use his authority under the Defense Materials Procurement Act to advance up to a hundred million dollars to Mossadeq against the future delivery of Iranian oil to the United States. He agreed to this, subject to his approval of the final plan." That would be disastrous, Raven thought. If Truman advanced that amount of aid to Mossadeq, the cartel would be finished in Iran, and other concessions would fall like dominoes. Fortunately for him, Truman and Acheson would be out of office in another few weeks, and he knew he could count on the Dulles brothers to reject this appeasement plan. He had already spoken to Allen about the Shah's willingness to go along with an American-sponsored coup. Now, all he had to worry about was

Truman's doing something rash during his last days as President. He didn't fully trust the Americans; they tended to be too sentimental.

He touched a button. Almost instantly, Hugh Leigh-Jones, his sixty-year-old secretary, opened the door with his familiar "Sir?"

"I want an appointment with Allen Dulles at the CIA tomorrow. Any time that's convenient for him," Raven ordered as he handed the older man the stack of papers on his desk. "And shred these immediately, Hugh."

"Yes sir."

"Also, call Franklin Bell at Standard Oil ..." he hesitated, seeing that Hugh had something to say. "Yes?"

"Sir Anthony, Mr. Bell is here at the airport. He says it is urgent."

"Fine. I also want to see General Schwartzkopf ..."

"Excuse me, sir?"

"Norman Schwartzkopf. He's retired somewhere in New Jersey. He was head of the U.S. Army Training Mission in Iran up to last year. I'm sure you can find him, Hugh."

"Yes sir. The pilot asked when you would be ready to disembark. There's quite a storm outside."

"Right away," Raven said, putting on his topcoat. He watched as his secretary shredded the last of the intercepts.

The pilot held a large umbrella for him as Raven walked to the terminal. Leigh-Jones tottered along behind, weighed down with Raven's three suitcases and portfolio, and blinded by the snow. "Damn it," Raven thought, "it snows wherever I go." He shouted over his shoulder, "Also, Hugh, see if you can find Chris. She's supposed to be somewhere in this damn country."

Whenever he went through customs, Raven always felt some queasiness, like the trace of seasickness he got whenever he boarded a ship, even if the sea was dead calm. He suspected that it came, in both cases, from not being in absolute control of events. For the brief moment that he stood before the customs inspector, he would never know what indignities he might be subjected to. As he now watched the inspector, who had what seemed to him one grotesquely stretched eye, rummage through his effects, he felt more queasy than usual. He told himself, trying to control the rising tremor in his stomach, that it was just a random spot-check as he watched the inspector carefully poke through his silk underwear.

Then the official demanded that Raven open the rectangular portfolio of drawings that he held tightly under his arm. Raven protested that they were only some worthless sketches that he had done for his own amusement, but to no avail. One by one, the sketches were laid out by the guard on the baggage counter. They were crude line drawings of a nude girl. The inspector's eye seemed to pop out of its socket as he held them up for scrutiny.

One showed a girl sitting on the edge of a couch, her legs crossed into a figure-four, her arms pinioned behind her, and her head thrown back. To Raven's utter disgust, the inspector leered at him as he went on to the next sketch. Scratching his head, he muttered, "This looks like smut to me," and then turned to Leigh-Jones, who was trying to avert his gaze from both the drawings and Raven, and asked, "What do they look like to you, mister?"

"See here, Inspector, you have no right to ask such things." Raven spoke in his highest and most intimidating Oxbridge accent—but at the same time he could see, in the large anticontraband mirror on the wall, that he had turned ash white. He suddenly felt an urge to have this prying one-eyed man killed.

"No right?" he officiously answered, displaying the sketch in both hands. "It is a violation of the law to import pornography into the United States. What flight did you arrive on?"

"Who the hell do you think you're speaking to like that, Buster?" a voice cut sharply across the room.

Raven looked up to see Frank Bell bearing down on the inspector with giant strides.

"This is Sir Anthony Raven, the Director of the International Oil Association, and, I might add, a guest of the Standard Oil Company while he's in America," Bell continued the attack. "If you're looking for a transfer to Nome, Alaska, we can easily arrange it for you."

The inspector reminded Raven of a turtle retreating into its shell. "Sorry, sir," he said, "I didn't realize who this man was."

Raven quickly gathered up the sketches and followed Bell out of the terminal. He had never had more respect for his American associate.

"I want that goggle-eyed idiot fired," Raven growled, seated in the back of the limousine next to Bell. Leigh-Jones sat up front with the driver before a soundproof glass partition.

"Don't let it upset you, Tony. He's only a moronic bureaucrat," said Bell, trying to soothe him.

"I'm serious, Frank. Use what influence you have. I don't care who you have to go to, but get rid of him."

"O.K., if that's what you want, but don't you think we should use our influence for more important things?" Bell changed the subject. "I've just come from a meeting at the State Department. Acheson had representatives from the nine largest oil companies there. Do you know what he wanted?"

Bell was just about to tell him what Acheson wanted when Raven interrupted: "He wanted the oil companies to provide tankers to transport Iranian oil to the United States."

"How did you know that?" Bell asked incredulously.

"We've been monitoring this whole business from London," Raven answered in a matter-of-fact tone.

"I never thought the State Department would ask us to deal in hot oil."

"Did any of the American companies show any interest?" Raven asked.

"No, not much. Acheson admits that they can't move Mossadeq's oil without our tankers. Thank God you suggested last month buying up all the short-term charters. I reckon we now control ninety-five percent of the available space on ocean-going charters."

"What else did Acheson offer?"

"He said that in this emergency, the national interest in protecting Europe's oil supply took precedence over the need to prosecute antitrust sections. He promised, if we cooperate, to have the Justice Department drop its International Oil Cartel case. Everyone was interested in that idea since it could save us a lot of embarrassment."

"There's nothing to lose by playing along. Tell the State Department you can't even consider working together with the other oil companies to transport Iranian oil until the antitrust action is dropped," Raven suggested. "Then when the Eisenhower administration comes in, we'll go ahead with our plan to save Iran's oil ... which won't include saving Mossadeq."

"Then you think we don't have to worry about Acheson?" asked Bell with an undertone of doubt in his voice.

"We always have to worry about Acheson. Never underestimate him. Luckily, he'll be leaving. Still, I don't trust the independent American oil companies when there's a profit to be made."

As the car passed under a streetlight, Raven caught a glimpse of concern on Bell's face. He had wrinkled his brow in a way that suggested to Raven that his last remark had offended Bell. He knew that Bell was sensitive to any intimation that the Americans might doublecross their European partners in a crisis.

"Don't worry about the American independents, Tony," Bell said firmly. "They know that they're in the same boat with the majors. If Mossadeq gets away with nationalizing the Iranian concession, none of their concessions will be safe."

"What about the companies that don't have concessions to risk, like Getty and Hunt? What do they have to lose?"

"They're not blind. They can see the big picture. They'll have their share after Mossadeq is dealt with," Bell said just a little less firmly.

"I am worried, Frank. Can we really be sure of Saudi Arabia holding the line?" He knew that Bell had been an executive of Standard Oil of California in the 1930s, when it had cut itself in on Middle East oil by bribing King Ibn Saud of Saudi Arabia.

"Did you ever meet their king, Ibn Saud?" Bell asked. "Quite a character. He must have been six foot six—he claimed he had shrunk with age—and he delighted in showing all his battle scars."

"And in demanding payoffs in gold sovereigns," Raven added.

"His fondness for gold caused quite a problem, all right," Bell agreed. "We needed permission to export gold from the United States, and who do you think we had to go to to get it? None other than our friend Dean Acheson. That was in 1933, when Acheson was Undersecretary of the Treasury, and he turned us down, would you believe it? Time was running out, and the Lord of the Desert was getting impatient."

"So what did you do?" Raven asked obligingly.

"What could we do? We bought thirty-five thousand gold

sovereigns on the black market—illegally. I personally escorted them to Jeddah and watched the King's finance minister count them out, one by one."

Raven tried hard to picture Bell twenty years younger, in his dapper, wide-lapeled suit and Princeton rep tie, standing behind an Arab in a white burnoose who was stacking smuggled gold coins into neat piles. "So he took your bribe, Standard of California finally got its hands on some Arabian oil, and the world oil structure was thrown into chaos."

"I'll admit it caused some temporary disruptions."

"It did more than that! It gave some Arabs the idea they could play us off against one another," Raven said.

"It all worked out, didn't it? We set up Aramco, took everyone in as partners, and joined the combine," Bell said, as the limousine skidded to a stop in front of the Park Hotel.

"Frank, the point is that we wouldn't want to see another American company, which had been lucky finding oil, take advantage of another opportunity. We can't afford to have another break in ranks over Iran. What we have to do this time is make sure that the independents know that they will get a cut of Iranian oil from us after we get rid of Mossadeq."

Bell nodded, knowing full well that he would have to do the negotiating.

Leigh-Jones was the first one out of the car. He gingerly guided an even more elderly bellboy to the luggage in the trunk. When Raven stepped out, he felt his shoe breaking through the thin crust of snow. The pool of slush that engulfed it reflected a rainbow of colors from the hotel's neon sign. He braved the indignity, thinking that American hotels were always full of unpleasant surprises. A tall black doorman in a silk hat unctuously held the glass doors open for him. He turned back and saw Leigh-Jones and the bellboy, with his handcart full of Vuitton luggage, walking in what seemed like slow motion up the icy ramp that curved around the side of the hotel.

Bell caught up with Raven as he entered the lobby and insisted on showing the Englishman to a suite of rooms on the top floor. It was a seven-room apartment that Bell's company maintained on an annual basis for important visitors. "Your secretary can use these two rooms for a bedroom and an office." Bell opened and closed closet doors as he gave his tour. "There are three private telephone lines, all quite secure." In the sitting room, Bell took great pride in demonstrating the mechanics of the bar. It was concealed behind an American decorator's idea of a bookcase, with fake leather-bound volumes, that slid open at the press of a button. "I think you'll find it well stocked, Tony," Bell said, pointing to the wrought-iron cages full of wine and liquor.

The bedroom was dominated by a four-poster bed, topped with a heavy velvet canopy. Raven knew that he would find it stifling, trying to sleep under this tent, but he felt too tired to complain. It was past midnight. "It's king size," Bell said, running his hand along the velvet fringe of the canopy. "If you ever feel you could use some company in Washington, I'll be happy to arrange it."

Raven said nothing. He watched as Leigh-Jones efficiently unpacked his suitcases and neatly arranged his clothes in the mirrored wall of closets across from the bed. "I think that will be all for tonight, Hugh," Raven said, dismissing his secretary with an imperceptible nod of his head.

"Feel like a nightcap?" Bell asked, moving toward the bar.

"Another time, Frank. I'm still on London time, and very tired." Even as Raven spoke he saw it was too late; Bell was already in the process of tilting brandy into a snifter.

"I don't want to keep you up. . . . I'll see you tomorrow,"

Bell said, leaving an opening between his declarations so that Raven could insist that he stay.

Raven began undoing his tie. "See you tomorrow then, Frank."

Bell moved toward the door, opened it, then turned to Raven, still lingering. "If you need anything, my office is at your disposal."

"Thank you," replied Raven, seeing that he still had not managed to dislodge Bell from his occupation of the doorway. As a last resort, he decided to send him away with a mission. "Do you know General Schwartzkopf by any chance?"

"I've heard of him." Bell closed his eyes for a brief moment to activate his memory. "He was the New Jersey State Trooper in charge of the search for the Lindbergh kidnappers, wasn't he? Yes. Then he was doing something in Iran."

"He was training the Iranian Imperial Gendarmerie during the war. He's back in America now, but he could be very useful to us. Do you think you could find a quiet way to bring him here for a meeting?"

"That should be no problem. . . ."

"Good." Raven cut him off in midsentence. "I hope to be hearing from you on it soon, Frank." Raven managed to back Bell into the corridor while shaking hands with him. Once through the threshold, Bell left.

Raven trudged back to his bedroom after bolting the outer door. He opened the portfolio to see if the customs inspector had damaged any of the sketches. He laid three of the crudely drawn pictures of Chris out on the bed. They were painful to look at, but exciting. He knew that Chris had made a fool of him. He also knew that he would continue his pursuit of her even if it cost him a painting worth over ten thousand pounds. She was not classically beautiful: he found her legs too thin, her breasts too small, her eyes too large, and when she laughed, he remembered, her cheeks reminded him of a squirrel.

It had taken him some time to find her weakness—Rossetti's "Portrait of a Virgin." She had seemed obsessed with that painting. When he offered it to her, he could actually see her quiver. It took her almost five minutes to look up at him and ask what he wanted in return. He realized that he could not be direct with her and ask her to trade herself for the Rossetti. He knew he had to be more subtle than that, to draw her in as he would a heavy salmon with a light line. First, he had to compromise her by making her trade something of herself for a valuable object. Then, he would humble her by stripping her of her privacy . . . the rest would follow. He knew that the initial offer had to be ambiguous enough so that she would accept it. He suggested a simple trade: he would give her the Rossetti if she would let him do a portrait of her.

"What sort of portrait?" she had asked.

"I'll dictate the pose," he had replied decisively. He knew his authority must be established from the start. He was the artist, and she—the subject of his whim.

Raven remembered her draining her glass of wine, still indecisive. Looking at the Rossetti, she had sighed, "When?"

"Here and now," he answered, helping her out of her indecision. "Why wait? You want your painting and I want mine."

"You're joking, of course. You wouldn't give a Rossetti away?"

He didn't bother answering. Instead, he took an easel from the closet and set it up a few feet away from her. He took a charcoal pencil in his hand. "Take your clothes off,

Chris ... I need to study you a little before I begin the sketch."

"Admit it, Tony! You borrowed the Rossetti from a museum just to tease me." She slumped down on the leather couch, waiting for his reply.

You're the tease, he thought as he watched her. You look into men's faces with your bright eyes, not giving a damn how you play on their instincts. Now I've found your weakness. "Do you want the painting or not?"

She nodded yes, accepting his challenge.

"Then off with your jacket."

She looked down at the blue velvet suit she was wearing, wondering whether she could really go through with this. Then her fingers undid the top button and went on to the next.

Raven turned and waited for Chris to slip out of the velvet. His pencil began slashing across the canvas, drawing her outline. It was very crude. Black hair on white skin. Long legs in a figure-four. Arms spread wide in the air.

Under the velvet jacket, she wore a white silk blouse. She unhooked her belt and stepped out of the velvet slacks. With grim determination, she looked up at him.

Raven had stopped sketching. The whiteness of her thighs, the crumpled blue velvet around her calves, the flicker of excitement in her eyes and her slow movements—it was all too much for him. He felt himself losing control. Beads of sweat began dropping from his forehead. His hands trembled. He couldn't keep his mouth closed, and he could hear the wheezing of his breath. The easel fell over as he collapsed, rather than walked, in Chris's direction.

With one deft movement, she slipped out of his reach. The fishing line had snapped, he realized. He could see himself in the mirror, panting like the forty-five-year-old fool

101

that he was. It took Chris only a minute to redress.

He wished she had run from the room. It would have been far better for his ego. Instead, she offered him a sip of wine from her glass. Using a napkin, she wiped the sweat from his brow, showing that she was now in control.

"You just need a little practice," she had laughed. "First try sketching me with my clothes on."

He tried to sketch her taut body three times. Each line drawing became more pornographic. The pressure became more than he could bear. "You're right, Chris. I do need some practice. Let's finish this another time."

That had been nearly three months ago. Raven knew that Chris still wanted the Rossetti painting, and would never let him off the hook that he himself had baited. In fact, he had received a letter from her just before he left for St. Moritz. It asked when and where they were to "consummate the trade." It bothered him that she had used the word *consummate*.

He put the inchoate sketches back in their leather case and changed into his pajamas. Even with the light out, he was unable to fall asleep in the canopied bed. He couldn't stop thinking of Chris. The phone must have rung twenty times before he found it. The transatlantic operator verified that he was Sir Anthony Raven, then told him he had a call from Nubar Gulbenkian in London. He looked at his watch. It was 5 A.M.

"Tony, I hope I'm not waking you." Gulbenkian never bothered to take into account time differences between continents. "I just had a call from our friend in St. Moritz."

"Which one?" Raven asked, trying to focus on Nubar's voice. He didn't know whether Gulbenkian meant Darius, or the Shah himself.

"My friend, of course."

Raven realized the message was from Darius. He fumbled

for a pencil and a pad of paper. He couldn't trust his memory at this early hour. "Yes?" he asked.

"He says—and I don't have any idea what it means—'The party must take place before August twentieth, or there will be no guest of honor.' "

Chapter X

OPTION B

"How was Christmas in Teheran, Mr. Steer?" asked Jasmine.

"It was a bit chaotic. It's impossible to find anything to buy. My father thinks the whole country is on the verge of bankruptcy," Steer explained, as he backed toward the couch in Jasmine's office.

"Well, let's get on with the tutorial." Jasmine looked at his watch, as if to emphasize that time was running out.

Steer let himself sink slowly onto the couch. "I've finished the paper I was doing ..."

"Why don't you read it aloud?" interrupted Jasmine.

"'The Politics of Usurpation in Iran,'" Steer began reading in a nervous voice. Then the phone rang.

It was Bronson Tracy. "I've got some good news ..."

"I'm just in the middle of a tutorial, Bronson," Jasmine tried to cut him off. "I'll see you in Washington tomorrow."

"Just two quick points," Tracy persisted. "I've found out that Yale is definitely going to make you an offer."

"That is good news," Jasmine said, trying to surpress his elation. He noticed that Steer was watching him out of the corners of his eyes, while pretending to sort through his papers.

"Second, Jake, we have given more thought to Option B." Tracy shifted to a more serious tone, which suggested that Option B, and not Yale, was the real purpose of the call. "I think you'll have to revise the scenario so that the blame for the assassination is put on the local Communists in Ajax."

"If we're going to play it out tomorrow afternoon, I'm not sure there will be time to figure out a plausible move for attributing the assassination to anyone."

"I understand the time bind, Jake. That's why I thought it would be best if you could catch a flight to Washington tonight. We could have breakfast . . ."

"It's a little short notice for me . . ."

"The last shuttle is at ten P.M. I'm sure it will give you enough time. See you tomorrow."

As Jasmine hung up the phone, he could see that Steer was wide eyed with curiosity. But rather than explaining to him that what he had overheard was nothing more than a hypothetical game, he decided to say nothing. He liked being thought of by his students as a man of mystery. Intrigue was a part of the business of teaching. "Sorry for the interruption, Mr. Steer. Let's proceed with your paper."

Steer's voice became more confident as he got into the details of Iranian politics. His father had apparently helped him, Jasmine thought as he listened. He couldn't, however, concentrate on Iran. He was still slightly bothered by Tracy's call. He puzzled over Tracy's usage of the first-person plural. Was he merely indulging in the royal "we" to refer to himself, or were there others involved in the design of the Ajax round whom he had not yet heard about? And why was Tracy so concerned about the details of Option B? Before, he had supplied only the most general guidelines for the game. The more Jasmine thought about Ajax, the more perplexed he became.

A sudden silence in the room uncoupled his train of thought. Steer had finished reading his report and was tilting his head to catch Jasmine's eye. For a moment he looked like a forlorn terrier whose trick had gone unnoticed by its master.

"That was an excellent summary, Mr. Steer," Jasmine said, throwing him a verbal biscuit. "The conclusion you are suggesting, I gather, is that political usurpation is a normal, rather than an aberrant, behavior in Iran." He had not heard Steer say anything quite so precise, but drew on his repertory of stock conclusions that roughly fitted almost anything his students were likely to say. If students disagreed, they could always argue with him. Steer, however, eagerly nodded his assent. He would make an excellent diplomat, Jasmine thought, as Steer backed out of the office.

Jasmine then stuffed the tutorial report in one file drawer and took the Ajax briefing book from another. Shuffling through the pages of the scenario, he stopped at the thirty-sixth move and scribbled across the top of the page, "Delete, substitute Option B." He put a fresh piece of paper in his typewriter.

The problem was how to make Option B "work," as Tracy would say. Making murders sound plausible was usually a problem for mystery writers, not political scientists, he thought, as he typed out, then ripped up, three pages of scenario. The bells on Memorial Chapel began ringing. He looked at his watch. It was five o'clock. Suddenly, he had an idea. He would have the King be away from Ajax when the assassination took place. Not only would this make it easier to assign the blame to the local Communists, who would be rioting in the streets, but it would also serve to lessen the suspicion that the King was in league with the chromium cartel. He quickly revised the thirty-sixth move, liking the elegance of his solution. It killed two birds with one stone. Like chess, scenario writing required the accomplishment of different objectives with the same move. Fully satisfied, he put the completed scenario in his briefcase and turned off the light in his office.

He was back at his apartment at 5:30 P.M. It was not a place of which he was particularly fond. He had rented it the night he arrived in Cambridge. The newly built highrise reminded him of a hospital. But it was faculty housing, and since his rent would be partly subsidized by Harvard, he instantly signed the lease. The next morning, he saw that the apartment had very little light, and he began spending more and more time in his office. He now found himself increasingly anxious to get to Washington. He moved around the room picking up the various things he needed for the trip—pajamas, slippers, razor blades, shaving soap, toothbrush, an extra pair of socks and underwear—and stuffed them into his briefcase.

He hunted through his bookcase for a suitably trashy thriller. Perhaps politics wasn't so different from mystery writing, after all. The phone rang. "Jasmine speaking," he said, expecting it to be Tracy.

"It's so nice to hear your voice, Jake," Arabella said. "Are you busy now?"

"What are you doing back so soon?" he asked. She and Tina were supposed to be visiting their father in Bermuda.

107

"Tina had to come back to find more paintings for her exhibit. Anyhow, it was too hot to play tennis, and there's nothing else to do on Bermuda."

"I'd like to see you, but I'm just on my way to Washington."

"Can't you catch a later flight?"

"The last shuttle is at ten and I can't miss it ..."

"Good. You have three hours. There's something Tina and I want to talk to you about."

What could Tina and Arabella want to talk to him about, he wondered, as he walked along the snowy street to their house. Arabella met him at the door, smiling in her enigmatic way.

"Has something happened?"

"Not really." She took his briefcase and overcoat from him and put them in the hall closet. Then, without turning around, she started up the stairs, assuming he would follow.

"What's so urgent?" he asked as he walked behind her. When she didn't answer, he said, in a tone of protest, "Really, I have a lot to do in Washington."

"I thought you went there to play games," she said over her shoulder.

"Hi," Tina called out, cupping one hand over the telephone receiver. "Be right there. I'm on a long-distance call to Washington." She resumed her conversation about some painting he had never heard of. She was wearing faded jeans, raggedly cut into shorts, and a loose-fitting sweatshirt. He could see that the sun had darkened her legs more than her face. Hanging up the phone rather abruptly, she caught his eye.

"I'm trying to arrange to borrow a painting from the National Gallery."

So she's going to Washington too, Jasmine thought.

"We have only two hours or so, Tina. Jake has to catch a plane," Arabella explained as she sat down at the table in the dining alcove and shuffled a deck of cards.

"That's *not* why you called me?" Jasmine asked, looking at the cards.

"But, Jake, you're the only other person in the world who knows how to play Conspiracy." Arabella was dividing the deck into three piles.

Tina slide into a chair across from Arabella, crossing her legs into a sort of "A." "Let's just play one game, then you can go to Washington."

"O.K., if you don't mind my leaving at nine," he agreed. He wanted to hear more about what had happened in Bermuda.

Jasmine picked up his cards, trying to remember the rules of the game. Arabella had taught it to him after one of their more amorous tutorials. The object, he recalled, was to get either all the spades in the deck, or none of them. Players had to follow suit, unless they were void, and—like Bridge—the high card won the trick.

"I should go to Washington this week," Tina said, leading the two of clubs. Arabella played the ten of clubs, and Jasmine, finding himself void in clubs, decided to drop the ace of spades on her trick. It counted fifteen points against her, unless she could get all twelve remaining spades.

"I can already see you're conspiring against me, Jake," Arabella said, leading the ten of spades. The game was called Conspiracy because there was a natural temptation for the players with the lowest score to combine to give the leading players as many spades as possible—short of all of them.

Jasmine threw the nine of spades on Arabella's ten without looking carefully at his cards. His mind wasn't on

109

Arabella's stratagem, but on his own. He was thinking how he could arrange it so that Tina's trip to Washington coincided with his own.

"You should have taken the trick, Jake," Tina said, throwing down the deuce of spades. "Can't you see Arabella going for them all?"

Jasmine looked at his hand. He had no other spades, which meant that the remaining eight were split between the sisters. He figured that if Arabella held the four high spades, she would simply have laid down her hand and won. He looked up at Tina. Obviously, she held one of the court cards, and was baiting her sister into a trap. "Sorry, I wasn't concentrating," he said, playing along with Tina's deception.

Arabella gave him a hard look. She was already suspicious. Then she shrugged and played the ace of spades, hoping that the jack would drop. Instead, Jasmine played a diamond, showing that he was now void in spades. Arabella stared daggers at her sister, who played another low spade. Arabella knew she had no chance of winning now.

"What stakes are we playing for?" Tina asked triumphantly.

"I'll decide later," Arabella answered. Her only hope now was to force her sister to lead a spade against her. She led a low club, forcing Tina to take the trick.

"When are you going to Washington, Tina?" Jasmine asked, as he sloughed another diamond.

"Haven't decided yet," Tina replied. She threw the lead to Jasmine with her last diamond.

"When you're down there, maybe you'd like to see the Gaming Center?" Jasmine caught a sharp glance from Arabella. He quickly played a high heart, hoping Tina would play a spade on his trick and ruin Arabella's plan to get all the spades.

110

"I still don't understand what political scientists are doing playing games in Washington," Arabella broke in before Tina could answer. "Sounds very corrupt to me." She played a low heart, as did Tina.

"Everything sounds corrupt to you. We're simply trying to develop a means of teaching diplomats what they call 'crisis management.' Jasmine found himself repeating the explanation that Tracy had given him. It somehow sounded less convincing coming from him. After hesitating, he changed his strategy, and played a low heart.

"I see. You play 'Let's Pretend,' or something similar," Tina said as she won the trick.

"Exactly what sort of crisis are you creating?" Arabella asked.

"A coup d'etat. Some nation cuts off the world supply of chromium, and we have to figure out, in thirty-six moves, how to get rid of that nation's government," Jasmine explained.

"Doesn't make much sense. Why would some country cut off the chromium supply?" Arabella was becoming increasingly argumentative.

"It doesn't have to make sense. It's just a hypothetical game." Tina was impatient to get on with the game of Conspiracy.

"Do you really believe the State Department would lavish all this money on something that was purely hypothetical?" Arabella said, arching an eyebrow at her sister.

"Are you suggesting that I'm being used?" Jasmine shot back. Arabella always made him defensive about his work.

"I'm just suggesting that the Game of Nations makes no sense," Arabella said in a conclusive tone. "Anyone want a drink?" She waited a moment, then got up and went into the kitchen.

"She's just trying to be provocative," Tina apologized when Arabella was out of earshot.

"If you're going to be in Washington this week, Tina, I'll show you the Capitol," Jake said in a quiet but persistent voice.

"Is that really what you want to show me, Jake?" Tina shook her head slowly, as if answering her own question. "If you think you can switch sisters so easily, you're mad."

He looked up, not believing his ears. Had she intuitively understood his interest all along? Or had he misheard her? He took some encouragement, if he had heard her right, from the fact that she had only suggested that it would not be easy, instead of impossible, to "switch sisters." He was looking straight into her eyes when Arabella returned with a gin and tonic.

"I can see you've both been cheating," Arabella said, picking up her cards. "I've decided on the stakes." She led another club.

Tina won the trick and led her final club. All she had left was the ten of hearts and her spades. She led the ten in the hope that it would be overtaken, but it held. She now realized that no matter which spade she led, her sister would win them both, and the game. "What are we playing for, anyhow?"

"We're playing for Jake," Arabella answered, laughing at her own joke, and showing her two high cards.

Jasmine felt Arabella pressing her hand against his knee under the table, and decided he didn't like her little joke. "I'd better call a cab," he said, jumping to his feet. "I can still catch the nine o'clock shuttle."

As he waited for the taxi dispatcher to answer, Arabella finished her drink and dealt out a hand of solitaire. Tina stood up and stretched. "See you when you get back."

He followed her out of the room with his eyes. The

dispatcher finally answered, and promised a taxi would be there within five minutes. "I'll wait downstairs," he said to Arabella.

"I'm sorry I annoyed you, Jake."

"It doesn't matter," he said, and left her sitting at the table.

While waiting for the taxi, he wondered what would happen if he left his briefcase behind. He could call Tina and ask her to bring it with her when she came to Washington. Suddenly, the taxi honked its horn outside and he rushed out the door—without his briefcase.

CHAPTER XI

SECRET AGENTS

"Have a seat, Tony . . . I'll be with you in just a minute," Allen Dulles wheezed. His yellow-tinged teeth were clenched around the stem of a thick briar pipe. Unable to get through on the telephone in his hand, he repeatedly jiggled the plunger, then looked up in frustration.

Raven settled into an overstuffed chair and waited for Dulles to complete his phone call. He had last seen Dulles in 1945, and he noticed that the thatch of gray hair on his head was much sparser and his mustache more closely cropped. Otherwise, he had hardly changed in the seven intervening years. He still huddled over his desk in the same scholarly way he had when they had reviewed Allied intelligence assessments during the war, and he still wore his rimless glasses on his head when he was not reading. Even though he was now the Director of the Central Intelligence Agency, he still reminded Raven of Mr. Chips. Looking around the cozily furnished office, Raven was able to recognize various pieces of Dulles' history in the photographs that almost entirely covered the wall behind the desk.

Directly over Dulles' head were photographs of all his relatives who had served the United States, including three secretaries of state and an ambassador to the Court of St. James's. To the left of these were pictures showing Dulles' progress from the playing fields of Groton to his graduation from Princeton. On the right were framed snapshots tracing his travels over nearly half a century. Raven's eye stopped on a photograph of Dulles standing in front of an innocent-looking villa in Switzerland. He recalled visiting him there during the war, when Dulles was using it as his base of intelligence operations against Germany.

"Kim, Tony Raven is in my office. Can you come right over?" Dulles said into the phone. Then he took the pipe from his mouth and turned to Raven. "You know Kim Adams, of course." He used the "of course" as a tactful question mark.

"I met him once in Cairo," answered Raven. In fact, he knew that Adams was the most trusted CIA operative in the Middle East, and that he was on a first-name basis with every important king, prime minister, and tribal chieftain in the area.

"You'll be seeing more of him. He's going to be our . . . liaison," Dulles said, hesitating to make sure he had chosen an innocuous enough term. "Yes . . . for the Iranian business," he continued as if Raven had asked a question. "By the way, I think, for the record, we should consider this one of those meetings that never took place."

"Of course, Allen," Raven agreed.

"We've never tried anything like this before in the Middle East. By all logic, this should be a British operation," Dulles said, as he tried without success to relight his pipe.

"The Shah, unfortunately, isn't being logical; he's insisting on Americans."

"Yes, I know," Dulles interrupted. "But we should be straight about one thing: we are not going to do this to help your oil companies. Eisenhower wants to do it to help Churchill." Dulles finally lit his pipe, then added, "Of course, there happens to be a certain coincidence of interests here. . . ."

"It will benefit everyone." Raven smiled. He wondered if Dulles knew that he had helped draft Churchill's plea to Eisenhower for aid in removing Mossadeq. Seeing the expression on Dulles' face, he assumed that he did. He also guessed that the "coincidence of interests" had at least been helped along by the more than two million dollars the oil companies had funneled into Eisenhower's election campaign.

"In any case, I think we've worked out an interesting . . ." Dulles again fumbled for an appropriate euphemism, "contingency plan." He shuffled through some papers on his desk, then lifted up a thin mimeographed book titled *AJAX.* Again, he searched the desk before realizing that his glasses were on his head. He smiled sheepishly and adjusted them for reading. "You've seen the AJAX plan, of course?"

"I saw an early draft," Raven answered.

"Here, take a look at the revised version," Dulles said. "Fortunately, we have someone quite gifted in contingency plans."

As he leafed quickly through the pages, Raven could see that it was an extraordinarily accomplished job. The coup was broken down into thirty-six distinct phases, each with a series of available options. As far as he could see the scenario seemed to take into account all the contingencies that might arise in Iran. "A remarkable talent," he concluded.

"Sorry to be late, Allen, but the Vice-President insisted on another round of squash," Kim Adams said as he burst through the door wearing slacks and a sweatshirt and carrying a squash racquet. Thrusting his square jaw in Raven's direction, he waved him back in his seat. "Hi, Raven ... don't bother getting up." Adams only called his superiors—and selected royalty—by their first names. Bounding into the chair closest to Dulles' desk and stretching his short legs out onto a convenient ottoman, he asked, with a trace of condescension in his voice, "How's the oil business, Raven?"

"Much the same as the politics business, Kim." Raven waited for the smile to set fully on Adams' bulldog mouth, then continued, "We both depend, don't we, on tacit influence over parts of the world where we don't have legal sovereignty." He thought of going on to draw a more specific parallel between the hidden operations of the oil combine and those of the CIA, but saw that Dulles and Adams had both grasped the point.

"You mean the Middle East, of course," Dulles interjected.

"Yes," Raven agreed. "Since the oil business shifted from the Texas Gulf to the Persian Gulf, the politics business must move there also ..."

"And Iran is our first stop." Adams completed Raven's thought. "Of course, it will take time to lay the groundwork there. I don't know if I should tell you this, Raven, but this is our first coup d'etat."

Dulles was obviously embarrassed by Adams' bluntness. He smiled as if it were all some joke. "I would prefer to think of this as ... er ... assistance ... we are rendering to the Shah of Iran, Kim." Looking down at the paper he was doodling on, he continued, "In any case, Kim is right, we must be well prepared."

"Yes, but time is running out. The Shah let us know in no uncertain terms that if we are going to act, it must be before August twentieth," Raven warned.

"That gives us . . ." Adams counted on his fingers ". . . eight months."

"Don't you think we should leave some margin? August twentieth is the last day," Raven argued. He made some quick mental calculations. Iran produced almost two million dollars a day in profits for the cartel. He estimated that the cartel would lose roughly sixty million dollars every month the coup was delayed. The stakes were enormous. "If we could move the target date up to March . . . or April . . . ?"

"That wouldn't give us enough time," Dulles answered flatly. "We can't set anything in motion before Eisenhower's inauguration on January twentieth. Then there will have to be a meeting of the National Security Council, and all sorts of briefing papers will have to be prepared for the White House. We'll be lucky if we get the go-ahead by March." Dulles paused, thinking of all the problems that were involved in such an undertaking. For one thing, the President would insist on having plausible deniability. Eisenhower would never want to be put in a position in which he would have to admit he had authorized the coup. Then there would be the task of getting agents in place in Iran. Of course, he could use the Iranian generals and cabinet ministers that Raven's group already owned, but he knew that the White House would want him to keep a safe distance between the CIA and the cartel in case everything exploded. And finally, there was the question of what to do if the Soviets heated things up by making threats. It was all an extremely risky business. He was lucky to have Kim to run the operation, he thought. Kim was a Harvard man, and he could be counted on to be sure that nothing went wrong. And if by chance things did go wrong, he would be just the person to take full responsibility. He knew that Kim always basked in his quixotic failures.

"In any case," Dulles continued, looking at Adams, "the less I know of the operational details, the better. Eventually I'll have to brief the President, and I won't want to tell him anything more than it is absolutely necessary for him to know." He turned to Raven. "Kim will work out an acceptable schedule, I'm sure."

"Right," Adams leaped in. "Let's have lunch tomorrow at my club, Raven. One o'clock, let's say."

Raven nodded.

"And take Tony to see the run-through of the scenario tomorrow afternoon, Kim. He'll enjoy that." Dulles advanced toward Raven with his hand stiffly extended. "Glad you could stop by, Tony. But remember—" He chuckled. "This meeting never took place."

Raven arrived at the Metropolitan Club promptly at one the next day. Adams had left word with the concierge that he would be late, and Raven was escorted to a corner table with an excellent view of the Christmas tree on the White House lawn across Pennsylvania Avenue. It was nearly two when Adams finally arrived.

"Hope you ordered the oysters, Raven," Adams said, without bothering to explain his tardiness.

Before Raven had a chance to reply, a smug waiter swooped down on him with a platter of oysters. At almost the same moment, a wine steward passed a cork under Adams' nose. Kim shook his head in disapproval, and the steward, with a look of utter admiration, produced a second bottle. After Adams opened this bottle, the steward filled their glasses. Then, without even perfunctorily consulting Raven, Adams ordered rack of lamb for two, saying, "Hope you like yours pink, Raven." He was by far the most imperious American Raven had ever come across, but—like the wine steward—he couldn't help admiring Kim's self-confidence. And both the oysters and the wine were indeed very good.

"I'm glad you're going to be working on this project, Kim," Raven began, noticing that Adams' head, like his own, was much too large for his narrow shoulders.

"I'm not glad to be involved in this adventure," Adams responded. "Don't really believe in it." He sipped his wine, silently judging it. "My view is that the world is too large a place for Americans to serve as the ultimate fixers everywhere. The British should never have pulled out of Iran until you had someone there running the show for you. Now we have to go in after Churchill's chestnuts."

"I couldn't agree with you more. We mishandled Iran," said Raven, thinking how appropriate was the phrase "Churchill's chestnuts." It was Churchill who, as Lord of the Admiralty, had forty years ago decided to convert the British Navy from coal to oil, and bought into the only concession available to the British—Iran. It was also Churchill who decided to drop paratroopers on the Iranian oil fields in 1942 and to expel the Reza Shah, who was giving the oil companies some trouble. Now Churchill had the same problem again, only this time he needed American assistance, Raven thought.

"But who cares what I think. We can't take any chances on losing Iran, so we, in what you call the 'politics business,' will retrieve your oil," Adams said, taking Raven's last oyster. With a flick of his hand, he gestured for another platter of oysters.

"Of course, it all depends upon the cooperation of the Shah," Raven added.

"Moushka?" It was Adams' pet name for the Shah. "He's young, maybe inexperienced, but he has nerve."

Raven smiled to himself. Who else but Kim Adams would call the Shah of Iran "Moushka"? He realized that Adams' close relationship with the Shah, even though it was a shade exaggerated, could be extremely beneficial to the cartel, not only for the purpose of the coup, but also afterward. If the coup succeeded, "Moushka" would be the ruler of a kingdom of oil for a very long time.

"Kim, the Shah needs to know that the Americans are fully behind him, and not just the oil companies. Would it be possible to have President Eisenhower signal such support?"

"No problem," Adams replied. "Ike is giving a speech on the state of the world in San Francisco next month. How would it be if I wrote a paragraph or two into the speech that pledged unqualified support to the Shah ... and I could add something like 'against all and any who attempt to subvert his legitimate throne.' Would that do the trick?"

"That would be perfect, especially if we alert the Shah in advance to watch for the signal," Raven answered.

The waiter brought over the loin of lamb, which though charred on the outside was blood rare on the inside. New glasses appeared, and after the appropriate ritual, red wine was substituted for white.

"Kings are always looking for signals from American presidents," Adams said, clasping both hands together and looking for a moment at the high ceiling, as if searching for inspiration. "I remember during the war, King Ibn Saud demanded that same sort of signal from Franklin ..."

"Franklin?" It took Raven a moment to realize that Kim was referring to Franklin Delano Roosevelt.

"Yes, Franklin wanted to build a pipeline across the

121

Arabian desert from the American concession on the Persian Gulf to the Mediterranean. Churchill was afraid that if the Americans bypassed the Suez Canal with their pipeline, Britain would lose control over the rest of the oil fields east of Suez, and he began pressuring King Saud not to allow construction of the pipeline."

Raven remembered the incident quite well. Churchill was then supplying Saud with part of his defense budget, and he was persuaded by Lord Tutman that it might be possible to finesse the Americans out of a part of the Saudi Arabian concession. He didn't interrupt Adams' version, however.

"Saud must have been over seventy then. Blind in one eye, and lame in one foot, but still Lord of the Desert. Whenever he heard whispers that he was losing his virility, he would ride across the desert to some tribal encampment and demand his right to the chieftain's wife for the night. When Churchill sent word through the British ambassador that his allotment of arms would be cut, and sent a detachment of British troops into his desert under the pretext of controlling the Arabian locust, old Saud leaped on his horse and rode alone all night to Dahrain, where the Arabian-American Oil Company was housed in Quonset huts. He saw it as just another tribal encampment and made quite a scene that night—half-blind with cataracts, roaring around on a horse, his sword flailing the air. He demanded that either their president send him a token of his esteem, or they leave his desert."

Adams motioned for the waiter to refill their plates with lamb, then continued, "You can imagine the bedlam it caused. The boys at Arabian-American begged Franklin to go to Arabia, arguing that Arabian oil was America's single greatest asset. At the time, Franklin was going to Yalta to meet with Churchill and Stalin. When he finally agreed to meet with Saud on his way back, everyone breathed a sigh of relief."

Except Churchill, Raven thought.

"The meeting was scheduled for February fourteenth 1945, at Suez. Franklin invited Saud aboard the U.S.S. *Quincy* for lunch. The problem was that the King insisted on bringing his entire harem with him to show off his virility, as well as his own coffee-servers, cooks, and Nubian slaves. He even brought goats and sheep aboard, since he refused to eat 'dead meat' for lunch. It was quite a meal. He gave Franklin a jeweled sword, and in return, Franklin gave him his spare wheelchair, which delighted the King, and Franklin promised to make Saudi Arabia eligible for American lend-lease arms. That ended the crisis."

Raven knew there was more to the exchange. In order to finance Saudi Arabia, President Roosevelt had arranged for American oil companies to deduct all royalties that they paid for oil from their United States corporate taxes. This meant that, in effect, the U.S. Treasury paid the costs of Americans doing business in Arabia in hidden aid. "Another case of the politics business and the oil business coinciding, I would say," Raven added with his own conclusion to Adams' story.

"You're coming to the Gaming Center at five, right?" Adams asked as he finished his wine.

"Gaming Center?"

"Yes. At the State Department. I've left a pass for you. That's where we play through the scenarios."

"I'll be there," Raven said, finally understanding.

"Right." Adams stood up. "I've ordered dessert for you and coffee. Sorry I can't stay, but I have to get back." Without shaking hands, he nodded to several other club members and left the dining room.

123

Raven took his time finishing his lunch and mulling over what Adams had said. He enjoyed the cherries jubilee that Kim had ordered for his dessert, finished a claret, and smoked a Havana cigar that Gulbenkian had given him in Switzerland. It was all going as planned, he thought.

When he came out of the Metropolitan Club, the limousine that Bell had provided for him was at the curb. He told the driver to take him to a nearby art supply store, where he purchased an easel and a sketch pad. Then the chauffeur took him back to the Park Hotel.

When he got back to his suite, his secretary handed him his messages. The first read: "I would be happy to serve in any way I can in this enterprise. Suggest that we meet in Washington on December twenty-first." It was signed "General H. Norman Schwartzkopf." Raven knew he would need Schwartzkopf in Teheran to make the necessary contacts among the Army officers.

The other message was a telegram. It said only I WILL BE IN WASHINGTON THIS WEEK. PERHAPS I WILL CALL YOU. It was signed "Christina." She had managed to leave him dangling again, he thought, as he crumpled up the telegram.

CHAPTER XII

AJAX

Jasmine held the phone receiver nervously in his hand and waited for a response. On the seventh ring, there was still no answer. He had been trying to reach either Tina or Arabella all morning, without success. The Game of Nations was due to be played in ten minutes.

What an idiot I am, he thought. With all his byzantine planning, he had not reckoned on the possibility that both sisters might be out when he called to retrieve his briefcase. Now here he was in Washington without pajamas, razors, or briefing book. He was about to hang up when he heard Arabella's voice.

"My God, where have you been? I've been calling you every ten minutes," Jasmine said, relieved that he had finally gotten someone.

"Oh . . . I guess I turned off the phone so I could study," she explained, then asked, "By the way, what are you doing for pajamas?"

"You found my briefcase?"

"The secret briefing book and everything." Then she added, "Of course, I read it."

"Arabella, I could get into serious trouble. Now listen . . ." He was about to ask her to bring it to Washington—knowing full well that she couldn't cut her classes—when she interrupted him.

"I found your Ajax scenario highly inventive, reminded me of one of your lectures. The only problem . . ." her voice faded.

"Was what?" he queried.

"The part about chromium doesn't make much sense, Jake."

"I've explained it to you before. It's a hypothetical game." His voice rose in intensity until he was practically shouting into the phone.

"Still, there's something fishy about it."

"Fishy about what?" He felt increasingly exasperated.

"For example, the special rule that any military action in Achillea will set the chromium export facilities on fire, and cause the world to lose a vital part of its chromium supply."

"So?"

"Chromium isn't particularly flammable, is it? And even if the port was damaged, it could be repaired, couldn't it?"

"What difference could that possibly make?" he growled. "As I keep telling you, the entire country of Ajax is hypothetical. We needed an export from Ajax that is vital to the West. We picked chromium. We could have picked any other material. The point was not to get bogged down in trivia, but to construct a certain type of international crisis."

126

"But why couldn't you have picked a flammable material, Jake?" she insisted. "There must have been some reason."

"I don't know why they picked material X rather than material Y. Look, I want to ask you a favor." He vainly tried to change the subject.

"You could have picked oil. It's a flammable substance. What would be wrong with that?" she continued.

"Maybe they use oil in another game," he said, still on the defensive. With mounting uneasiness, Jasmine recalled that he himself had suggested using oil rather than chromium, but Tracy had vetoed it, saying, "Oil's old hat." He would never admit it to Arabella, but he too had thought the choice of chromium slightly puzzling.

"They must have had some logical reason for wanting to use chromium instead of oil," she persisted.

"What could the logic possibly be?" Jasmine asked, his own curiosity finally aroused. It was put in as a red herring to conceal the real purpose of the exercise. Jasmine suddenly was aware of a sinking feeling in the pit of his stomach. He didn't need her to tell him that chromium might be a diversion. Up until now, he had actively suppressed the idea that he and the other game players were deliberately being duped. But she was right. Chromium did have an implausible ring to it.

Suddenly, Jasmine became aware that someone was watching him. Turning his head, he saw Bronson Tracy standing in the doorway, beckoning him into the Gaming Room. Tracy pointed at the clock. "We can talk about this later, Arabell. The game is scheduled to start now," he said, trying to conclude the conversation. "Oh, yes, about my briefcase . . ."

"You're in luck," Arabella cut in. "Tina had to go to Washington today. She'll bring it over to the State Department—pajamas and everything—on her way to the Mellon Collection. Call me later." She hung up. He tried to digest the fact that his plan had actually worked. As Tracy shouted for him to hurry, he called the front desk and left a pass for Tina to come to the Gaming Center when she arrived.

Jasmine hurriedly took his position at the head of the gaming table. He saw that all fifteen other players had already slipped into their places behind placards identifying their roles. The King of Ajax, Wilmot Abraham, poked a pudgy hand in the air to ask a question.

"One moment, Professor Abraham," Tracy said as he impatiently toyed with the rheostat that dimmed the room's lights. "We have observers coming again tonight. We'd like them to hear all the questions."

"I just wanted to know what time we would finish?" Abraham persisted.

"Before midnight, I hope ..." Tracy looked up toward the door. "Ah, here they are now," he said, rushing over to shake hands with Kim Adams.

"Jake," Tracy said as he shepherded the other men to three chairs directly behind Jasmine, "I'd like you to meet Kim Adams."

"Heard about you, Jasmine." Adams did not bother to shake hands. "Hear you have some sort of talent for these games."

When Adams moved his head, Jasmine noticed another man standing behind him, staring at the game with the scrutiny that a gem collector applies to precious stones.

"Oh, yes, excuse me for not introducing you two. Jasmine ... this is ..." Adams hesitated before introducing Jasmine to Raven, then smiled. "Tony Black, another observer at the Game of Nations." He half-introduced Jasmine to a third man standing behind "Mr. Black" as Mr. Moffat. Moffat was short, bald headed, and smelled of a very strong perfume.

"We're ready now for the second round of Ajax," Tracy announced as he lowered the lights. "The moves have all been punched out on separate IBM cards," he whispered to Adams, holding up a pack of the cards for him to see. He then inserted the first card into the computer.

On the screen flashed #1. CHROMIUM MINES IN AJAX CLOSED DOWN BY CARTEL. Different-colored lights blinked on the display screen in front of Jasmine, indicating the pattern of the negotiations. At the same time, the UNIVAC computer began printing out, on Jasmine's teletype, the resources available to each player. But Jasmine could not concentrate on the mechanics of the game; he was thinking too hard about chromium.

His mind raced through the thirty-six steps in the Ajax scenario. Why chromium? he asked himself at each step. It still made no sense. He then scribbled down on a yellow pad in front of him what the logic of the game required of whatever material was selected. "Must be (1) flammable; (2) controlled by worldwide cartel; (3) dependent on transport that could be cut off by handful of companies; (4) *not* dependent on native work force; (5) vital to the West." Chromium met none of these five conditions. Then why did Tracy insist on using chromium? he asked himself again and again. Was there a real purpose that transcended the Game? He looked back down at his list. Only one material seemed to fit all five criteria: oil. Oil certainly was flammable. He remembered Professor Wiley had mentioned something about an antitrust case being filed against the international oil cartel. And of course oil required virtually no native labor force—after the well was capped, the oil flowed by gravity through pipelines into storage tanks and then onto tankers. He also realized that oil required the special sort of transportation facilities, such as ocean-going tankers and pipelines, that were owned by a few large oil companies. Finally, oil was a vital commodity for the West.

One by one, he checked the five points off on his pad. He again mentally ran through the scenario. There was no doubt in his mind. The Ajax round was designed for oil, not chromium. But why conceal the fact? He could see no reason for substituting chromium for oil in the scenario, unless the State Department really was planning a coup d'etat in some oil-producing nation. That would explain why Tracy had insisted on using chromium. But where was Ajax?

The eighteenth move flashed on the screen KING ASKS PRIME MINISTER TO RESIGN. Negotiations took place against a ticking clock, "action plans" were typed into the computer, the UNIVAC whirled, and the distribution of resources on the giant board was electronically changed. "The King has few resources left in Ajax," Raven whispered to Adams.

Jasmine kept trying to unravel the real plan—if there was one. If it's a major oil-producing country, it must be one with a legitimate throne, he thought, or the whole scenario won't work. He began listing the major oil producers on his pad. He could only think of Venezuela, Indonesia, Saudi Arabia, Iraq, Kuwait, Libya, and Iran. He crossed out Venezuela and Indonesia, since they didn't have thrones. That left the five Middle Eastern kingdoms.

PRIME MINISTER REFUSES KING'S ORDER. CALLS PARLIAMENT INTO SESSION, read the twentieth move.

Jasmine thought for a moment about that move. There had to be not only a king, but a parliament as well. And Saudi Arabia, Libya, and Kuwait were pure monarchies, with no form of parliament. He crossed those three off his list. Now he was down to two countries. Either Iraq or Iran was Ajax. They both seemed to fit equally well into the scenario. Then he began to remember something that Steer had muttered during their last tutorial. He wished now he had paid more attention.

PRIME MINISTER ASSASSINATED. COMMUNISTS BLAMED, read the thirty-fifth move.

They were playing Option B, Jasmine realized. If this was now scheduled to take place somewhere in the Middle East, he would be responsible for planning an assassination. He looked behind him. "Well done," he heard the man he was introduced to as "Butch" say to Tracy. The computer again arbitrated the "action plans" and awarded almost all of the resources to the King of Ajax and the chromium cartel. Both the local Communists and the Soviet Union were judged to be without any remaining resources in Ajax.

The screen announced FINAL MOVE: KING RE-TURNS TO AJAX IN TRIUMPH. Then the clock stopped. Everyone applauded. Jasmine figured the players were especially happy they had finished the game in less than four hours. They all had time now for an expensive dinner in Georgetown at the State Department's expense. He noticed the three observers slip out as quietly as they had entered. Tracy stood up and held both his hands over his head for quiet.

"Thank you, gentlemen. It was a brilliant game, brilliantly played. I think we owe a special debt to Professor Jasmine, who designed the Ajax round ..." he waited for the smattering of applause to die out before continuing, "We, of course, will send each of you the computer analysis of the game for your comments ..."

As Tracy continued to speak, a guard passed Jasmine a note. It stated: "8:03 P.M./ Miss Tina Winchester/ Waiting: North Anteroom." He didn't wait to hear the rest of Tracy's praise. He had to tell Tina what he suspected. Without a word of explanation, he dashed from the table through the double doors. He hoped they would all assume he had received some urgent message.

When he ran into the anteroom, he couldn't believe what he saw. The observer with the heavy eyebrows was shaking Tina violently by both arms. "Who do you think you are?" he yelled at her.

"She's with me, Mr. Black!" Jasmine shouted across the room. For a moment he thought it was some security precaution—perhaps Tina did not get the proper pass to be in the Gaming Center. Then he saw the man raise a clenched fist as though he were about to hit Tina. It took Jasmine only four long strides to cross the room. "What in hell do you think you're doing?" he yelled, spinning the man around and grabbing him by both lapels. As he looked back at Tina for a split second, he felt a heel crush the bridge of his right foot. The pain was excruciating. Struck under the left eye, Jasmine toppled to the floor.

"Damn you, Chris!" he heard the man shout at Tina. "I've had enough of this! You can't back out now."

Using a table for support, Jasmine had just managed to get to his feet when McNab, the security officer, rushed in. "Don't you know fighting is not allowed in the Gaming Center, Professor? I'll have to report you." Wilmot Abraham and Myles Smithline came over to help him, and he saw Tracy rush across the room to his assailant.

"Tony, I'm terribly sorry. This is unforgivable," he could hear Tracy apologizing.

"My God, look at your eye," Abraham was saying. "What on earth happened?" Jasmine couldn't answer. He realized that he had no idea what had happened. He watched Tony Black leave, with Tracy following at his heels like a pet dog.

He wondered why he was so solicitous of this stranger. Then he saw Tina coming toward him, carrying his briefcase.

"I'm sorry, Jake," she said, putting an arm around him for support. "Can we go somewhere and talk?"

He clung to her as he hobbled down the corridor. His foot hurt horribly every time he put pressure on it. He could hear Abraham and Smithline following closely behind, chattering about the Ajax round. He knew that Smithline was probably admiring Tina from behind, while snickering at his own clumsiness. The moment they were outside, his hand automatically shot up at the sight of a passing taxi. The driver skidded to a stop. He had luck with taxis, if nothing else, he thought, as he pushed Tina in and slid in close to her.

"Where shall we go?" he asked her.

"Wherever you say." She touched his hand gently.

He swallowed hard and told the driver "Hay-Adams Hotel." He looked at his watch. It was only a quarter past eight. Then he turned to Tina. In profile, her features stood out like etchings in an ivory cameo. "What were you doing with Tony Black ... or is that an indiscreet question?"

"Who?"

"The man who was shouting at you ... Tony Black," he repeated.

"That was Sir Anthony Raven."

"He was introduced to me as Black."

"It's a long story, Jake, too long for tonight."

"But who is he? Why was he at the State Department tonight?"

"I have no idea. I didn't expect him to be there."

"But ..." Jasmine tried to make sense out of the situation. Raven had come as an observer of the Ajax round. He was introduced under a pseudonym, because he was part of the

133

group involved in the real coup d'etat. That would explain why Tracy was so oversolicitous of him, and why Adams smiled so conspiratorily at him after each move in the Ajax round. Tracy, Adams, the bald-headed man who smelled of perfume, and Raven were working together on the coup, Jasmine decided.

"Sir Anthony Raven, huh. How did he get knighted? Does he work for the British government?"

"I don't know much about him."

"Tina, I need to know."

"All I know is that he's an art collector ... and he's on the board of a number of corporations."

"Which ones?" Jasmine pressed.

"I only heard him mention one, when he was talking with Nubar Gulbenkian ... Anglo-Iranian Oil. He was going to Iran for them."

He squeezed her hand tightly. Oil, Iran, the Company—it fit perfectly into the scenario. The King of Ajax was, in fact, the Shah of Iran; the Prime Minister was Mossadeq; the Ajax chromium cartel was the Anglo-Iranian Oil Company.

"What's wrong?" She looked at him as if he were suffering from some fever-induced madness.

But he lapsed into silence as she stroked his hand to calm him. Perhaps I am overexcited, he thought.

When they arrived at his hotel, Tina followed Jasmine out of the cab and wove her free arm through his. He still had trouble walking. "Let's get something to eat," he suggested.

"Let's get sandwiches sent up to your room," she said decisively.

As they got into the elevator, he remembered that the briefcase Tina was clasping contained his pajamas. He still couldn't believe that the plan had worked.

134

Chapter XIII

THE MAN IN THE BLACK PAJAMAS

"Let me tell you a story, Ambassador," Mossadeq said with a serious look on his face. He sat on the edge of a small couch in black pajamas and a purple robe. His shoe-button eyes, which could glimmer with joy, were now moist and sad. The Iranian premier made no effort to disguise the fact that he had been weeping before the American ambassador was ushered into his residence.

"You wanted to see me about some urgent matter, Your Excellency?" replied Ambassador Steer. Steer, a tall, gaunt diplomat, had served America in some of the most difficult trouble spots in the world—Moscow during World War II, Athens at the time of the Greek civil war, Belgrade at the time of Tito's break with Stalin, and New Delhi at the time of India's independence—but he found the situation in Iran

135

especially trying. He couldn't help liking Dr. Mossadeq, a prince who had entered politics at the age of seventy-four and who had become a living symbol of nationalism to the Iranian people. But on the other hand, he knew from the Embassy's intelligence reports that Iran could remain solvent for only another few months without oil revenues. Something had to give—Mossadeq or the oil companies.

"My story will take only a minute of your time," Mossadeq whispered in a frail voice, "and I think it will help you understand why the prospect of negotiating with the British makes us ... how shall I put it? ... uneasy."

Steer obligingly sat down across from the Premier. He could hear a crowd shouting something in Persian through the closed windows. He noticed that Mossadeq clutched a bottle of heart stimulant in his left hand, as if he were expecting an attack at any moment.

"Twelve years ago my nephew, Ali Reza, received his commission in the Iranian Navy. Of course, we only had three ships, but he was made the captain of a small vessel, the *Palang.*" Mossadeq pronounced *Palang* with a heavy nasal twang. "The *Palang* had little to do. It simply sailed back and forth in front of the British refinery at Abadan to protect it from any surprise attack by the Germans."

"This was in 1941, I assume," Steer said knowingly.

Mossadeq's face was perfectly divided by a long vertical line. "It was a time when Iran was neutral in the European war, and looked on the British as friends. Of course, we didn't understand the politics of oil in those days. In any case, the *Palang* was at anchor in front of the refinery at Abadan, at peace with the world, and my nephew was at watch on the bridge. Through his binoculars, he saw a British cruiser approaching. It was the H.M.S. *Shoreham.* He waved to the British officers on the deck and they waved back—very friendly. Why shouldn't he think the British were friendly?" Mossadeq asked rhetorically, then continued. "When the *Shoreham* was practically next to the *Palang,* its gunners opened fire with five-inch guns. Some of our sailors' arms were blown off while they were still waving to their British friends. Can you imagine that, my friend? The *Palang* sank in less than five minutes."

"What happened to your nephew?" asked Steer, thinking instinctively of his own son.

"His body was found washed up on the beach a week later. By that time, British paratroopers had our oil fields, and, together with the Russians, they had divided our country—but you know all this."

"I can't say that I understand it, except that it was wartime and the British were afraid that Reza Shah would collaborate with the Germans."

Mossadeq, unconvinced, shook his perfectly bald head. "But why sink a ship without warning?"

"Perhaps the British feared that the *Palang* would fire on the refinery at Abadan when they landed troops in Iran." Steer chose his words carefully.

"What it tells me is that the British will go to any length in order to keep control of their oil supply in Iran. When it comes to oil, Iranian lives don't mean a damn thing. Do you disagree, Ambassador?"

"My interpretation of history is not particularly relevant now. The problem, if I may put it bluntly, Dr. Mossadeq . . ."

"Please be candid. It is the quality I respect most in Americans."

"You're right in saying that the British desperately need Iranian oil—but Iran also desperately needs the money from Iranian oil. You cannot survive without it. Therefore, there must be an accommodation—"

"Yes, we need the money that is ours," Mossadeq interrupted, thrusting his arms in the air like a prophet. "The oil is Iranian. We will compensate the British for their investment, and sell them as much oil as they want at a fair price."

"They have a lease that runs for another forty years. They will not accept nationalization as a matter of principle. There must be some middle ground."

"We will not compromise if it means giving away an inch of our sovereignty. They will never again find Iranian sailors waving to them when they come to invade our country."

"They do not have to invade Iran. They can prevent Iran from selling any oil. They know that you cannot let Iran collapse into bankruptcy . . ."

"Nor can you," Mossadeq said, with a dry smile on his face. He changed instantaneously from a demagogic prophet railing against British imperialism to a cunning diplomat finessing a difficult point. "If the British were to succeed in destroying my government, who would pick up the pieces? It might be the Communists, then the Soviets would move in. You can't allow that, can you? Just imagine, if the Soviet Union controlled the Persian Gulf, where would Europe get its oil from then? No, America could not allow Iran to collapse." He had played his trump card and now sat back in his chair, awaiting Steer's response.

"You're playing a dangerous game, Your Excellency. The United States is caught in a complicated situation . . . among allies . . . the British might prefer to take their chances with another Iranian government. There are other Iranian leaders. . . ."

Using an old shepherd's cane for support, Mossadeq propped himself up and walked to the window. "I want you to hear something, Ambassador." With a burst of strength, he flung open the double windows and stepped onto the balcony. Again, he was the prophet.

Steer could feel the room shaking as the crowd shouted
"Mossadeq zindabad!"—"Long live Mossadeq!" Mossadeq
bowed humbly to his supporters and the crowd fell silent.
Steer couldn't understand what Mossadeq was saying, but
there was no doubt in his mind that the hearts of the people
of Iran belonged to Mossadeq.

The Premier, now standing erect, stepped in from the
balcony and closed the doors. "Don't count on another
leader, my friend. The young upstart who calls himself Shah
has no following in this country. I keep him around only
because he is a symbol, and at this point Iran needs symbols.
I am the man you must deal with. And if I go, it will be the
Soviets who take my place."

"We have a new President . . ."

"Eisenhower. I have never met him."

"He wants peace in the Middle East," Steer said, trying
not to sound pious.

"Everyone wants peace, but Britain wants a piece of
Iran—its oil fields."

"As a friend and a man I respect, let me warn you, Dr.
Mossadeq, that President Eisenhower will never betray the
British. That must be the assumption on which you base
everything else."

"Are you suggesting that he might even collaborate with
them to replace me?"

"I said nothing of the kind." Steer turned away from
Mossadeq. He wondered how much the old fox already
knew.

"My friends tell me that Sir Anthony Raven and his
associates are making certain plans with the American CIA.
Of course, my friends could be wrong . . .?"

"Raven? I've heard of him only in connection with the
Anglo-Iranian Oil Company. I know of nothing between
him and the CIA," Steer answered firmly. He did not want

139

to mislead Mossadeq. He had, in fact, been told nothing about a CIA intervention in Iran. Under Dean Acheson he knew he would be told—but under Dulles, he was not so certain.

"Of course, it's possible that certain parties in London are making claims just to intimidate Iran. But didn't Raven work with Dulles during the war?"

"Allen Dulles was in the OSS. I have no idea about Raven."

"In any case, I just wanted you to know the sort of things that are being said—whether they are true or not."

"I am glad you are keeping me informed." Steer realized that Mossadeq wanted him to let Washington know that he was on to their plan. But was there really a plan? he wondered.

"Any United States intervention into our internal politics would be disastrous, as you must realize. Iranians consider the Americans our friends. We still wave to your sailors when they come into our ports. We don't expect treachery."

"What do you expect?" Steer interrupted. He could feel that the moment was right to press Mossadeq.

"We expect American aid. I am writing a letter to Eisenhower asking for a loan of one hundred and fifty million dollars to see us over the next six months. By that time, if the British don't accept our terms, we can arrange to sell the oil to American companies." He made a few hasty calculations with his fingers. He was now acting like a Persian businessman.

"Oil is a very complicated business, Your Excellency. The international oil companies might not want the American independents to have the oil."

"We can't worry about their problems, can we, Ambassador? I want this letter to be hand delivered to your President. That is why I asked you here. I do not even want to use an Iranian to translate it. If it got into the hands of my opponents . . ." Mossadeq took a typed, three-page letter out of his briefcase and handed it to Steer.

"I will use my personal translator, Dr. Sallah," Steer offered.

Mossadeq nodded. "This loan is of vital importance."

"I'll do my best—but you mustn't underestimate the strength of the alliance between the United States and Britain, Doctor." Steer stood up.

"Yes. Churchill and Eisenhower. I'll keep that in mind." He ended the interview with a wave of his hand.

On his return to the Embassy, Steer found an EYES ONLY telegram for him. It was from the new Secretary of State, John Foster Dulles. He read with some concern that Kim Adams, Dulles' personal representative, would be arriving in Iran on February first. Steer was to provide him with "all and any support he requests, on a no-questions-asked basis."

Chapter XIV

ROOM SERVICE

"Now tell me about Raven," Jasmine quietly asked Tina, as she delicately maneuvered a swab of damp absorbent cotton around the dark orbit of his wounded eye. The cool alcohol felt good. So did the warmth of her hand as it brushed his cheek. He sat on one of two twin beds. The hotel room, heavily padded in a golden plush, reminded him of the interior of a jewelry box.

"Be still for a moment," Tina said, standing over him and supporting his head with one hand. As she bent over him, he could see the shadow between her breasts. He felt paralyzed by her nearness as she removed the last vestige of dried blood.

"When did you first meet Raven?" he asked.

She paused for a moment, then sat beside him and looked

into his pale eyes. They were very demanding. She decided it would be best to give him a carefully censored version. "I met Raven first on a boat in St. Tropez, and then again in England. We talked about his paintings. I must admit, I found him intriguing. Then he asked me to have dinner with him and another man that I might recognize, but I wasn't to let on that I knew who he was. He even told me what to wear: a blue velvet dress, which he bought for me. The three of us dined that night by candlelight in Raven's home. I recognized his guest instantly as Anthony Eden."

"The British Foreign Minister?"

"Yes. They talked about empire and power, looking at each other all the time as if I weren't even at the table. Every once in a while, Raven would touch me—like he owned me ..." She stopped, frowning slightly, then continued. "After dinner, he took me home in his Rolls-Royce and said he wanted me to become his mistress. I didn't say anything. But I wanted to see him again. The next week he invited me to another dinner, and paraded me around as if I were already his. He sat me next to a blue-bearded Armenian with a spidery orchid in his lapel, and practically offered me to him for the night. And suddenly, I no longer felt awed. I was only amused by his assumption of such power over me. I laughed out loud and he got very angry, then turned away. I didn't hear from him for almost a month, until he took me to his house in Chelsea to see a painting he had just acquired. It was Dante Gabriel Rossetti's portrait of his sister. He knew it was a painting that I particularly loved, and he told me that I could have it if I would pose for him. I left, planning never to see him again. Then, tonight, he was leaving the Gaming Center when I came in." She rested her head in her hands as she completed the story.

"What did Raven ask Eden for, at that dinner?"

"He was telling him, not asking him."

"What?"

"He wanted Eden to do something about someone. He said something like 'Unless he goes, England will be looking down the barrel of his gun.' "

"Whose gun, Tina? Whose?"

"Mossadeq's."

"Then that's the man whose assassination I've just planned."

He was interrupted by Room Service, pounding on the door. Tina leaped off the bed and vanished into the bathroom. He was impressed with her discretion, but it served little purpose, since he had ordered for two. He opened the door, and a short waiter with long, simian arms pushed a cart into the room without even looking up. "Two club sandwiches, french fries, a bowl of fruit, and a pitcher of coffee." As he ticked off each item, he produced it from one of the various compartments of his cart with a magician's flourish. The top of the cart opened into a small table, and the waiter proceeded to set it for two. Jasmine scribbled his name across a bill and slipped the waiter three crumpled dollar bills. The waiter backed out of the room, conspicuously putting the "Do Not Disturb" sign on the door as he left.

The bathroom door opened almost immediately, and Tina, who had taken off her shoes and stockings, dashed to the table. Before she even sat down, she managed to scoop up a handful of french fries. Neither she nor her sister were inhibited eaters, Jasmine thought, as he seated himself across from her. Dipping a french fry into some ketchup on her plate, she wolfed it down, leaving a red smudge on one corner of her mouth.

"Of course, it's all guesswork," he puzzled out loud, "but

Raven did use a false name. How can you explain that without being conspiratorial?"

"Maybe he's simply a man of mystery," Tina said between mouthfuls of her sandwich. She could see that Jasmine was headed down the track of a conspiracy. Oddly enough, it amused her in some perverse way to be involved with two men who were both part of the same mystery.

Jasmine watched Tina plunge the last wedge of her sandwich into her mouth. He noticed that the top three buttons of her blouse had come undone, and he could see where her honey-colored tan halted abruptly at the periphery of her pale breasts.

She bit into a peach in her hand, and in a moment reduced it to a pit. She couldn't understand why she was suddenly so hungry, but she knew it had something to do with Jasmine.

Jasmine poured himself a cup of coffee, still pondering the problem of the coup d'etat in Iran. Was he being logical? Had he inadvertently excluded some alternative explanation? And why was Tina looking at him so directly?

"Watch out, you're spilling your ..." She motioned toward his coffee cup.

Her warning made his hands tremble even more, and he felt the hot coffee soaking into his clothes and scalding his knee. It had been a day full of pain and surprises. Then, as she leaned over and tried to wipe the pool of coffee from the table, he took her hand.

When she opened her mouth to speak, he kissed her lightly on the corner of the lips. He could taste the peach juice as he moved his mouth from one corner of hers to the other.

She slid into his coffee-stained lap, and shut her eyes. She waited for him to relax his embrace, then, using both hands for leverage, pushed him away so she could look into his eyes again. "Don't worry about Arabella. She should have told you that she is involved with someone in England."

He felt a sudden flush of jealousy. He had never thought of Arabella as having another lover. But why not? She was certainly proficient at lovemaking, he reflected. And why should it bother him? If anything, it would simply make it easier for him to be with Tina. Nevertheless, it did bother him.

Tina kissed him on one cheek, then the other. "Everyone else at Harvard bored Arabella—you excited her. You were the only one who would play her conspiratorial games. She believes everything in life is a conspiracy."

"Let's not talk about Arabella," he implored. He quickly undid the remaining buttons on her blouse, then put his hands between the silk and her skin, sliding his arms around her thin back. "Stay," he whispered.

Jasmine carried her over to one of the beds, and turned out the lights. She shed her slacks by undulating her long legs.

"You take the tops," he smiled, pulling his pajamas out of the briefcase. Jasmine slowly took off his own clothes. He could see Tina in the mirror, slipping into the pajama top with one graceful movement.

A moment later, she slipped into bed beside him. She felt his hand brushing her hair from her neck, but she froze, wondering whether she were betraying her sister.

Why isn't she responding, Jasmine thought as he kissed her face. He tried hard not to make incestuous comparisons with Arabella, but found himself touching Tina in all the same places. Finally, she moved slowly toward him.

"I told you you couldn't expect to go from one sister to the other so easily."

He didn't loosen his embrace until he fell asleep. After

he'd stopped tumbling into sleep, he began to dream that he was trying to read some writing on a metal surface. It was silvery and very shiny. First, he thought it was some foreign language that he didn't understand, then he realized it was simply inverted English. But whenever he tried to turn a word backward in his head, it faded. In the distance he heard the ringing of bells. He could make out one letter in the first word—*X*. The bells grew louder and a hand tapped him on the back. He woke up, realizing that the word was *AJAX* and that the phone was ringing. Tina answered it before he could stop her. He heard her say, "Arabella, I'll speak to you tomorrow." Tina sat frozen, with her head in her hands. Jasmine realized that Arabella had called his room, and now she would know everything.

Chapter XV

WALTZ NIGHT

Jasmine's first stop the next morning was the Gaming Center. Flashing his State Department pass, he breezed by the double set of guards. He walked briskly up the main corridor, turning left as usual at the research library, and took the elevator to the fourth floor. Then down the empty, windowless hallway that led to the Center. As he expected, the double doors were locked. Picking up the red phone, he asked for John McNab. Then he waited. Last night, while lying next to Tina, he decided that he had no choice but to get to the bottom of this absurd Game of Nations.

"What can I do for you, Professor?" McNab said as he ambled down the corridor. With his bad teeth and lean, pointed head, he reminded Jasmine of a ferret.

"About the misunderstanding yesterday ... I thought I

148

owed you an explanation, John," he answered, hoping to
establish a first-name camaraderie with the security officer.

"I was wondering about that," McNab said.

"You see, I thought Raven was breaking security, being
here . . ."

"He had a pass," McNab answered, lighting his Sherlock
Holmes pipe with a single match.

"But he's on the operational side," Jasmine bluffed. He
picked the phrase "operational side" out of a spy movie he
had recently seen.

"Is he now?" McNab smiled. He inserted a quarter-sized
mint in his yellow teeth; it dissolved into a brown smudge.

"I didn't think Kim should have brought him here. It
could compromise the Game," Jasmine fished again with his
movie-spy lingo.

"If Kim brought him here, I wouldn't worry about it,
Professor."

"I guess you're right, John," Jasmine said, giving up the
fight. McNab was simply parroting everything he said. He
turned to go.

"Kim is one of our shrewdest operators, Professor. I served
with him in the OSS . . ." McNab continued.

Jasmine wheeled around and looked into McNab's blood-
shot eyes. He knew a little bit about the OSS—the Oh, So
Social, as they used to call the intelligence agency when he
served in Venezuela. They were all Harvard, Yale, and
Princeton boys in Venezuela, who considered themselves the
crème de la crème, and liked to jump behind enemy lines.
McNab sounded like Notre Dame or some Big Ten college.
He wondered how he had wormed his way into the OSS.
"In the Middle East, I'll bet." Jasmine took a stab in the
dark.

"In Iran. We bounced around for a month on camels with

Qashqai tribesmen. Kim had those beggars map out the oil fields for us."

"It must be a lot duller for him now at ..." Jasmine hesitated as he saw McNab's mouth open.

"The Agency has its moments. Kim seems to think that Ajax is going to be one of them."

"What ... ?" Jasmine started to ask, before swallowing his question in a single gulp. He realized that the only "Agency" McNab could mean was the "Agency" that had succeeded the OSS—the Central Intelligence Agency. Now it all made sense—the elaborate security precautions, McNab's sweeping the room, the expensively programmed computer, Kim Adams, Tracy and his professors. This wasn't the State Department. The Gaming Center was a CIA front. He didn't have to ask McNab anything anymore; he had no doubts for whom he was playing the Ajax scenario.

"Too bad you won't be going over this time, John," Jasmine said, giving McNab a fatherly pat on the back.

"Going over?"

"To Iran." Jasmine smiled. He began walking back. McNab trailed a few feet behind him.

"The walls have ears, Professor. You can't be too careful these days, never know where a limpet might be concealed." He caught up with Jasmine at the end of the corridor. "Anyhow, no more riding with the Qashqai for me. I do security these days. Only action I get now is from playing chess. Sad." McNab disappeared around a turn.

Jasmine took the elevator back down to the main floor and on a sudden impulse ducked into the research library. It was empty, except for a hairy man sitting at a long table flipping through a foot-high stack of papers and a short, buxom redhead of about thirty, who shifted her weight nervously from one leg to the other as she stared at him. "Can I help you, sir?" she finally asked.

Jasmine displayed first his official pass, then his unofficial smile, and finally, when she looked up, his most beseeching glance. He had learned from long experience that women found him most attractive when he appeared helpless. "Sorry to bother you ..." he stammered meekly, going into his distracted-professor routine. "I'm Doctor Jasmine ... from the Gaming Center on the fourth floor...."

"No bother at all. That's what I'm here for, Doctor." She crossed her white arms defensively over her chest, a habit of long duration, and awaited his request.

"We're doing contingency planning ... crisis management, you know?" She didn't, but nodded anyway. He knew that his penetration of the library had been successful—so far. "I thought I'd better look at some of the reports on the oil industry in Iran." He had a good deal of experience with librarians, and knew how to maneuver them to the card catalogs. "Could we take a look?"

He followed closely behind as she walked to an alcove marked "Authorized Persons Only Past This Point." When she reached the wall of small sliding drawers, she asked, "Do you mind waiting back there?" She pointed back to the entranceway of the alcove.

"That's all right. I'm authorized." He smiled. "And I wouldn't want you to have to pull out more documents than is absolutely necessary."

She acquiesced and pulled out a long wooden drawer under the label "IR–IT." "Israel, Ireland, Iraq"—she worked backward to Iran. As she thumbed through the cards, she gave out short sighs of exasperation. "Now exactly what was it you wanted to see?"

"What do you have on the Iranian oil industry?" he asked, peering over her shoulder.

"Here is the report you want, I think, Number 811, 'The Nationalization of Iranian Oil: Economic and National

Security Implications.' " She lifted the card out. "Oh, it's been withdrawn."

He could see the handwritten note at the bottom of the card, which read: "Withdrawn from circulation, November 1, 1952, by order of Secretary of State." The date November first stuck in his mind. He strained to recall it, then remembered it was the date that Tracy asked him to begin working on the Ajax round.

"I'm sorry, all of the reports on the Iranian oil industry seem to have been withdrawn," the librarian said with a shrug of her shoulders.

"Is that usual?" he asked, pressing closer against her to have a better look for himself.

"I wouldn't know. I've just been working here for a week. Miss Sloane, the chief librarian, should be back from lunch any moment."

He retreated a step, bowing his head in defeat, and looking at her with sad eyes.

"Just a minute ... there is one report we just got in this morning on oil in the Middle East or something like that ... I was just about to catalog it."

He followed her back to the table of neatly stacked documents where he had originally encountered her. She plucked one report from a stack in the corner. "We're not supposed to make it available before we catalog it, but ..."

"Just let me take a quick look at it to see if it's what I want." He took it from her hand, and the title leaped out at him: REPORT BY THE DEPARTMENT OF JUSTICE: INVESTIGATION OF THE INTERNATIONAL OIL CARTEL. It began: "Following cancellation of the wartime suspension of antitrust investigations and prosecution of the oil industry, investigation of the worldwide cartel activities was resumed." His eyes skipped to the next paragraph, attracted by the mention of Raven's company, Anglo-

Iranian Oil. "Investigative efforts reveal the outline of a world petroleum cartel formed in 1928 by Anglo-Iranian Oil, Royal Dutch Shell, and Standard Oil of New Jersey. Over the succeeding years, four other American companies joined the cartel—Standard Oil of California, Mobil, Texaco, and Gulf. It appears that the uninterrupted extension of this basic cartel agreement has resulted in a worldwide pattern in which seven of the major oil companies (1) control all major producing areas outside the United States; (2) control all foreign refining operations; (3) effectively divide world markets; (4) maintain noncompetitive world prices for oil; and (5) control all foreign pipelines and world tanker transportation facilities."

So this was why the government needed the cooperation of the cartel in Iran, and why the cartel case now had to be shelved. He had just reached the section titled "National Security Implications" when the report was suddenly whisked out of his hands. He looked up into the bulging eyes of a tall, plain woman wearing heavy horn-rimmed glasses. She did not look as though she would be amenable to any male's charms, at least not like the redhead quaking beside her.

"Doctor Jasmine, this is Miss Sloane," said the redhead, withdrawing as fast as she could.

"This is a classified document, sir," Miss Sloane said, clenching the report tightly in her hand. "It has not even been cataloged yet. May I see your clearance?"

Backing away, he again displayed his pass. But it obviously had no magic for Miss Sloane. "I'm working at the Gaming Center." He again tried bumbling his way out.

"This pass is not valid for the research library," declared Miss Sloane in a voice directed at the redhead, who shrank back even farther. "I'm afraid I'm going to have to report this to Security." She carefully copied his name on a sheet of paper. "We have to respect the rules, you know . . ."

He didn't wait for her to complete her sentence. He shot a baffled look at the redhead, turned, and dashed out the door. He quickened his step as he passed the guards. He knew that Miss Sloane would report him to her security officer who would, in turn, get in touch with McNab. He pictured the look of horror on McNab's face when he discovered that Jasmine had no security clearance whatsoever. McNab might figure out then that Jasmine had conned information out of him about Adams and the CIA. He would immediately call Tracy.

There was a lone taxi waiting in the circular drive in front of the State Department. Jasmine dived in, his mind still trying to track the chain of events that he had set in motion in the library.

"Mr. Calvin, right? You ordered a Yellow Cab?"

"Right," lied Jasmine, "we're going to M and Eighteenth Street."

"I thought you wanted to go to the airport?"

"Change of plans," he said, spying a man whom he presumed to be the real Mr. Calvin trying to signal the cab. "Let's go."

The taxi dropped him a few minutes later in front of Sam's Sartorial Shoppe. A red-lipped dummy in black tie and tails smiled rigidly through the plateglass window. Jasmine checked that he had his wallet, which he automatically did whenever he was on the verge of spending money, and proceeded inside.

"Hello there, I'm Sam," said a short, spunky man with a heavy Jewish accent.

"So you want to look handsome?" he asked, measuring Jasmine as he talked.

"I need to rent a tuxedo for tonight. Do you have one for about twenty dollars?"

"Don't worry. I'll fix you up. How tall are you?"

"Six foot four."

The short man pulled his tape measure around Jasmine's waist and shoulders. "Have just what you need," he said, handing him a tuxedo to try on.

It fit well enough, Jasmine thought, as he looked at himself in a full-length mirror. "Jasmine the Gigolo," he mused, mocking his own good looks. He was pleased with himself for having gotten a few morsels of information out of McNab and the assistant librarian. He rehearsed a number of variations of the knowing look he hoped to employ that night at Tracy's dinner. Then he paid the deposit on the rented tuxedo and rushed back to the hotel to meet Tina.

He half-expected to find the room empty except for a note explaining that she had gone back to Cambridge. He would not have really blamed her. But the moment he opened the door, he was reassured. Tina was wearing a silky green taffeta dress that left her shoulders bare. Her freshly dried hair flowed down her back. She modeled the dress for him with a few twirls that sent the skirt sailing in the air. "Are you surprised to find me ready?" she asked with a dazzling smile.

She stepped into his shadow and straightened the black bow tie around his neck. "Not on the lips," she said, tilting her head back and offering him her neck to kiss.

In the elevator, he pulled her to him by both wrists and pressed against her. He could hardly feel the elevator going down. He let her go only when the door opened on the second floor and two Midwestern businessmen got into the elevator. He knew Tina did not like public displays of affection.

The taxi driver took almost an hour to find Tracy's secluded home in the Virginia suburbs, and then another five minutes to negotiate the winding driveway to the front door. The rambling white house was nestled on the top of a hill, and partly hidden on one side by an overgrowth of rhododendron bushes. On the other side, a lawn, still covered with drifts of snow, led down to the bank of the Potomac. Between the house and the river was a tennis court and a Victorian-style greenhouse. Jasmine could see that the taxi driver was impressed with the estate.

Tracy met them at the door. "Jake, glad you could make it. And this must be . . . ?"

"Christina Winchester," Jasmine filled in the blank, then added to Tina, "This is our host, Bronson Tracy."

Tina gave Tracy an enchanting smile as he helped her off with her coat and handed it to a Filipino servant. Jasmine threw his own coat over the man's outstretched arm, then followed Tracy and Tina into the party. ". . . About time someone revived the Viennese waltz . . . We just don't know the meaning of romance anymore," Tracy was saying.

They plunged into semidarkness, the rooms being lit only by candlelight. As Jasmine's eyes gradually adjusted to the flickering light, he could dimly discern black-suited men whirling gowned women around a circular dance floor as a string ensemble played a Strauss waltz. A moment later, he saw a ring of café tables around which people sat eating their dinner. Tracy lifted two chilled glasses of champagne for them from a passing waiter's tray, then led them to an adjoining room where a queue of guests waited patiently in front of a long buffet table. "Food," Tina whispered delightedly in his ear.

"Jake, I'd like you to meet a friend of mine from Yale," Tracy said, tugging Jasmine toward a stocky man with owlish circles under his bloodshot eyes. "Professor Lassbloom, this is the young political scientist from Harvard that I was telling you about, Jake Jasmine."

Lassbloom smiled by wrinkling his nose and opening his

mouth wide. "Ah, you wrote the paper on Praetorian Politics for the Council. Very good indeed. What brings you to Washington, Jasmine?"

"I came here to plan a coup d'etat." Jasmine deliberately spoke in a loud, drunken voice. Confrontation was to be the final test of his theory. He'd find out soon enough whether or not this conspiracy was anything other than a figment of his imagination.

Lassbloom wasn't smiling. His lips clamped closed, his eyes narrowed, and he retracted the hand that he had extended a moment before. Nor was there any sign of amusement on Tracy's face. Tina broke the stony silence, gagging on a gulp of champagne.

Tracy muttered, "Jake, be careful . . ."

"Have you seen the Ajax scenario, Professor?" persisted Jasmine. "The CIA did a pretty good job, I'd say."

"I am here to advise the Department of Justice on an antitrust matter that I don't think would interest you." Lassbloom pronounced each word slowly and distinctly, allowing a slight Teutonic accent to creep through.

"The International Cartel Case?" Jasmine punted again. "No doubt it will be called off to facilitate the coup in Iran."

"How do you know about this matter?" Lassbloom demanded, looking at Tracy.

"He doesn't. He's drunk," Tracy shot back defensively.

"Dance with me, Jake," Tina intervened. Winning a brief tug-of-war with Tracy, she pulled Jasmine onto the dance floor. On their first turn around the waxed floor, she realized that he was not overly proficient at the waltz. He improvised as he went along, imitating the other dancers.

"I'm sorry," he said, stumbling over her foot. "I thought I could prove something by confronting Lassbloom. All I managed to do was lose the possibility of a tenured job at

Yale." He pressed her into a deep dip, as couples were doing on either side.

"On the contrary, Jake, I'd say they gave themselves away."

"But they didn't say anything ..."

"It doesn't matter what they *said*. Didn't you see the expression on Tracy's face when you mentioned the CIA? It was as if you had mentioned his secret mistress. His jaw began trembling, his eyes turned white—the pupils began contracting so fast, he turned pale. And the Professor—I could see he understood everything you said. He was furious at Tracy; he thought that he had told you about the plan." She pressed her hand against the back of his neck as he turned her, and she could feel that it was moist.

He looked at her, wondering if she could detect the panic in a man's face as easily as she could detect fraud in a painting. Did he now have to rely on her intuition for his evidence? He tried to reconstruct Tracy's expression in his mind, but couldn't. Then he looked past Tina's shoulder and saw Kim Adams. "Let's give it another try, Tina," he said, taking her by the hand and leading her toward Adams.

"Kim, nice seeing you. ... This is Christina Winchester ... Christina ... Kim." Adams stood there, penguinlike, arms folded behind his back. "I'm Jasmine ... from the Ajax game ..." Jasmine began again, extending his hand.

"Right," Adams replied, without bothering to shake hands.

"When will you be leaving for Iran, Kim?"

"Not sure yet," Adams said in a bored voice, then turned toward Tina.

"But you will have to go to Iran at some point."

"Why me?" Adams looked distractedly around the room as if he didn't want to miss anyone important.

"You will have to persuade the Shah to follow the Ajax

scenario. . . ." For the scenario to succeed in Iran, Jasmine deduced that it would be necessary to have the Shah in on the game.

Adams looked at Jasmine with evident distaste for a minute, then turned to Tina again. "Would you like another glass of champagne, Miss Winchester?" He handed her a glass from a passing tray without waiting for her answer, then added, "Not very good champagne, and your friend has unfortunately had one too many. I hope he gets home all right." He began to walk away. "Please excuse me now." As he passed Jasmine he said through clenched teeth, "Learn to shut up, you bloody fool." Then he passed through a group of guests and disappeared into the semidarkness.

Jasmine took Tina's glass of champagne from her hand and finished it. Then he pulled her back onto the dance floor. "What do you think of Kim Adams?—the Lanny Budd of the CIA."

"He's certainly in control of himself. He hardly batted an eye when you mentioned the Ajax scenario, Jake. I couldn't read anything at all on his face—except contempt for you."

Jake turned just then and saw Professor Lassbloom, Tracy, and Adams sidling up to him. For a moment they stared at him like three doctors consulting on a serious case. Then Tracy spoke. "Jake, I think there has been some sort of misunderstanding." He smiled and hooked his arm through the crook of Jake's elbow. "Can we talk about it?" With a gentle pull, Tracy separated him from Tina. "If you could spare him a moment, Miss Winchester? Something important has come up." He smiled at her as he guided Jasmine to a small porch off the main room.

The porch was even darker than the other rooms. Jasmine sat on a wicker glider. Tracy pulled up a chair facing him; Adams and Lassbloom stood off to either side. "Now what's all this nonsense about the CIA and Iran?" Tracy asked.

"And the international cartel case," Lassbloom added.

"There's not much I can tell you that you don't already know," Jasmine said, trying to sound confident. He knew he was in too deeply now to try and do anything except continue his bluff. "It's obvious that the CIA is going to use the Ajax scenario to stage a coup d'etat in Iran and get rid of Mossadeq for the oil cartel." He watched Tracy as he spoke, and he understood what Tina meant about how his panic showed in his face.

"That's an idiotic idea, Jake," Tracy said.

"If it were really idiotic we wouldn't be sitting here now, would we? And you wouldn't be sweating, Tracy," Jasmine responded.

"Jasmine, it's clear to me that you are confusing a hypothetical game with your own personal fantasy of power," Lassbloom suggested in a husky whisper.

"If it's only a fantasy, then you gentlemen won't mind if I tell it to *The Washington Post,* will you?"

"I would mind, Jasmine," Adams cut in roughly. "You would compromise a national security operation, damn it! I always thought you would figure it out," Adams sighed. "Someone who was clever enough to design the scenario would also see through it. We should have let you in on it from the beginning. You might as well explain it all to him, Tracy ... and also explain why he can't tell anyone." Shaking his head, Adams left the other three men on the porch.

Tracy walked to a cabinet at the far end of the porch, poured himself a stiff drink, then returned to his seat and began, adopting a humbler tone. "Kim's right, of course. We had no business trying to fool you, Jake. If you had been told what the real problem was in Iran, I know you would have *willingly* cooperated ..."

"In an assassination?" queried Jasmine, decisively shaking his head no.

"In an effort to restore democracy, Jake," Tracy continued in a pious tone, although he was obviously still rattled.

"Democracy ... or oil?" Jasmine needled. He found Tracy's pretense of idealism nauseating. It was bad enough that they had tried to dupe him once, he thought, and now they were trying to do it again.

"Look, Jasmine," Lassbloom intervened, "let's not play the part of a naive civics teacher. Of course, oil is a part of it. Mossadeq's government is bankrupt. No one will buy his nationalized oil, and even if Iran found a customer, the oil cartel wouldn't provide tankers to ship the oil. The country has no other source of revenue. In the best of all possible worlds, a thing like this wouldn't happen. But the fact that the United States government is faced with is that the Mossadeq government will collapse sometime in the next one hundred and fifty days. If we do nothing, the country will be thrown into chaos, and the Communists will take over. Some twenty million Iranians will lose their freedom, and Western Europe and Japan will lose their main source of oil. That could lead to a wholesale collapse of NATO. Are those facts clear enough for you, Professor Jasmine?"

Jasmine squirmed slightly in his seat under Lassbloom's gaze. "Those are your facts, Professor. You can marshal them however you like. All I know is that you are planning to murder an old man to please the oil cartel—and I won't have any part of it."

"Murder Mossadeq?" Lassbloom screwed up his entire face with exaggerated repugnance. "Do you think I would have any part in an assassination? Be reasonable, young man. You yourself worked out the scenario for the coup—it's bloodless as far as I know. The Shah makes a gesture of dismissing Mossadeq, then flees the country, there are a few staged demonstrations, the army intervenes and restores the Shah to his rightful throne. After that, there will be free elections ..."

"What about Option B?" Jasmine played his trump card.

"Option B?" Lassbloom opened his hands in a gesture of bafflement.

"Option B was a contingency plan that I asked Jasmine to draw up," Tracy explained. "The National Security Council decided to drop it from the scenario, so I didn't bother telling you about it, Professor." Tracy then turned to Jasmine, "No one wanted to see old Mossy killed. I just wanted to see what repercussions there might be if the worst happened, so I asked you to run it through the game."

"You've definitely decided to drop it ...?" Jasmine repeated.

"Christ, yes, that was decided three weeks ago. I couldn't tell you, of course, because you weren't supposed to know Ajax was anything but a game."

"In any case, I don't see why even a bloodless coup is necessary. There must be other means ..." Jasmine argued on, but felt himself slipping slowly from his pinnacle of moral righteousness.

"I don't understand everything that happens either, Jake," Tracy said softly. "The National Security Council simply ordered us to prepare this contingency plan to prevent Iran from going Communist. Perhaps we'll never use it. That's up to Eisenhower, not us. We have to be good soldiers."

"You might have to follow orders, but I'm not in the CIA and I don't work for the government!" Jasmine shouted, trying to regain the initiative.

"Jake, you present us with a bit of a problem. The Ajax scenario has already been approved by the National Security

Council and by Eisenhower. It is also classified 'Top Secret.' We need your cooperation. . . ." Tracy now spoke in a very authoritative tone.

"That's too bad. You should have been more discreet." Jasmine stood up to go.

"Please sit down," Lassbloom said, with a note of desperation in his voice. "If you act recklessly, Mr. Jasmine, you could wreck your whole academic career."

"Are you threatening me, Professor?"

"Of course not," Lassbloom said. "Just consider the situation."

"It's your decision, Jake," Tracy piped in. "Think it over at least. Maybe tomorrow things will seem clearer. If you change your mind, come over to the Gaming Center, and we'll arrange a security clearance for you. If not, no hard feelings." Tracy walked over to the door and clasped Jasmine's right hand in both of his.

"O.K., I'll sleep on it and call you in the morning," Jasmine agreed, retracting his hand. He thought it best to leave on amicable terms. In the morning, he would call and refuse them flatly. He stepped quickly through the porch doors into the living room.

I've got to get out of here, he thought. He assumed that Tina, always hungry, would be gorging herself at the buffet table, but there was no sign of her there. He began methodically weaving in and out of the ring of café tables, thinking she must have sat down somewhere, but he completed the circle without finding her. Next, he made a rushed inspection of the periphery of the room, then the anteroom, both without success. Even though he felt it totally implausible, he couldn't entirely suppress the idea that the CIA, or someone, had seized Tina as a hostage. After another twenty minutes of rushing over to thin women in green who turned out, on closer view, to be total strangers, he began to panic.

163

When someone tapped him on the shoulder, he spun around.

"Your taxi is waiting," Tracy said, smiling graciously.

"Have you seen Tina ... I can't seem to find her." For some reason, he was out of breath.

"She seems to be having a lovely time," said Tracy, pointing to the dance floor.

Jasmine instantly recognized the green taffeta. Tina was being moved very gracefully around in circles by a gray-haired man a few inches shorter than she whom he also recognized—Raven. Keeping his eyes on Tina, Jasmine waited on the edge of the dance floor for the music to stop, then moved forward.

Raven returned the still smiling Tina to Jasmine's outstretched hand. "Sorry about the other day, old man.... Thought you were some sort of a thug ... Automatic reactions, commando training in the war, and all that. Tina's been telling me about you. Let's have a drink."

"Some other time. I have a cab waiting now," he said, not wanting to get entangled any further. "Let's go," he demanded, and whisked Tina off. "I'll explain in the cab, but we have to get out of here," he added when they were out of earshot. He managed to get her into her coat and almost through the door when she stopped dead in her tracks.

"Please, Jake, can't we get something to eat? I haven't had anything all night and I'm famished." She had learned at school in England it was always effective to use hyperbole, so she added, "Unless you want to see me shrivel away with malnutrition...."

Jasmine rushed back to the buffet and filled a plate with an enormous mound of crabmeat salad. Then he scooped up a handful of scampi and threw them on top of the crabmeat. As several people looked on, he put two large drumsticks in his overcoat pockets, and proceeded to the fruit bowl, where he plucked out three pears and stuffed them into his already bulging pocket. "It's for my cat," he explained to an open-mouthed woman with a diamond tiara in her grey hair.

He got into the cab with Tina at one hand and the plate in the other and headed back into Washington. "No silverware," he apologized, handing Tina a drumstick. She was not deterred. She ignored the curious looks the driver gave her and treated it all like a summer picnic. She gnawed through the drumstick, devoured the scampi, and dipped her fingers into the crabmeat salad. While she ate, he tried to tell her what had happened on the porch.

"Could they really get you fired?" she asked while sucking the last bit of flavor from a scampi shell. "You could always get another teaching job, couldn't you?"

"It wouldn't be that easy." He passed her a pear, seeing that she had finished with the seafood. "But I figure they can't really complain about me without revealing their own role in the coup—and I don't think they'll do that."

When they arrived back at the hotel, there was a hand-delivered envelope waiting for Jasmine. He didn't open it until they were safely in their room. Tina searched his pockets for remnants of the feast, and found the other drumstick, which she chewed on while she undressed.

The manila envelope contained a typewritten note, which stated in block letters, "DISCRETION IS THE BETTER PART OF VALOR," and seven glossy eight-by-ten photographs. For a moment, he thought that someone was trying to sell him some very explicit pornography. Then he realized that the naked girl was Arabella, the naked man himself, and the setting, the leather couch in his office. As he quickly shuffled through the pictures, he could see Arabella going through her acrobatic act with him. It was like an old flickering movie. In the last picture, he could even see the

165

fawnlike expression on her lips. He wondered where they had hidden the camera. There was no question in his mind that these pictures, if shown to anyone, would completely wreck his chances of ever teaching again—even in a high school. The rules of the game were very strict: if you seduce a student, don't get caught.

"What are you looking at?" Tina asked. She was now wearing nothing but the green shoes. He slipped the photographs back in their envelope and took the drumstick out of her mouth. He felt her kick her shoes off as he held her tightly against him. In the morning, he knew, he would send her back to Cambridge alone—but he couldn't help wondering if they would be photographed that night.

CHAPTER XVI

LIE DETECTION

"Is your name Jacob Jasmine?" McNab asked, one word at a time.

"You know damn well it is, John," snarled Jasmine. Turning around, he could see McNab nibbling a chocolate, and Tracy chain smoking.

"Please, Professor, just answer yes or no to each question ... and please look straight ahead at the wall, and be very still—otherwise, it throws the machine off," McNab instructed him.

Jasmine sat very still and stared at the blank wall in front of him. A cloth cuff, which reminded him of what doctors use to take a patient's blood pressure, was wrapped around his right wrist. A corrugated rubber tube, which looked like a vacuum cleaner hose, was coiled around his chest. A metal

167

plate was pressed fast against the palm of his left hand. McNab had already patiently explained that the cuff would measure changes in his breathing pattern, and the metal plate would measure changes in his perspiration rate. As he answered questions, these measurements would be recorded by three pens on a slow-moving roll of graph paper. Supposedly, these wavering lines would then tell McNab whether he was telling the truth or lying. "Do you really think this lie detector works, Bronson—or is it just supposed to intimidate me?"

"A polygraph test, of course, requires interpretation, but it does seem to be very good at catching the sort of emotional stress that is frequently associated with lying," Tracy explained, slightly frayed by Jasmine's questions. "In any case, everyone in the CIA gets fluttered once a year with the polygraph—it's standard procedure."

"Only I'm not in the CIA—I don't even know what I'm doing here."

"We have to give you a special security clearance ... and as I explained to you on the phone this morning, that is going to require you to take a lie detector test twice a month until Ajax is over. ... And you agreed, Jake." Tracy snuffed out one cigarette and lit another.

"You mean you blackmailed me into it."

"Who blackmailed whom, Jake?" Tracy retorted. "It was you who threatened to tell *The Washington Post* about Ajax. Now I suggest we proceed."

"Is your name Jacob Jasmine?" McNab repeated patiently. He knew that the prime virtue required of a security officer in the CIA was neither intelligence nor imagination, but patience.

"Yes."

"Did you know your father?"

"No." Jasmine knew they were trying to get a jiggle out of him by asking about a father whose name he never even knew. His mother had concealed his father's identity from him.

"Did your mother use the name Julie James?"

"Yes." That had been her stage name, and then her movie name. She lived in lights—from neonrise to neonset, she once told a Broadway columnist. Jasmine had learned to live in her flickering shadow. And now that he had just begun to make a name for himself, he was threatened by scandal. No matter how far he progressed, it seemed he was always being driven back to a secret life.

"Did you graduate with honors from UCLA?"

"Yes."

"Did you work for the Coordinator of Information in Venezuela during the war?"

"Yes." It was there that he had learned the trick of turning shadows into reality. He could still hear Nelson Rockefeller, the coordinator, outlining the problem to the psychological warfare staff: the German community in Venezuela must be discredited. Jasmine had come up with the solution: to produce a fake Nazi propaganda film that would enrage the Venezuelans. He had quickly assembled it, intercutting a real Nazi film, which depicted American exploitation of Venezuela, with some counterfeited scenes that purported to show leading Venezuelan politicians being corrupted by blonde American prostitutes. The film, titled *Yankees Abroad,* was then posted to German cultural clubs and business establishments in Caracas and, as planned, was intercepted by the Venezuelan police. When the Minister of the Interior saw himself edited into a sex party, he ordered the immediate expulsion of three hundred Germans from Caracas. Everyone in psych warfare complimented Jasmine

169

on his success, and he suddenly realized the ease with which
governments could be manipulated. He found it a bit ironic
that it was now he who was being blackmailed by sexual
photographs.

"Should I repeat the question?" McNab asked Tracy. A
twang of emotions had registered on Jasmine's graph. Tracy
examined the graph personally, then ordered McNab to
proceed.

"Have you ever been a member of a subversive organization?"

"No."

"Have you ever had a homosexual experience?"

"No."

Tracy then intervened. "I think that's a sufficient number
of test questions. Let's get on with the business at hand."
McNab flipped over a few sheets of paper and Tracy
indicated to him what he should ask.

"Do you have a student named Arabella Winchester,
Professor?"

"Yes."

"Did you make love to her on several occasions?"

"Yes." He felt himself flush. He knew the machine would
be recording the stress he felt. He also knew he had to
control his emotions. He couldn't have them knowing all his
secrets.

"Did you ever tell Miss Winchester about the Ajax
scenario?"

"No," he lied. It was time to experiment. He could hear
McNab whisper to Tracy. They had obviously found a
squiggle on the graph. He realized that he needed some sort
of strategy to outwit the machine. How could he distract his
mind enough to muffle his emotional responses? Then he
thought of a device he had used with great success to control

his own sexual excitement: he would recite one of his own political science lectures to himself.

"I am going to repeat the last question." McNab now adopted a very professional tone, like the master of ceremonies on a quiz show. "Did you ever tell Arabella Winchester anything at all about the Ajax scenario? Please think carefully before you answer."

Jasmine threw a switch in his mind and began rehearsing the lecture he had planned for Thursday. "A coup d'etat is not an assault from outside the system, but from inside. It has become increasingly feasible as a mechanism for change because modern states, even democracies, depend more and more on the control of vital data." When he felt himself comfortably imbedded in this private track, he answered the other question, "No."

He could hear Tracy telling McNab, "That's much better. No wiggles." He smiled, realizing that he had outwitted them.

The rest was easy. He told the truth about making love to Tina. He even confessed to various unusual acts of lovemaking. But when he was asked if Tina knew anything about the conspiracy, he answered negatively. He could tell by the routine rapidity with which they asked the questions that they believed him. In fact, by the time the three-hour session ended, he was sure that he had succeeded in convincing Tracy that he was the only person outside the CIA and the oil cartel that knew about the plot in Iran.

As he unstrapped him from the lie detector, McNab cautioned Jasmine, "You should be more careful, Professor. The other day you tried to trick me. You should never try to fool a professional." He had a hurt look on his face.

"I'll remember that in the future, John." Jasmine scrambled to his feet, stretched his arms, and started for the door. He wanted to get back to Cambridge on the next plane—he had to make sure that neither Tina nor Arabella would give him away by saying anything about Ajax. He had also had enough of Washington, with its computer games, candlelit waltzes, lie detectors—and everyone calling everyone Doctor, Professor, or by a first name that sounded like a last name. Tracy intercepted him before he reached the door, however.

"Do you mind if I drive you to the airport, Jake?" he asked, holding the door open for Jasmine. "There are still a few things I'd like to explain."

"Why not?" Jasmine followed Tracy through a maze of doors and corridors, eventually emerging into an underground parking garage. Tracy led him to his Mercedes. When they got outside, Jasmine was surprised to find it was a bright sunny day. He had left his hotel early that morning, after shredding the photographs to pieces and flushing them down the toilet.

"I was afraid you might have already told someone about Ajax—that would have been very serious—but the polygraph was most reassuring," Tracy explained as he steered the car. "Now all we are asking is that you don't mention anything about Ajax, Iran, or oil for the next few months ... and that you come to Washington for a few more tests—at our expense, of course. That's all you'll have to do. No one will ever know about your ... shall we say, indiscretions?" Tracy fell silent as they passed the obelisk dedicated to George Washington, and then sped onto the highway. "I'm really doing this for your own good, Jake. You have a real genius for political science. Lassbloom still hopes to get you at Yale. You have to realize intellectuals can't cop out of the Cold War—we're involved whether we want to be or not."

"You're sure it's going to be a bloodless coup?" Jasmine interrupted. He had suddenly remembered that the coup in

172

Venezuela that he had witnessed was supposed to be blood-less—until friends of his began disappearing. Their birth-dates also disappeared from the records.

"Absolutely. You heard what Lassbloom said last night. We're going to restore not only the Shah, but free elections in Iran. What we're working out is a blueprint for democracy in the Middle East—you might even find you would want to consult on it."

"Mossadeq isn't going to get killed—even by accident?" Jasmine persisted, still trying to satisfy himself.

"Absolutely not. He might be forced into exile, but you can be sure there will be no attempt on his life. Ike wouldn't stand for it."

"And Option B is out, right?"

"Damn it, Jake. Why should we lie to you? We have enough on you to make sure ..." Tracy checked himself, seeing that it was unnecessary to finish his sentence. As the car rolled to a stop at the Eastern terminal, Jasmine leaped out and rushed to catch the four o'clock shuttle to Boston. He waved good-bye in the continental style, using only the tips of his fingers.

The flight to Boston took almost two hours, and by the time Jasmine reached his apartment in Cambridge, it was completely dark. Before he even turned on the lights, he hurriedly dialed Tina's number. No answer. He began sorting through his mail, which was mostly unpaid bills. But the thought kept gnawing at the back of his mind that Tracy—or Raven—might try to get to Tina. After all, he had mentioned Ajax in front of her at the waltz. They might be curious to find out whether she had understood anything. He tried her again on the telephone without success. He then typed out a short note on his typewriter: "Tina/ Arabella. It is very important that you don't talk to strangers until you talk to me. J." and ran with it out to his car.

173

When he got to their house, there were no lights on, and he slipped the note under the door. Next he drove to Ken's Delicatessen and ordered his usual three-decker sandwich. Between each quadrant of his sandwich, he made four more calls to the unresponsive number.

On his way home, he stopped by his office. There was a message that Professor Lassbloom had called him, a recommendation form for a Rhodes scholarship that Steer had left for him to fill out, and an invitation from Professor Wiley to a faculty poker game. For lack of anything better to do, he typed out the lecture he had mentally composed earlier in the day. Then he retrieved Steer's paper from his file and read it. He couldn't concentrate. His eyes wandered around the room, trying to extrapolate the angle from which the spy camera had taken the compromising photographs. When the campus bells rang ten o'clock, he decided it was time to leave.

On the way home, he again drove past the house on Sparks Street. Seeing a solitary light on the top floor, he brought the car to a halt in a dirty snowbank. Jumping from the car, he saw someone—either Tina or Arabella—silhouetted in the window. Lights began descending from floor to floor. Before he even touched the bell, the door opened. It was Arabella. She was wearing a Chinese-style bathrobe.

"I hope I didn't get you out of bed," he apologized, seeing that he had. "I know it's late, but I've been calling you all night."

She stepped back and let him pass her into the foyer, but made no effort to break the uncomfortable silence. She just looked at him, pursing her lips.

He felt, as he had in their tutorials, that her eyes were judging his every movement, and he squirmed for a moment. He could see even in the dim hall light that she was

174

not wearing anything under the sheer robe. "Where were you?"

"I turned the phone off again," she said, her words fading into cold silence.

"Is Tina home?" he asked, avoiding her eyes.

"She left for New York this afternoon. Some emergency about a forged painting at the Met, she said. I'll have her call you when she gets back. Good night, Jake." She rushed through the news as though it had little import, turned abruptly and walked to the spiral staircase.

"New York?" he asked, with a baffled look on his face. He was confounded by Tina's unexpected trip. She always seemed to disappear when he was searching for her. "Wait a minute," he called, with a tinge of panic in his voice. She stopped on the third step. The light from the top of the staircase made her gown completely transparent. "Did you get my note?"

"Don't worry. I don't intend to speak to any strangers or ... traitors." She turned halfway around, letting a faint smile rise to her lips—then ebb.

"I must talk to you and Tina before—" He hadn't finished the sentence when she turned and continued up the stairs. He hesitated for a moment, then followed her up "—before anyone else tries to question you."

"They already have." Arabella said without looking back. "A Professor Tracy called for Tina a half-dozen times. That's why I turned off the phone." She reached the landing and proceeded into the kitchen. "Would you like some coffee?"

"Sure." He could never remember turning down a cup of coffee. Perched on a high stool, he watched her grind the fresh beans and then pour the powdered coffee into a paper cone.

"Well, what happened?" she asked as she put the kettle

on the stove to boil. She glanced quickly at him and saw that he had the hunted look on his face that she had seen before.

"Didn't Tina tell you?"

"No. She was dashing off to the airport. Anyway, I assumed you would tell me—sooner or later." She waited, leaning against the formica counter.

As he tried to explain how he had confirmed that the Game was in fact a conspiracy, he looked up into her eyes, but couldn't tell whether she approved or disapproved of what he had done. He carefully censored from his story any hint of his romantic involvement with Tina, and omitted mentioning the pornographic photographs. Just as he was describing the lie detector tests he had agreed to, he was interrupted by a whistle from the kettle. She went over and poured the water through the paper cone, waiting for the coffee to filter through.

"Do you really believe that they are not going to murder Mossadeq?" she said.

"That's what they tell me."

"And you believed them? What else could they have told you?"

"Perhaps I shouldn't have confronted them so directly. . . ."

"You really like to think of yourself as some sort of accidental man, don't you? Things just happen to you: me, Tina, a job at Harvard, an offer from Yale, Bronson Tracy, the Game of Nations, a murder plot, a consulting position with the CIA, lie detector tests . . ." Her tone changed from flip to serious. "You don't even want to take responsibility for an assassination that you planned yourself."

"Don't be ridiculous. There are things I haven't told you. . . . What you don't know is that they're blackmailing me."

"Our tutorials?" She gave a loud, throaty laugh of embarrassment.

"I'm glad you're amused." Again he felt growing frustration with Arabella.

"Anyhow, it's your decision. Mine is to go back to bed." She turned out the kitchen light and left him sitting in the dark. "Good night, Jake," she said with an inflection that reminded him of the Harvard bells.

He looked at his watch—it was almost midnight. He nursed his lukewarm coffee for another half-hour while debating what to do. He had never wanted Arabella more than he did tonight. He wondered whether she had wanted him to follow her to her room. Then he suppressed the thought. It had been a long, hard day.

BOOK TWO

Early Summer, 1953

CHAPTER XVII

THE *SANSI* INCIDENT

June, 1953, Iran. The port of Abadan had no visible signs of life. The fifty-foot-high rotary pumps looked like carousels turned on their sides. No longer were they turning to create pressure to suck the oil from the wells in the interior of Iran to the storage tanks at the refinery. The great cylindrical tanks, which sounded like giant teakettles when they boiled the toxic fumes from the oil, were now deathly silent. So were all the other enormous pressure cookers that once refined half of Europe's oil.

It was far too quiet for Captain Ambros. He poured himself another drink of ouzo as he watched Iranian soldiers struggle to connect a hose to his ship, the S.S.*Sansi.* He was not inherently a brave man, and it was only the gold coins, which he could use to buy land back in Greece, that had induced him to make such a dangerous run. The smaller tanker he commanded was owned by a syndicate of Panamanians, but chartered to a Swiss corporation for this particular voyage.

As the oil gurgled into the tank of the S.S. *Sansi,* the ship slowly sank in the water until its gunnels were barely three feet above the water line. She was carrying her maximum load—one thousand tons of oil. Ambros looked at his pocket watch. It was past midnight and time to finally open his sealed orders. They were not particularly surprising. He was to head directly for the Suez Canal, stopping nowhere, and keeping at all times in international waters. Once through the Canal, he was to deliver his consignment of oil to the ENI refinery at Callagia, Sicily, and receive his bonus— $5,000 in gold for a week's work was not bad pay, he thought, as he ordered the lines cast off.

He stayed on deck all night, guiding the *Sansi* through the Straits of Hormuz and out of the Persian Gulf. He was worried about the squadron of British warships stationed at the Tunb Islands, but they seemed to take no notice of his tiny ship. The next day he sailed around the horn of Arabia without incident. Just as he began the passage into the Red Sea, he heard the drone of airplane engines. On his right was the British colony of Aden, which he had been ordered to avoid at all costs; on his left were the shoals of Africa. Straight ahead—and almost within reach—was the Suez Canal.

Squinting into the bright sun, he could see planes circling lazily overhead. They reminded him of birds of prey. Through his field glasses, he could see the Royal Air Force markings on their wings. By his count, there seemed to be eight fighters. A minute later, the lead plane rolled out of the formation and flew directly across the bow of the ship. The pilot motioned him to turn right—toward Aden.

Ambros carefully checked his charts to make sure the *Sansi* was still in international waters. It was. Thinking of the bonus waiting for him in Sicily, he ordered the helmsman to continue on his course to the Suez Canal.

The planes widened their circle overhead. Then, one by one, they fell out of formation and opened fire with their machine guns at the water five hundred yards ahead. The bullets raised a foot-high barrier of water in the path of the *Sansi*. Ambros kept on course for another five minutes, but with the wall of machine-gun fire coming closer, he realized that he had no choice. One stray bullet could explode his highly flammable cargo. Throwing up his hands in a gesture of mock surrender, he ordered the helmsman to make a ninety-degree turn to starboard. Despite his orders, he would be landing at Aden.

It was a far cooler day at the Queens Club in London. Nubar Gulbenkian lobbed the ball high over Raven's position at the net. "Good show in Aden, Tony," he chatted as he watched Raven race back on the grass court. It had been too high a lob.

Raven was well behind the base line now. He measured the high bounce carefully, then sliced down on it. Gulbenkian, he knew, would never rush in to return a drop shot. "We couldn't let the *Sansi* get to Italy. Who knows what the Italians might be tempted to try next?"

Gulbenkian saw the drop shot coming, and accepted his defeat graciously. He knew if he rushed in to retrieve it, Raven would just lob the next one over his head. "Your game," he conceded. "Let's have something to drink."

In the bar, Raven seemed impatient about something. "Just pour it over the ice, American style," he instructed the barman, who couldn't quite accept the propriety of Scotch-on-the-rocks at the Queens.

"Quite a feat getting the *Sansi* into Aden yesterday—or was it just luck?" Gulbenkian asked, still wanting to know what had happened to the consignment of Iranian oil. The barman brought him a Gin-and-Schweppes, his usual order.

"Like all things, it required some tinkering." Then Raven went on to explain, "We had a court order impounding the oil—damn it, it is still Anglo-Iranian oil, even if the Italians refuse to recognize our ownership of it."

"But you had to get the ship into British territory to give the order any force. Wasn't that a bit tricky?"

"Just required a few RAF planes—nothing much." Raven saw no need to give all the details on the interception on the high seas. Churchill had been reluctant to violate international law when only a thousand tons of oil were involved. Raven had argued that the Italians were violating British law in buying oil from Iran, and, unless the *Sansi* was stopped dead in her tracks, the Italians would be taking ten tankers a week into Abadan. With the blockade broken, the Americans might decide to call off the coup over there. Without even bothering to reply, Sir Winston picked up the phone in 10 Downing Street and asked for the Commander of the Air Squadron in Aden.

"If nothing else, the Italians will think twice before they try to steal our oil again," Gulbenkian continued.

"Perhaps so, but they will try again. Time is against us, and we might as well face that reality."

"Unless we change the government in Iran."

"That's our only hope," Raven agreed. "And even that won't solve anything permanently. But it will give us a few years, maybe even a decade, to find something better." He looked up sharply. Gulbenkian's blue-tinted beard looked ridiculous contrasted against his tennis whites, but Raven never underestimated his wily intelligence. He was truly his father's son when it came to understanding conspiracies.

"But it may not be as easy as getting some Greek captain to heave-to in Aden ..."

"Tell your friend Darius not to worry. Everything is arranged." Raven ordered another round of drinks.

"With the Americans?"

"Yes, but ..." Raven waited while their drinks were replaced.

"But ... ?" Gulbenkian smiled.

"But the Americans are so inexperienced in this kind of business ..."

"Even your chum Dulles?"

"You won't believe this, Nubar. They have a college professor planning this whole coup as if it were some damn board game."

Gulbenkian did believe it, however. He knew instinctively that it would be useful for him to find out who this professor was. "A board game? I don't quite follow you, Tony."

"I told you you wouldn't believe it. They constructed an elaborate game of Chinese Checkers or something with electric lights on it."

"The Americans make games out of everything, even sex. Some girl from California was teaching me to play something called 'strip poker' last night. All very strange. But where I still don't follow you is why they needed this professor in the first place?"

"Well," Raven shook his head incredulously, "believe it or not, this is their first coup d'etat, and they have never developed the capacity to deal with this sort of thing. At least, that's how Dulles explains it."

Gulbenkian threw back his head and laughed. "But then ... why a professor?"

"It seems he teaches a course on coup d'etats. Did you ever hear of anything so absurd?"

"What college would give such a course?"

185

"Doesn't really matter, does it?" Raven stopped short. He didn't want to give Gulbenkian too many details. "And don't tell Darius that the Americans are virgins at this activity—until after the coup. Why give the Shah anything extra to worry about?"

"I'm going to see Darius next week in Monte Carlo."

"Reassure him, by all means. Tell him Dulles got a resolution through the National Security Council in Washington authorizing him to do whatever is necessary to protect Western interests in the Persian Gulf. He interprets this as carte blanche authority to back the Shah. The Shah can also expect an old American friend of his in Teheran soon."

"I see," Gulbenkian answered, seeing that the subject was now closed. "Do you have a plan for dinner? If you like, I could ask my California friend along . . ."

"I have work to do tonight, Nubar. Some other time." He had had enough of American game playing, he thought, as he excused himself from the table.

Gulbenkian shouted after him, a satyric smile on his face, "By the way, how is Chris?"

"She's still in America. Fallen in love with some American—temporarily."

The chauffeur sprang to open the door as Raven approached his Rolls. Without saying a word, he slumped back in his seat and thought about Chris. He wondered how he could be so successful in the world of men, and so unsuccessful with women. He could change the fate of entire nations, but he couldn't persuade one girl he fancied to sleep with him. It hurt even more to think that he had lost her to another schemer—Jasmine.

Gulbenkian watched Raven's Rolls drive off, then, finding a quiet phone in the wood-paneled locker room, he placed a transatlantic call to John Pfisster in New York. Although

Pfisster handled the Gulbenkians' business in the United States, Gulbenkian called him only on important occasions. He didn't find Pfisster amusing at all, but in legal matters he had shown himself to be both competent and discreet.

"Pfisster," he began, "there is a private matter I want you to pursue for me."

"I'll try to be of service, Mr. Gulbenkian," Pfisster responded, assuming that his eccentric employer had again involved himself with some scheming woman.

"There is a professor somewhere in America, probably in the East, who gives a course on the unlikely subject of coup d'etats. I want you to find him."

"Do you know where he teaches?"

"No. Nothing more than I told you. Employ as many people as you like, but I need to know his name, college, and background by the end of the week. Is that clear?"

"Can you tell me how this involves you . . .?" Pfisster hesitated. He wondered why Gulbenkian would want to find such a professor.

"If you must know, Pfisster, he's living with a woman who . . ."

"Say no more. Not really my business," Pfisster said, greatly relieved. "Call you back when I have something definite." Even as he spoke, he began calculating how many college catalogs would have to be reviewed. Fortunately, he was paid by the hour.

Chapter XVIII

GRADUATION

Jasmine felt faintly ridiculous in his scarlet gown. Among other things, it was several inches too short. But, as he had found out earlier that day, academic gowns came in only one size at Harvard.

"Stunning fit," Tina concluded sarcastically. She stretched out her leg from where she was sitting, touching the gap between the hem of the gown and his dark socks with the toe of her bare foot. She did like him in red, his pale eyes reflecting it like sparks in a fire. "You might as well try the cap on." Swinging it by the tassel, she flipped it over to him.

He put on the four-cornered cap, looked in the mirror, and quickly took it off. "I can't wear this. Let's forget graduation and go take a walk around Walden Pond instead."

"Nonsense." Her voice broke into laughter. "I like you like this: medieval." With both hands, she pressed the square cap back on his head. "Anyhow, we promised Arabella we'd see her graduate."

"Then you'd better get dressed. It starts in ten minutes." He watched in the mirror as she drove her long legs, one after the other, into her body stocking. He never ceased to be amazed at this ritual, though she had been with him for four months now, more or less. More, because on the nights she slept over, she usually managed to excite every nerve end in his body. Less, because she spent every other night at her own apartment on Sparks Street. "I don't like men to become a steady habit," she explained when she began alternating residences. She also made occasional trips out of town to find paintings for her pre-Raphaelite exhibition. He didn't really object to these absences as much as he pretended to, since they gave him a chance to finish his book on coup d'etats.

Leaning on his shoulders with both hands, she stepped into her blue pumps, which raised her almost three inches. "Ready," she said, as the bells in Memorial Chapel began caroling, signaling the beginning of the procession.

Harvard Yard was overflowing with students in black gowns and their proud parents. Neither would find glory so easy to come by again, thought Jasmine, as he reflected on his own parentless graduation from UCLA twelve years earlier. The procession was just forming in front of Harvard Hall.

"Why are you in red, Jake?" Tina teased. "Are you some sort of a Communist?"

"Just a Ph.D. We have to differentiate ourselves from the uninitiated." Only five days before, at the Gaming Center in Washington, McNab had also asked him whether he was a Communist, while he was plugged into the lie detector

189

machine. He had answered "No," and passed his eighth consecutive lie detector test. Tracy finally seemed satisfied that he was "secure." That particular nightmare appeared to be coming to an end. "Wait for me over there," Jasmine said, pointing Tina toward a section of reserved seats. He then joined the contingent of other crimson-robed professors who were marching by.

"Hear your offer from Yale came through," Professor Wiley whispered to Jasmine as they marched past President Pusey standing on the reviewing stand. "Lucky man, getting tenure at the age of thirty-five. How did you swing it?"

Jasmine didn't answer immediately. He would like to have seen the expression on Wiley's haughty face if he could tell him the truth—that he had gotten the offer of tenure by planning a coup d'etat for the CIA. Of course, he couldn't— at least not without jeopardizing his career and maybe his life. "I can only assume that the Political Science Department there thought my course on Political Pathology had great potential," he finally said.

"Henry tells me that it was Lassbloom that fixed it for you . . . ?" Wiley nodded to Henry Kissinger, who was marching two rows ahead in the procession.

"Possibly," answered Jasmine noncommittally. Kissinger taught a seminar on International Relations that competed directly with his lecture. Months ago, he had asked for and received a draft of Jasmine's book. Kissinger still, however, had not commented on it. It suddenly occurred to Jasmine that if Lassbloom had told Wiley about the offer, he might also have told him about the circumstances behind it. As the procession snaked its way into the front row of seats, he managed to separate himself from Wiley so as to avoid any further embarrassing questions.

After the professors came the students. Tina watched her sister take her Summa degree from President Pusey, shake hands with him, and move on in the line. Arabella showed no emotion in her face; she never had, not even as a child. She was the most brilliant member of the family and rarely lost a competition—except for Jasmine.

The whole ceremony ended with merciful speed once the degrees were handed out. Adlai Stevenson, Edward R. Murrow, and R.E. Steer received honorary doctorates. The selection secmed designed to show disdain for the attacks of Senator Joe McCarthy on Harvard, since Stevenson, as the Democratic candidate for President, had gone out of his way to ridicule McCarthy; Murrow had used a full hour on television to depict the Senator as a demagogue; and Ambassador Steer had just recently been denounced by McCarthy as "the center of a pinstriped conspiracy in the State Department." Jasmine loudly applauded the choice, regretting for a moment that he would leave Harvard. Finally, the Harvard choir sang a Bach oratorio. Everyone rose, and the procession, reforming row by row, snaked its way back toward Harvard Hall, then dispersed.

Both gowned and conventionally clothed participants moved across the street to the Law Quadrangle where long tables were set up under red-striped canopies for a festive lunch.

It took Jasmine almost ten minutes to find Tina and Arabella. They were already seated and busily eating the cold chicken that had been set in front of them—and was intended for the whole table. "Excuse me," he said as he slid in next to Tina, noticing that directly across the table from him, speaking with great excitement to Arabella, was his student, Brixton Steer.

"Professor Jasmine, how kind of you to join us," Steer half stood up, still thankful for the "A" that Jasmine had given him. "I'd like you to meet my father . . ."

Jasmine looked to his right. Ambassador Steer, the distinguished-looking man he had seen on the podium moments ago, was seated next to Tina. He met his hand midway across Tina's head, while she looked up at the set of clasped hands. "Glad to meet you, sir." Jasmine had the same tone of solicitation in his voice as his student had had toward him a moment earlier.

"Brixton has told me a great deal about your course on Usurpation. Sounds fascinating . . ."

"That was the paper I did, Father. The course was on Political Pathology . . ." interrupted young Steer.

"Yes, of course," the Ambassador continued, ignoring his son's correction. "It involved usurpation in Iran, didn't it?"

"You must know Mossadeq," Arabella quickly interjected. She glanced across the table and saw that Jasmine was giving her a hard look. His eyes pleaded with her: Not that subject again.

But why make it easy for him, she thought. It was that very subject that they had had their last and most bitter argument about—his unwillingness to take responsibility for what he had planned for Mossadeq. Then, as if to purge himself of all memory of it, he had moved on to her sister. Even now, Arabella could see from the corner of her eye Jasmine stroking Tina under the table—like she was a Siamese cat. Leaning forward intently, Arabella asked, "Is Mossadeq really the demagogue he's supposed to be?"

"Arabella," Brixton cut in diplomatically. He knew his father had strong feelings on the subject of Mossadeq and would prefer not to discuss them in public. "When do you leave for England?"

"Later." Arabella flicked away the distraction without even turning to Brixton. "Now I want to hear about Mossadeq."

Jasmine couldn't help admiring Arabella's perseverance. He knew there would be no stopping her until she got her answer. He could also see that Steer was keenly interested in her, and felt a pang of jealousy—even though it made no sense to him.

"You're quite right to be interested in Mossadeq. He is an extraordinary man," Ambassador Steer began. "He didn't get involved in politics until he was an old man—seventy-four. Then he decided to enter on the side of the poor. Of course, he himself is one of the wealthiest men in Iran. As heir to the previous Qajar dynasty, he owned more villages than the Shah. But he saw that there was a need for land reform, and . . ." he paused, searching for the right words.

"So he joined up with the Communists," Arabella suggested.

"No, no. That's only what the American newspapers reported." The Ambassador tapped the table as he spoke. "He never joined with the Communists. They tried to use him, and perhaps he played along with them."

"He did nationalize British oil," Tina chimed in.

"Right. His entire policy is to drive the British out of Iran, get control of the million barrels of oil a day the country can produce, and use the revenue to build a nation. In theory at least, it's a fairly logical policy."

"Yet you wouldn't say he has a very promising future, would you?" Arabella pressed.

"It all depends."

"On what?"

"On whether he can sell Iranian oil. It's that simple."

"What about the *Sansi* incident?" the younger Steer interjected. He wanted to show both his father and his professor that he understood the power plays of *Realpolitik*. "Doesn't that prove that the British are prepared to enforce their blockade against the sale of Iranian oil?"

"Only against a Panamanian tanker with a dubious charter. They would hardly have dared intercept an Amer-

193

ican tanker—and Mossadeq's only real hope is America."
Ambassador Steer discreetly looked around, and then continued in a low voice, "Mossadeq has made a very serious application for American aid. If it is accepted by Eisenhower . . ."

"It won't be," Jasmine interrupted.

"What?" the Ambassador said, taken aback by the assuredness of Jasmine's tone.

"Eisenhower will reject the application with a loud bang of publicity." Jasmine hadn't meant to say this, or even to get drawn into the conversation, but in his mind he saw Move Two in his revised scenario light up on the screen in the Gaming Room: PRESIDENT REJECTS AJAX BID FOR AID. HUMILIATES PREMIER.

"That's a most extraordinary assertion, Mr. Jasmine. I dare say that the President himself hasn't made up his mind yet." Perhaps I am being too hard on my son's professor, the Ambassador thought. What do political scientists know of the real world, anyhow? Trying to moderate his last remark, he asked, "What's your opinion of what will happen in Iran? Brixton has told me of your interesting mode of analysis . . ."

"I don't think Mossadeq will last two months. Once everyone realizes that the United States won't be coming to his aid, his government will weaken. Then the Shah will move . . ." Jasmine hesitated, realizing he was on the brink of disaster. He backed away. "At least, that's my guess—but it's sheer supposition."

"The Shah move against Mossadeq? . . . hmmmm." The Ambassador always added a long "hmmmm" to ideas that he thought were worthless or stupid; in that way, he at least gave the appearance of considering them deeply. "The problem with that idea is that the Shah is a figurehead. He has no power."

Jasmine watched the Ambassador turn to his lunch and

delicately cut a piece of chicken for himself. He obviously considered the subject exhausted. So be it, Jasmine thought, relieved that he hadn't entirely blown the secret.

"Suppose some power backed the Shah?" Arabella continued.

"Who would? The British have already tried—and failed," Steer said, suspending a forkful of chicken above his plate.

"The Americans," Jasmine found himself saying. Then he stopped short.

"Americans in Iran? . . . hmmmm. Certainly, Professor, you must know how unlikely that is." In the silence that followed, he finally managed to get the piece of chicken into his mouth.

Brixton, feeling repressed, took advantage of the silence. "I see that Churchill is taking over the Foreign Office while Eden's in the hospital." He had read the story about Anthony Eden's illness in the *Economist* that morning, but presented it as though it were inside information.

"Will you all excuse me? I have a plane to catch to Washington this afternoon. It was nice meeting you, Professor, ladies . . ." Ambassador Steer moved away from the picnic table with both grace and speed. Thirty years in the diplomatic service had taught him how—and when—to escape from social situations. Brixton followed his father across the Yard, hoping for an introduction to President Pusey.

"I think I made a fool of myself," Jasmine said as he walked Tina and Arabella to Sparks Street. This was Tina's night with her sister.

"Nonsense. You did very well with Ambassador Steer—he is impossibly pompous," Tina said.

"Thought you'd like talking to him about Iran," Arabella added, with a sadistic smile on her lips.

"You mean you liked the idea of provoking a little scene," Jasmine retorted, but couldn't help smiling as he thought

195

about the conversation. The Ambassador seemed to have no idea of what was about to happen in Iran.

"Wait until the Americans put the Shah back into power in Iran." His thought surfaced. "At least Steer will have a new respect for political scientists."

"More likely he'll assume you're in on the coup, which you are, of course," Arabella said, tossing her mortarboard cap in the air, and catching it by the tassel.

"Don't start that again, Arabella." He swatted at her cap in midair as if it were some annoying insect, and slapped it firmly into her hands. "And stop acting like a precocious child. You were graduated from Harvard today, remember."

"Be nice, Jake," Tina said, coming to her sister's defense. She knew Arabella would be returning to England at the end of the week, where she would quickly forget Jake—and the whole Iranian business.

"Sorry to be so unserious, Professor," Arabella said, putting her cap back on her head with an exaggerated concern. "But you did plan the coup."

"Don't exaggerate. I wrote a scenario for Ajax. That's all. If they use some parts of it for other purposes . . . there's not much I can do about it."

"Other purposes like an assassination, you mean?" Arabella cut in.

"Arabella, please," Tina begged. "You know how they trapped Jake on this. Now shut up about it—once and for all."

"Anyway, there is no assassination. . . . The Americans are just giving the Shah some support in a very complicated situation. They probably have an entirely new scenario by now." Jasmine wiped the beads of perspiration from the back of his neck as he talked. Arabella always seemed to hit him where he was the most vulnerable.

"How are you going to feel if old Mossadeq is butchered in the back of a truck, just like you planned in Option B?"

196

Arabella persisted. "And you know damn well there is something you can do about it: tell Mossadeq."

"The world is not as simple as you make it out to be." As he spoke, Jasmine wondered whether, even if he believed the assassination were certain, he would risk everything he had to save the life of an old man he didn't know. Then he remembered his friends in Venezuela, disappearing in 1948. All that had remained were empty streets, stained with blood.

"Your friend Raven will be in America next week, won't he?" Arabella asked Tina, bringing up another painful subject.

"Raven?" Jasmine looked sharply at Tina.

"I had a letter from him, asking to see me. He said he would be in Washington the first week in July."

"Probably the first dress rehearsal for the coup," Jasmine commented bitterly.

"I don't plan to see him," Tina volunteered.

"Someday I'd like to meet him again," Jasmine mused. They were at 11 Sparks Street. Jasmine left Tina at the doorstep without kissing her good night. He never could in front of Arabella.

He took a roundabout way home, walking down Brattle Street, stopping at the Paperback Book Store in the Square. After browsing for an hour without buying a book, he continued around Harvard Yard. His mind kept locking in on names—Mossadeq, Raven, Adams, McNab. To divert himself, he played the pinball machine at Tommy's, winning a free game he didn't use. Again, he was thinking of Raven.

It was midnight when he opened his front door, and the phone was ringing. He caught it on the tenth ring.

"Professor Jasmine?" the operator said. "Please hold on for Long Distance. New York calling."

Jasmine waited while the operator made the connection.

197

"John Pfisster here," a voice said authoritatively. "My firm is representing Oxbridge Press in London. You're familiar with it?"

"Yes," Jasmine answered, although he had never heard of it.

"They are very keen on publishing your book on coup d'etats as part of their political series. You do have a book on coup d'etats?"

"Well, of course, it's not exclusively on coups."

"Of course." Pfisster breathed a sigh of relief. This was his eighteenth call. Finally, he had found his quarry. "Would you be interested in letting them publish the section on coups?"

"It's not really finished. I should have it done by the end of summer. If Oxbridge could wait ..." The idea of having his book published in England appealed to him.

"Oxbridge has a pretty tight schedule for the series. Would you be willing to fly over to London, at our expense, of course, to talk to them about it, Jasmine?"

"Fly to London?" Wouldn't Arabella be surprised if he turned up in London, he thought.

"We usually put our authors up at the Connaught. I'll make the arrangements. Call me back at KL-5-1852 when you've decided on a date."

Jasmine hung up the phone. The thought of a free trip to London managed to distract him only for a moment from the names that kept flashing through his mind. After each name, a series of moves lit up. He couldn't get away from the Game of Nations.

Jasmine set up the pieces on the chessboard on his desk. Except for one postcard match, he had stopped playing with other players—he was too good for most amateurs, and didn't like losing to professionals. But working out the endless permutations in a chess problem relaxed him. He always hoped the principles in chess would coincide with those in life. There was, for example, the basic principle of noncommitment. Two pawns in a parallel formation on the fourth rank constitute a far stronger position than that which results when either of the pawns is pushed to the fifth rank. Once committed to an advance on either side, the back pawn becomes a target and the front pawn becomes a dependent part of the chain. Yet he knew the pawn would have to be committed at some time. Genius in chess involved delaying the commitment as long as possible. It was more complicated off the chessboard. Flicking the pieces over with his finger, he returned to the telephone and called Tina.

"I've been thinking about Raven," he began.

"Jake, it's two in the morning . . ."

"I'm sorry to wake you. But I think maybe you should see Raven in Washington."

CHAPTER XIX

RAISON D'ETAT

Nine serious-looking men, all wearing charcoal suits, jumped to their feet when John Foster Dulles burst through the double doors of the situation room. The two senior officials only half-rose at the round table. "Let's get down to business, gentlemen." Dulles exuded energy and confidence with every word he spoke. He looked around the table: these were men he could count on in a pinch—R.E. Steer, the State Department's best troubleshooter in the Middle East; Bronson Tracy, the CIA's top political action man, whom Dulles' brother Allen had lent him for this operation. Passing over the junior men, all specialists in some field or another, his eyes focused on the empty chair at the end of the table. "Where's Kim?"

"Right here," Kim Adams said, smiling with both rows of

teeth as he made his way toward the empty seat. "Sorry to be late, Foster. Had to see Allen."

Steer marveled at the way Adams operated. His consistent lateness, his first-name acquaintanceship with the powerful, and his imperious tone were the levers he used to manipulate less secure diplomats. By mentioning "Allen," for example, he made it clear to the State Department people that the CIA was somehow behind this meeting, and that only he and "Foster" knew its precise role.

"The first thing you should know, gentlemen, is that the President has just made an irreversible decision on Iran: not one penny of American aid until Mossadeq is kicked out," Dulles began. "How do you think this will affect Mossadeq, Steer?"

"The announcement, if and when it's made public, will humiliate him—it could pull the rug right out from under him unless we're careful."

Adams spoke up. "We've already leaked Mossadeq's plea for aid and Eisenhower's rejection of it to *The Washington Post.* If that sends him flying out of office, it'll just save us the trouble."

Steer tried to digest what Adams had just said. Humiliating foreign leaders was not his kind of diplomacy. And humiliating Mossadeq at this critical juncture could destabilize the entire Middle East, he thought. Obviously, decisions had been made to which he was not privy. Oddly enough, and somewhat disturbing to him, his son's professor at Harvard had managed to predict this exact course of action through some curious form of political analysis. "Hmmmm ..." he said aloud. "Am I reading you right, Kim? Are you suggesting that our policy should be to destabilize Mossadeq?"

"That's the President's decision," Dulles answered for Adams. "You might as well know the full story. On April ninth, the National Security Council, after considering the threat that Mossadeq's control over Europe's oil supply posed to the Western alliance, unanimously decided that the current government in Iran must be replaced by one more amenable to Western interests. The Council—and President Eisenhower—authorized the necessary action no later than August twentieth."

"Hmmmm," Steer commented again. "What sort of action are you contemplating, Mr. Secretary?" Ever since Adams had stopped in Iran in February, Steer had suspected something was brewing, but hadn't known what.

"We intend to aid Iran, not Mossadeq. It's that simple," Dulles answered. The men in charcoal suits nodded in unison.

"Yes. But Mossadeq is the head of the government of Iran," Steer persisted.

"Leaves us only one alternative, right? To get rid of Mossadeq. Right, Steer?"

"Mr. Secretary, I don't think it's that simple. If Mossadeq goes, how can we guarantee that the Communists won't move in to pick up the pieces?" He glared for a moment at Dulles, refusing to be bullied into accepting their decision. Then he continued. "The last thing we want in the Middle East is a power vacuum. With Mossadeq gone ..."

"Good point, Steer," Adams interrupted. "But we don't intend to leave a vacuum for the Communists. We're going to move the Shah in the moment Mossadeq is gone."

"I see," Steer murmured, thinking that his son's professor had also been right about the Shah. Something funny seemed to be going on. He objected half-heartedly, saying, "The Embassy hardly has the resources for anything like that ..."

"Right," Dulles cut in. "It won't be the Embassy that

does it. Kim and Tracy have worked out the necessary steps." He signaled Tracy with a wave of his hand.

"The code name for the operation is Ajax," Tracy began, opening his briefing book.

"Am I correct in understanding that this is going to be a CIA operation?" Steer looked squarely at Dulles.

"Right. It's Allen's show."

"Then, with your permission, I think it best if I don't hear any details. The less I know, the better . . ."

"Kim will be in Iran to work out the nitty-gritty. Until then . . ."

"Until then, Mr. Secretary, I think it best if I absent myself from Iran. Been planning to take a home leave, anyway. Kim can handle things, don't you agree?"

"Right." Dulles glared back at Steer. He was not used to being challenged by his subordinates. But perhaps it would be best if Steer were out of Iran during the coup. It would give Kim and the CIA a freer hand in case things got sticky.

For a moment Steer stood awkwardly at the table, assessing where his duty lay. A CIA coup was not what he had bargained for when he flew in from Teheran. He firmly believed that what the Middle East needed was stability. And it seemed clear to him that sticking an unknown quantity like the Shah on the throne of Iran would only lead to instability. He felt an obligation to make his case as cogently as possible. All the chips had to be out on the table. "The one thing I would like you to carefully consider, Mr. Secretary, is whether the problem is Mossadeq himself—or oil."

"Not easy to separate them, Steer. When Mossadeq seized the British oil concessions, he made himself the problem." Dulles stopped, satisfied that he had made his point.

"But the British can't hold on to Middle East oil forever—

that's the real problem. They can hold on only as long as their fleet dominates the Persian Gulf . . ." Steer could see he was losing the argument.

"Churchill intends for that to be a very long time," Adams interrupted.

"Whatever he intends, the British military position depends on their holding the Suez Canal—and all our intelligence indicates that the Egyptians will kick them out in a matter of three to four years. That certainly is Nasser's intent."

"Nasser is an old friend," Adams said. He had helped bring Nasser to power only a year before. "We can persuade him to go slow on his timetable for the Canal and buy time. Of course, eventually . . ."

"Eventually, we'll all be dead." Dulles banged his hand down on the table. "Too much long-term planning vitiates the will to act. Let's not forget why we are here. Some demagogue in Iran is testing the will of the Western alliance."

Steer saw no use in continuing the argument. Dulles had turned Mossadeq into a moral issue—one of his favorite ploys. And in moral issues, there could be no compromise. Slowly, Steer walked from the room, thinking that he would never return to Iran.

"With a little guidance from us, the Shah is going to turn out to be quite a force in the Middle East," Adams said after Steer had left. "He's young, but he's as shrewd as his father was."

"The date is August twentieth. Let's have the basics, Tracy," Dulles demanded, impatient with the arguing that had been going on.

"It's all clean and simple. The Shah will dismiss Mossadeq. Mossadeq, of course, will refuse to step down as Premier. Then we will neutralize his political base. Meanwhile, we'll keep the Shah out of harm's way until Mossadeq is gone. It will all take three days, and almost no bloodshed."

"How are you going to neutralize Mossadeq?" Dulles asked.

"That's a detail I think you'd rather not know," Tracy answered.

"Kim, you'll be my personal representative in this business. Make sure nothing goes wrong. Eisenhower can't be embarrassed. Right?" Dulles spoke as though he were coaching a college football team.

"Right, Foster."

"Good. We're all agreed then. I'll tell Allen to take over from here. Thank you, gentlemen."

The meeting ended within seconds of Dulles' exit. The young men in the charcoal suits filed out after the Secretary, content that they had seen history being made. Adams stayed behind for a moment with Tracy.

"When do you plan to do the final runthrough on Ajax?" Kim asked.

"Allen wants to do it in Switzerland. August thirteenth is the most convenient date. Supposedly, he'll be taking his summer vacation. He thinks it's best if the Director of the CIA is out of the country, in case there's any flap."

"I don't expect there will be any flaps," Adams answered. "The American press will buy the story. It's a romance made to order for them: SHAH RETURNS TRIUMPHANTLY; USURPER FLEES . . ."

"Or is killed trying," Tracy added.

"I still don't like that part. Unnecessary."

"I take it the British end of the operation is all set?"

"We'll see. Raven will be here on July fourth. Curious character. Can't really figure him out."

"But we need the resources of the oil companies in Iran.

205

And you have to hand it to him—he has delivered."

"I guess so," Adams said, striding from the room. Rubbish, he thought to himself as he left the State Department. Sure, the oil companies made it all easier by providing a few agents in place and several million dollars. But given a month, and a few parachute drops into Iran, he could line up all the assets he needed himself. After all, he had the Shah in hand, and it wouldn't take much to buy enough Iranian generals for the coup. He couldn't see why the Dulles brothers had given in to Churchill on Mossadeq. Though he couldn't say so in the meeting and embarrass Foster, Steer was dead right: the British would be out of the Middle East in a few years. Then America would have to act alone. Still, who was he to go against the President's decision? If Ike wanted the oil cartel to call the shots, so be it. His job was to make sure it worked.

Tracy sat alone in the situation room. He had even less confidence in the plan than Adams. He began counting on his fingers all the things that could go wrong. First, there was Jasmine, who could go off half-cocked again.

Chapter XX

TINA'S LETTER

Jasmine instantly recognized the flowery handwriting on the envelope as Tina's. It was postmarked Washington, D.C., July 5th, 1953, and attached to a fairly bulky package wrapped in brown manila paper. Ripping open the letter, he read:

Dear Jake,

I took great pleasure in watching the rockets bursting in air over the Washington Monument last night. Quite a fete—the Fourth of July. And all seen from the penthouse of Sir Anthony Raven.

Since it was your suggestion, it should come as no surprise. Enclosed are a few documents from Raven's safe that should satisfy your—and my clever sister's—

curiosity about Iran. I'll leave the details of what happened last night in his penthouse to your imagination. Suffice to say that I posed for him as he wanted, got the Rossetti in return, and took the papers for you after he fell asleep. No doubt he will miss both me and the documents by the time you read this letter.

I can just see the quizzical look forming on your brow. Are you shocked? I hope so, my darling. I was shocked when you proposed that I see Raven again. At first, I couldn't believe my ears. I thought you must have been joking. You knew—quite well—how he had lusted after me in London, like a starved child after chocolates, how he'd even dangled a Rossetti worth ten thousand pounds in front of me. Yet, you were willing to use me to find out about your silly game in Iran. Did you really think I could get the information without paying his price?

And, of course, my cunning little sister provoked this all. She has never understood that there are questions that need never be answered. Nor has she learned that something is lost when a mystery is completely unraveled. As for me, I am attracted by what I don't fully understand, and repelled by what can be fully explicated. Logic has always left me cold. What drew me to you was your universe of mystery—the knight errant, racing off to wherever, to play a game involving the kingdom of Ajax. Who cared whether it involved the world's oil, or the world's chromium? But dear Arabella had to have her answer—and so did you. So now it's all reduced to a rather sordid document, which explains everything.

None of this, of course, really explains why I came to be with Raven last night. Certainly, I didn't do it for

you, or for Arabella, or even for the Rossetti. Let's just
say that it was the challenge that intrigued me. Raven
dared me to sit naked in front of him, and you dared
me to elicit a secret from him. Well, I accepted both
challenges.

I ordered a magnum of champagne for the fete, then
turned out the lights and hoped he would be drunk by
the time I finished my striptease. But he finally did
pass out in my arms, and I waited until I heard him
snoring, then fished his keys out of his pocket and
opened a half-dozen locked drawers—until I found
what you wanted.

By the time you get this letter, I'll be on a plane for
Rome. Another collection to authenticate: this time for
the Aga Khan.

I think it's best if we don't see each other for a while.
For me, the mystery is gone. But don't worry—Arabella
still is infatuated with you.

TINA

Jasmine read the letter over, unable to bring himself to
believe that Tina had left him. His head buzzed with pain,
which made it difficult to focus his attention on the letter.
Somewhere in the back of his mind, he had always known
that she would leave and go back to her world of art
collectors and millionaires. Arabella had warned him that
Tina liked to taste everything that life offered her—then
move on to the next delicacy. But even accepting that, he
couldn't believe he had judged the situation so wrongly.
And it was this question about his own judgment that was
gnawing away at his mind like a hungry termite.

He had never thought Tina capable of seducing Raven,
or as a femme fatale. Yet, she had proved herself perfectly

capable of getting what she wanted from any man—and she made it sound like it was nothing more than one of her piano exercises. Jasmine couldn't help thinking that if she could play Raven so adeptly, she had also toyed with him. But why? Was he just another challenge? Had it been because of a tacit competition she had with Arabella?

His eye focused on the word *mystery* in the middle of the letter. He didn't understand what she meant. He decided then that he would never really understand Tina.

He looked for a moment at the brown manila parcel to which Tina's letter had been attached. He shook his head slowly to clear it, then tore open the wrapping paper. Inside, he found an inch-thick sheaf of documents fastened together in a green plastic binder. The cover page was titled simply *The Ajax Scenario.*

He read through it quickly. He could see that the thirty-six rudimentary steps that he had designed for the Game of Nations had been meticulously developed into an operational plan for the overthrow of a real government. The date for the coup d'etat was August 20, 1953—less than six weeks away. Oil had been substituted for chromium in this version, and Iran for Ajax. He flipped quickly to the thirty-sixth move. As he had feared, it was Option B—the assassination of Mossadeq. He was to be killed by his military aide in the vehicle that had been arranged for his escape.

Jasmine could see that Raven had scribbled handwritten notes on the typed pages of the scenario, giving dates, places, names, and his evaluation of the likelihood of success for each of the steps. On the last page was the list of Iranian officials secretly in the pay of the oil cartel. Raven noted on the top of the list "AWD might be able to use some of our helpers listed below." Jasmine easily guessed AWD was none other than Allen Welsh Dulles.

210

Attached as an appendix at the end of the scenario was Raven's detailed analysis of the effect of the coup on world oil. Raven concluded that Mossadeq's nationalization could not be formally repealed. Any attempt to do so would only "provide kindling for a future revolutionary barn fire." Instead, Raven proposed: "the Shah, on his return to power, will nominally endorse the nationalization, and thus mollify the local nationalists. At the same time, he will make a de facto agreement with the cartel to produce, refine, and market Iranian oil at world prices." In order to conceal the real interests behind these arrangements, Raven suggested that it be disguised as "an international consortium, with token shares given to a number of oil companies not in the cartel." In order to avoid "the chaos of competition," he maintained that the cartel would control the amount of oil produced in Iran through clauses in the "consortium agreement," which would not be made public.

Jasmine realized immediately the brilliance of Raven's scheme. How could a man clever enough to mastermind such a strategy make such a fool of himself over Tina, he wondered. Raven would have realized by now that this document had been stolen from his safe—and that Tina had taken it. Suddenly, the danger of Tina's situation dawned on him. Raven might go after her—or, he might put two and two together, and figure out that she had sent the document to Jasmine. After all, Raven had seen them both together the night that he had made the scene about the CIA at Tracy's party.

Raven might already be trying to recover the document. Jasmine picked up the telephone and dialed Arabella. He hoped she might know how to get in touch with Tina. After three rings, the operator came on the line and told him that the telephone had been disconnected. So they had both moved from Sparks Street.

Fumbling through his pockets, Jasmine found his address book. He quickly looked up Arabella's dormitory number and dialed it. No answer. Then his eye fell on another name in the book: Fletcher Foxcroft.

Chapter XXI

THE KING-MAKER

From the air, Teheran looked like any other city in the Middle East. A few scattered minarets poking through the purple dust, a few large buildings, and a sprawl of mud houses fanning out in all directions. Looking down on the capital of Iran, Kim Adams wondered—Is this where the future of the Western world's oil is going to be decided? To him, Teheran meant dust, open sewers running beside the narrow streets, noisy bazaars, and frustrating traffic jams.

As the Pan American flight came in for a landing, he checked his calendar watch. It was 6:00 P.M., July 22nd, 1953. In just one month, if his mission was successful, the Shah would be returning to this same airport in triumph. And why shouldn't it be successful? he asked himself as the wheels hit the tarmac.

The Embassy Cadillac took him directly to the Park Hotel. His usual suite on the top floor was ready the moment he walked through the doors. Red Murphy, whom he always requested for tough operations, was sprawled on the couch, his .45 automatic showing through his checkered jacket.

"Red?" Adams barked without breaking stride. "I want a direct line to the Shah's palace put in today, and another to the Embassy, though I'm not sure those fools will do much except get in the way."

"Right," Red answered, not bothering to move from the couch.

"And I want six messengers standing by at all times."

"Should I have their tongues cut out for security's sake?"

"Be serious, Red. We only have thirty days."

"To do what?"

"I'll fill you in later. First get the phones and the messengers. Then get Norm Schwartzkopf over here ..."

"I wondered what that goon was doing in town."

Adams wheeled around and looked sharply at his executive officer. No manners, no culture, no schooling—but Red had nerve, intelligence, and could be counted on in any pinch. "And we're going to need a printing press," Adams added.

"No problem. I'll just rub my magic lantern once or twice. By the way, what about dinner tonight?"

"Fine," Adams answered, and went into the bedroom to unpack.

Less than an hour later, Red banged on his door and shouted, "Schwartzkopf's here."

Emerging from his bedroom, Adams saw that the living room was now total chaos. A half-dozen Iranians were in a corner trying to install one of the direct phone wires. Another half-dozen were jammed into the front corridor.

Schwartzkopf was pacing back and forth, followed by two sinister-looking bodyguards. Red was back on the couch, reading a magazine and ignoring the confusion.

Pointing to the six messengers, Adams asked, "Are they dependable?"

"Absolutely," Red answered. "Just got them out of prison—and they want to stay out."

"Fine. But can't you have them wait downstairs, or, better yet, get them their own suite."

Red spoke a few words of Persian to the group, and they disappeared through the door. "They're next door. Just thought you'd like to look them over, Kim."

One of the workmen picked up the phone and gestured wildly. Adams walked over, picked it up, and said casually, "Just tell His Highness Kim's in town, at the Park." It was the direct line to the Shah.

"The printing press will be installed tomorrow—a few blocks away," Red said, sitting up.

"General Schwartzkopf, terribly sorry to keep you waiting." Adams extended his hand.

"I know you're busy, Mr. Adams." Schwartzkopf was a short, solidly built man in his late fifties, and looked very much like the policeman he was. Twenty years earlier, as a captain in the New Jersey State Police, he had handled the search for the kidnappers of Charles Lindbergh's child, and had become internationally known for his tenacity. During the war, he served in the OSS as a liaison with the military police. Then, in 1945, the Shah offered him the job of training the Iranian Imperial Gendarmerie, and he had spent the next three years in Iran—where he got to know all the key police officers involved in internal security. It was Raven who had coaxed him out of retirement for this operation.

"Do you know Murphy? Good. Thought we might all

215

have dinner tonight. You're free, General, I hope?" Without waiting for a reply, Adams threw on his rumpled white jacket and headed for the door. "Let's go. I hope you like roast pig, General. They do the best pig in Asia about fifty miles from here up in the mountains. Hope you don't mind taking a little ride."

Red Murphy and the two bodyguards followed Adams and Schwartzkopf out the door, and down to the car.

Even with Red driving, it took nearly two hours of weaving through donkey carts to get to the village of Sultana. Towering over the tiny mud houses were the ruins of a Mogul fort.

"Have you heard about General Adfanazov?" Schwartz-kopf was asking as the car pulled up in front of the enormous ruin.

"Announced that he had a list of all the American and British agents in Iran, or some rot like that. I heard about it in Washington. What happened to that fool?" Kim asked.

"He seems to have disappeared—with the list," Schwartz-kopf answered, with the smile of a cat who had just eaten the proverbial canary.

"Didn't know we had any agents in this country," Red muttered as he got out of the car.

"I think you'll find we have some friends well placed in the Iranian police—some very old friends," Schwartzkopf answered, motioning for his bodyguards to remain in the car.

Adams led the group down a narrow path, under the remains of a Mogul arch, and into a courtyard lit by torchlight. In the center was a huge pit lined with white-hot stones. Off the end of another half-collapsed arch that looked like a giant question mark against the moonlit sky hung about a dozen pigs of varying sizes.

"That one will do," Adams said, pointing to one of the

more succulent pigs. Two Iranians sitting at the far end of the courtyard thrust a bamboo stake through the animal and carried it to the pit. "Sit anywhere." Adams pointed to some primitive benches set around a stone table.

"Interesting place, Mr. Adams ... but they don't seem to do much business," Schwartzkopf said, seating himself next to Red. He was furious that Adams had made him ride for two hours and risked all their lives on mountain roads to please his own eccentric tastes, but he said nothing. This was his last operation, and he looked up to Adams as someone who could help him back in America. Yellow flames were leaping high in the air as the pork fat hit the sizzling stones.

"Knew you'd like it, General. Now, how many 'friends' in the Iranian police are in your pay?"

"Hard to say. I've kept contact with about ten, but they are very well placed. One is chief of counterintelligence—about a hundred men work under him. Perhaps if you could bring me into the picture a little bit more..."

"Nothing to hide, General. All very straightforward. On August twentieth, we're going to throw Mossadeq out of his little palace."

"No wonder you need two telephones and six messengers," Red quipped.

"Do we have enough resources for an operation of that magnitude?" Schwartzkopf asked. He was beginning to regret he had come out of retirement.

"Sure. We have your ten agents—and two bodyguards," Red answered. He had confidence in Adams, even though his last operation, trying to establish a Billy Graham sort of Holy Man in Iran, made him wonder if the CIA was still the sane organization he had joined in 1947.

"We don't need much manpower," Adams continued. "Basically, this is a deception operation. If we can get control of the Army Communications Center, we can make Mossadeq think there is a tribal uprising in Shiraz."

"Then we'll send all the units loyal to him out into the desert," Schwartzkopf interrupted.

"Exactly. Of course, we'll need to seize a few points—the radio station, airport, parliament—and put a few tanks on the highway for roadblocks."

"That's going to require troops, isn't it?"

Adams ignored Schwartzkopf's question. He motioned to the Iranians, who plucked the pig out of the fire and set it on the stone table. "Yes. We're going to need some sort of diversion in Teheran—an anti-Shah riot or some other mess. That will be our pretext for bringing troops in from the North." He carved a piece of pork with a knife one of the Iranians put in his hand, and tasted it. "Superb. Better than anything you'll find in Paris."

"Let's say then that you'll need some help from me in provoking the disturbance."

"Try a piece, General. It's marvelous."

"And in seizing the Communications Center."

"And in making sure that Iranian counterintelligence does nothing to upset our timetable," Adams added.

Just then, Red looked up. His gun automatically came out of its holster. A dozen or so Iranian soldiers in olive-green uniforms entered the courtyard. "They have American carbines," Red said quietly and professionally.

"Nothing to worry about. Just tell the chef to put the rest of the swine on the fire," Adams said, chewing his pork.

"This looks bad," Schwartzkopf muttered.

"The pork? Oh, you mean the soldiers. Don't worry. Friends of mine."

After the soldiers had positioned themselves around the courtyard, a white-haired general made his way toward

Adams' group. "Kim, you're here already," he called out in a distinctly French accent, then embraced Adams.

"General Zahedi, I'd like you to meet two of my associates, General Schwartzkopf and Mr. Murphy." After making the introductions, he motioned Zahedi to join them at the table.

"It's a great honor seeing you again," Schwartzkopf said. He now understood the purpose of the long drive through the mountains. Zahedi had his own private army, which could be counted on against Mossadeq. The trick was getting his troops to Teheran, and that was where the diversion would come in.

"And how is Raven?" Zahedi asked. "I hear he's coming to Iran next month."

CHAPTER XXII

SCOOP DECLINED

It took only one clap of thunder to panic the rowers in Central Park Lake. Picnic lunches were thrown overboard, passengers lurched from side to side as they tried to change places, oars splashed in the water, and everyone began yelling at each other. With the first drop of rain, the brightly colored boats raced for the dock as if pursued by Moby Dick.

Jasmine continued to nurse his eighth cup of coffee as the rowers scrambled ashore carrying in their hands shoes, socks, sun reflectors, picnic baskets, and children. He marveled at the way New Yorkers could both assume and abandon the pretense of bucolic romance in the course of an afternoon. The drizzle was beginning to bother him, but there was nothing he could do about it. Why the hell did Foxcroft have to pick an outdoor cafeteria for their meeting—and why was he an hour and a half late? Jasmine pondered. Then he ordered another cup of coffee from a waiter dressed in a sailor's uniform.

"Sorry to be late," Fletcher Foxcroft apologized. He was by now two hours late. "Took longer than I thought to check out the story."

"Doesn't matter, Fletch. I knew you would want to verify what I told you yesterday." He watched Foxcroft wipe his seat dry with the newspaper he carried. Then Fletch took out a small notebook and peered at his handwriting through his horn-rimmed glasses. The glasses made him look even heavier than he was, Jasmine decided.

When Jasmine had first met Foxcroft in Venezuela, he was lean and hard looking. He also didn't wear glasses, perhaps because he did very little reading. They were then both working for Nelson Rockefeller's propaganda machine—the so-called Office of Coordination of Information for Latin America. Foxcroft, who had been trained by the Associated Press, turned out to be a whiz at manufacturing stories about German terrorists. All the Rockefeller staff would have to do was give Foxcroft a headline, ARMS CACHE FOUND IN ——, and in three minutes he'd spin out a story about suspected German saboteurs operating in the designated area. It was always the same story, of course, but what mattered was that he knew how to write it so that it was always acceptable copy for the wire services. After the war, he went to work for *The New York Times,* and although Jasmine didn't hear from him, he read his byline from Cairo, Teheran, Beirut, Jeddah, Jerusalem, Amman, Baghdad, and every other city in the Middle East that was in the news. Now, with two Pulitzer Prizes under his belt, he was the *Times'* roving diplomatic correspondent.

"It's an incredible story, Jake—if it's true," Foxcroft said, still reviewing his notes.

Jasmine squirmed slightly as he heard Foxcroft slip into the conditional tense. He had given the reporter every-thing—the Ajax briefing book, Raven's notes on the future of the oil cartel, the names of the players in the Game of Nations, the exact date of the assassination. It was the biggest scoop Fletch had ever had. Why the note of doubt? "What do you mean, 'if it's true'?" Jasmine asked.

"I'm not questioning your integrity, Jake. But the story has to be checked out."

"You read the scenario?"

"Yeah—but I can't write a story about the country of Ajax, can I?"

"It's Iran, obviously."

"Nothing's obvious in this business. I called Myles Smith-line in the State Department . . ."

"He confirmed the Game of Nations, I hope."

"He said you invented it. Sold it to the State Department as some sort of crisis-management training tool. They paid you four thousand dollars and expenses—is that true?"

"They paid me as a consultant, sure, but I didn't invent the Game. They fed me the facts . . ."

"Smithline says you made it all up. Never worked. Suggests you're using it all to publicize your book on coup d'etats."

"He's obviously lying. Covering up for the CIA."

"Nothing's obvious. He has always been a reliable source in the past."

"What about Professor Abraham? Did you speak to him?"

"He confirms Smithline's story. Says you got into a fistfight with Tony Raven over some English girl. True?"

"Irrelevant. He must be in cahoots with Smithline."

"And what about Bronson Tracy?"

"You promised not to call him, Fletch."

"I didn't. But would he back Smithline?"

"Of course. I told you, he's CIA."

"Thought he was a Yale professor. ... Anyhow, that's three sources disputing you. Do you think any editor in the country would take your word?"

"I gave you Raven's report. He spells it all out. The plans for controlling Iran's oil. How could he write that unless he knew a coup was in the works?" He looked at Foxcroft and wondered how he could have spent five years in the Middle East and still understand nothing about its politics. He probably worked just as he had done in Venezuela, pumping up press releases into stories from "informed sources," Jasmine concluded.

"Raven is known as a brilliant planner. This memo only suggests that he foresees the eventual collapse of Mossadeq, not a coup."

"Fletch, you read Option B!"

"So?"

"Look at Raven's copy. He's written the name Ramses next to it. Colonel Ramses is Mossadeq's bodyguard. Explain that away." Jasmine tried to censor the anger out of his voice without success.

"How do I know it's Raven's copy—or handwriting? Or for that matter, what Ramses means? It might be a very common Iranian name." He handed Jasmine back Raven's briefing book.

"You mean you don't want to write the story, Fletch."

"No one else will write the story, either, Jake. Suppose everything you say is true, just for argument's sake. Suppose the CIA is about to overthrow some demagogue in Iran. It must have the President's approval, right?"

"Probably."

"Do you think any responsible newspaper in the country

223

would undermine American foreign policy for the sake of a scoop?"

"You're telling me that a story that goes against the CIA can't get printed?"

"I'm telling you no one gives a damn who's on top in Iran—just as long as it's not the Communists."

"What about Mossadeq? He's going to be assassinated."

"So you say. Anyhow, as far as the American public is concerned, Mossadeq is a crybaby, a thief—and a Communist."

"That's just the stereotype that's been created for him."

"We couldn't print newspapers without stereotypes. Why make a fuss about it? Go back to Harvard, Jake. Finish your book. Who knows? It might even be a best seller." He had always liked Jasmine. In Venezuela, he would come up with an idea a minute—some good, some bad. He had too wild an imagination for a journalist, but he might make it as a professor if he'd just drop this Ajax business, Foxcroft thought to himself.

"Do you think anyone would be interested in publishing a chapter from it on how a murder was planned in Iran?"

"Only the Iranians." Foxcroft smiled bitterly. "Nice seeing you again, Jake." He pushed himself up from the table, pumping Jasmine's hand.

The sun was coming out again. Rowers were once more boarding their crafts, and waiters were taking orders for coffee again.

Only the Iranians, Jasmine thought, as he ordered another cup of coffee.

Chapter XXIII

PRESS RELATIONS

Bronson Tracy swiveled back and forth in a large Eames chair in his office at the CIA. He held the telephone a few inches away from his ear.

"Pretty sure I cooled Foxcroft down," Myles Smithline was saying. "I made Jasmine sound like a pretty unstable opportunist."

"You completely denied his story, of course."

"Of course. And Wilmot Abraham backed me up."

"Well done." He knew that even if Smithline hadn't been able to dissuade Foxcroft from pursuing the story, Dulles had friends at the *Times* who would make sure the story was never published. Nevertheless, it could have been embarrassing.

"Only problem, Tracy," Smithline continued, "Jasmine

seems to have gotten hold of some list of American and British agents in Iran. Foxcroft mentioned someone called Ramses. I told him he was probably a figment of Jasmine's imagination." He began to chuckle.

"Good grief—Ramses. Sit tight, be back with you in a minute." Tracy slammed the phone back into its cradle. He couldn't believe what he had just heard. How on earth could Jasmine have obtained those names? And if he had Ramses' name, he knew about the assassination. Christ—he knew everything. If the information were published—or somehow managed to get into Mossadeq's hands—it would blow the entire network in the Middle East. No doubt about it, that fool Jasmine could blow everything: the coup, the assassination, all the agents, the Shah—everything.

He picked up the phone again. "Get me Adams in Teheran. Superpriority."

"Do you know what time it is in Teheran?" Adams' groggy voice bounced back five minutes later. "The master list? I burned it, of course, the moment I memorized it. Do you have some security problem at your end? In the future you might remember there is an eleven-hour time difference." Adams hung up without waiting for Tracy's reply.

Tracy knew there was only one other copy of the master list—the draft that Raven had originally prepared. He caught Raven at his office in London, just as he was leaving. "Tony, remember that draft you did for Kim? Did you destroy it?"

"Destroy it," Raven muttered. He found all this cloak-and-dagger talk inherently off-putting. "Have a copy in my attaché case. Perfectly safe, you can be sure. . . . Hold on, I'll have a look."

Tracy held the phone for five minutes, silently cursing Raven's breach of security.

"Seems to be missing. . . . Can't understand it. Someone

must have broken into my hotel room. . . . Oh, God—" He stopped short. Chris. That's why she'd come that night—and that's why his keys had been on the floor.

"It was Jasmine," Tracy said.

"Yes. I know. You've got to stop him. He'll ruin every-thing—that's his damned talent." Raven was thinking more of Tina than the Iranian oil fields.

Pacing back and forth across his office, Tracy tried to get up the courage to report the event to Dulles. He knew Dulles would probably call off the entire operation, rather than take a chance that it would explode in the CIA's face. All these months of work he had put in would go down the drain. The British would feel betrayed. And it was all his fault, he thought as he wiped the perspiration from his brow. He should never have used Jasmine without compro-mising him first—and when he'd proved insecure, he should have locked him up for the duration of the operation, rather than trying to bribe him with a job at Yale. He had created the problem. Now he would have to solve it.

Tracy picked up the phone again. "Get me McNab. Superpriority."

Chapter XXIV

PAWN'S GAMBIT

It was 1 A.M. by the time Jasmine found a parking spot in Cambridge. He was so tired he could hardly keep his eyes open as he walked the three short blocks to his apartment house. It had been an exhausting day: the long wait for Foxcroft in Central Park; being politely told that he was either a liar or a fool; then the six-hour drive back from New York in a rainstorm. Fearless Foxcroft was right about one thing, he thought as he made his way to the front door. It was a waste of time trying to get a story published on the coup in Iran. No newspaper would touch it with a ten-foot pole, even if he could substantiate the plot.

There wasn't a single light on in his apartment building. He assumed the other members of the faculty had already left town for their summer vacations. The only sign of life he could see was a flicker of light in the phone booth across the street—some pervert making an obscene call, he assumed—as he turned the key in the front lock.

His mailbox was jammed with bills, advertisements, and postcards from students wanting their final grades sent to their summer addresses. There were only two letters of interest.

The first, postmarked London, July 12th, 1953, said: "Sorry I can't wait for your triumphant return back from Washington. I got a charter flight to England, which leaves tomorrow. Hope you've solved the mystery of Ajax. By the way, what have you done with Tina? She's missing. I'm summering in Oxford. Love, my tutor. A."

The second letter was postmarked New York, and neatly typed. It read like a telegram: "My client advises it best that you meet him in London on August 1st to discuss immediate publication of your book. Reservation made for you at the Dorchester. Enclosed please find roundtrip air ticket to London." It was signed "John Pfisster, Pfisster & Pfisster."

The last thing Jasmine wanted to think about at this late hour was his book. He stuffed the ticket in his jacket pocket, along with the other mail.

He could hear a phone ringing as he dragged himself up the three flights of steps to his apartment. Who could be calling so late—and so persistently? He counted eighty-eight rings on his way up the stairs. Only when he reached the third-floor corridor did he realize that it was his phone.

It didn't stop, as he hoped it would, when he opened the door to his apartment. He wearily started walking toward the phone, past the chessboard set up on the dining room table. Suddenly, he stopped.

Something was wrong. Before he had left for Washington, he had set up a Smothered Mate. It was a chess problem that had always interested him. The White King was

229

completely surrounded by its own pieces, leaving it no breathing space. A Black Knight could then mate, in the next move, by simply putting the King in check. The problem was blocking the impending mate. Now, he could see, a pawn had been moved forward, giving the King a space to move.

He hovered over the chessboard, totally perplexed. Who could have moved the piece—and ruined the Smothered Mate? When he moved the pawn back, he noticed a smudge of chocolate on his finger.

The phone continued to ring. Putting his hand on the receiver, he was about to pick it up when he felt the same stickiness—the same chocolate that was on the misplaced pawn. The phone kept ringing, but some instinct told Jasmine not to answer it. He looked back at the chessboard. The person who had moved the pawn was not a beginner. He understood the Smothered Mate. Nor was he any real expert. The pawn's move could be easily countered. A mediocre chess player had recently been in his apartment—but who? And why?

Someone had entered the room, stopped at the chessboard, considered the problem while he put a chocolate in his mouth, moved the pawn, and then picked up the telephone. Then Jasmine remembered the flicker of light in the telephone booth when he turned his key. Why would anyone let the phone ring so many times—unless they knew he was headed up the stairs? His chocolate-eating chess adversary was in the phone booth outside. But who was it?

Jasmine closed his eyes. A jumble of pictures flashed through his mind: McNab popping a chocolate mint into his ratlike teeth at the Gaming Center; McNab saying he played chess; the person in the phone booth across the street. McNab ...

I'm being paranoid, he thought. But just because I'm

paranoid doesn't mean someone isn't trying to kill me. It took him only seconds to fasten a cord to the telephone receiver. Then, carefully unwinding the cord as he walked back to the door, he retreated into the hallway. From a crouching position, he gave a quick tug at the line. The receiver lifted off its cradle and fell to the floor.

From the phone booth across the street, McNab watched the blue-yellow flame light up in Jasmine's apartment. A thousand darts in a half-pound plastic explosive. Jasmine had no chance, McNab thought, as he bit down on the mint between his teeth. One nice feature about remote-control telephone bombs is that the target is verified before the bomb is detonated—and they kill without doing excessive property damage. McNab licked a trace of chocolate off his lips and slipped the beeper he had used to detonate it with back in his pocket.

In the distance, he could hear sirens. He would explain to Cambridge police that Jasmine had been under surveillance for months as a pro-Iranian terrorist. They would search his apartment then—and find the guns, grenades, and propaganda leaflets McNab had planted in the linen closet. He wouldn't have any problem convincing them that Jasmine had been manufacturing bombs—and that one had accidentally gone off.

He called Tracy. "Problem solved," he said tersely.

"Good work. Now make sure you get the list." Tracy hung up the phone and looked at the luminous dial on his alarm clock. It was 1:19 A.M.

"Who was that?" his wife called from the adjoining bed.

"Just a wrong number," he answered. For a moment he felt sorry about Jasmine—but he had become such a nuisance.

Chapter XXV

COVER STORY

"No body?" Foxcroft wiped the fog from his glasses and looked at the shambles of Jasmine's apartment. He could still smell the stench of sulfur. "What's that supposed to mean, Captain?" He had known Captain Burke briefly when he was the Boston Bureau Chief for the *Times*.

"Apparently, Jasmine wasn't here when the bomb went off. ... Could have been a time bomb," Captain Burke answered. His mind was not on Foxcroft's questions. It was on the cache of automatic weapons his men were pulling out of the linen closet.

"Hell, the story's already gone out on the wires that Jasmine blew himself up." Foxcroft had been having a nightcap at Sardi's with the night editor when a cub reporter rushed in with the news that a Harvard professor had blown himself up. "Wouldn't be named Jasmine," he had asked, and the reporter looked at him as if he were some sort of genius. Foxcroft's first guess was suicide—Jasmine had looked at his wit's end that afternoon. He didn't know if there was much of a story in the suicide of a professor—but maybe it could be tied into Joe McCarthy's persecution of academics. Anyhow, he had had the last interview with Jasmine—and that could be a peg for the story. Stepping out into the street, he had hailed a cab and said "Boston." It had cost two hundred dollars on the meter, and now it seemed Jasmine wasn't even dead.

"Who did you say had him under surveillance?" Foxcroft slightly squinted his right eye at Burke. It was his way of saying he was suspicious of something.

"That's not for publication. I said the FBI—purely for your background."

Foxcroft tightened the squint by half-smiling. He knew it wasn't the FBI. Hoover was a publicity hound. If his men had a terrorist under surveillance, he would already have announced it in a press conference. "Sure it's not another government agency, Captain ... the *Times* has information that it is the CIA."

The smile froze on Burke's face. "Well, as long as you heard it from someone else. But don't print it before checking with them."

"O.K.—I'll let them brief me on the case. Thanks for the tip, Captain." His technique never failed. He simply put his guesses in the form of "the *Times* has information ..."

Foxcroft was in Tracy's office the next morning. "This has to be very deep background, Fletcher—no quotations, no attribution—national security is involved."

"You make the rules, Mr. Tracy. If I can't play by them, I'll give you fair warning," Foxcroft replied, trying to make himself comfortable on the couch.

"There are, of course, matters I can't discuss—we don't want the Soviets to know we're on to their game." Tracy stopped to light his pipe.

"Are you trying to say Jasmine is a Soviet agent?"

"Well, this is one matter I can't go into ..." Tracy watched Foxcroft swallow the bait. A few gentle tugs on the line, and he could lead him wherever he wanted.

"The *Times* has information that he was trying to steal secrets about a CIA operation in Iran."

"The *Times* has a well-deserved reputation for accuracy. As I'm sure your source has already told you, it is a purely defensive operation."

"Defensive? Not sure that's our understanding."

"Deep background, then. Only to be used to correct information you already have. Agreed?"

"Agreed," Foxcroft repeated, taking out his notebook, and discreetly placing it on his lap.

"As you know, the Soviets control the Tudeh Party in Iran." Tracy decided it was best to begin with a trite but true fact. It would help assure Foxcroft's confidence in him.

"Right. We know the Tudeh has been snuggling up to Mossadeq. What does that have to do with Jasmine?"

"Then you also probably know that the Soviets plan to assassinate Mossadeq and put the Tudeh in power."

Foxcroft's mouth opened slightly, but he said nothing. His first rule of journalism was: never admit ignorance. "Yeah, that's one of the rumors floating around," he said.

"It's more than a rumor, but please don't print anything about it. Sensitive sources are involved." He waited for Foxcroft to nod his approval, then continued: "The CIA has been trying to penetrate this conspiracy—but it's highly

234

sensitive since our allies are not exactly enamoured of Mossadeq."

"Yeah. They probably are rooting for the Soviets to succeed."

"Well, you see the problem."

"And Jasmine," Foxcroft began to squint.

"He's one of the most ingenious Soviet agents we've come up against. A mole. Infiltrated the CIA, stole a top-secret contingency plan to stop the Soviets in Iran."

Foxcroft thought back to Jasmine in Venezuela. He did have brilliant moments. He just rubbed Rockefeller's staff the wrong way. Not impossible he was an agent. Foxcroft's second principle of journalism was: nothing is impossible. "But if Jasmine was a Soviet agent, who tried to kill him last night?"

"All we know for sure is that the bomb was manufactured in East Germany. Why someone put it in Professor Jasmine's phone—and why it failed to kill him—well, we just don't have the answers."

"Why would the Soviets try to kill their own agent—that's what you're hinting at, aren't you?" His half-squint increased to a full squint.

"That's your surmise. I can't stop you from making it. The fact that it was an East German bomb is not conclusive."

"No. Might have been your boys, trying to stop a Soviet agent before he passed on secrets. That makes more sense, doesn't it?"

"Don't be melodramatic, Fletcher. You've been around long enough to know that we don't murder people." Tracy snorted a laugh, as if it was too ridiculous to consider.

"Anyhow, it wouldn't be printable—CIA TRIES TO MURDER PROFESSOR," Foxcroft mumbled.

"Foxcroft. From your reputation, I know you're a serious

journalist. You've been around the world and I daresay you know more about Communist intrigue than most diplomats." Tracy relit his pipe. He knew flattery never hurt when dealing with the press. "The reason I've consented to this briefing is that I wouldn't want you going off halfcocked in the wrong direction."

"Don't worry about that," Foxcroft said, closing his notebook. "You don't, by the way, know where Jasmine is now?"

Tracy laughed heartily. "Ask the FBI. They are coordinating the search." He walked Foxcroft to the door thinking that the briefing had gone rather well. At least he had planted the idea in Foxcroft's mind that Jasmine was a Soviet agent. Now all he had to do was fabricate a few bits of confirming evidence—and leave them out for Foxcroft to stumble on. With a little luck, and help, Foxcroft might win another Pulitzer Prize for revealing that the Communists killed Mossadeq. "If I can be of further help, Fletcher, don't hesitate to call."

Foxcroft pumped Tracy's hand, thinking, "This guy is lying through his teeth." It wasn't anything Tracy said that struck him as false or mendacious. It was simply his third rule: No one tells the truth—entirely.

A half-hour later Foxcroft was back at the National Press Club. He ordered a double martini. Across the room, reporters were moving along a wall of cubbyholes in which were distributed the press releases of various government agencies. It reminded Foxcroft of a beehive, reporters swarming over the releases like honey. He had rewritten press releases himself his first three years on the *Times,* but now something more was expected of him. He began reviewing his notes—everyone had told him a different story: Jasmine, Professor Abraham, Smithline, Tracy. And he only knew one thing for sure—everyone was lying. He ordered another double martini in anticipation of the trip to Ann Arbor.

He arrived at the University of Michigan that evening and found Professor Abraham at the Faculty Club. "I'd like you to read this story before the *Times* publishes it tomorrow," he began.

It took only a few minutes for the Professor to scan the three-page "story."

"This is wrong ... deeply wrong," Abraham said, his body shaking like putty.

"Which part ... the part about you being a CIA agent, the part about you being involved in the internal politics of Iran, or the part about you collaborating on a cover story with Myles Smithline."

"I'll sue the *Times. ...*"

"No need to sue for libel, Professor. We're giving you every opportunity to correct any errors in it." Foxcroft had written the story on the plane down to Detroit. It was never meant for publication.

"There's not a shred of truth in this. The Game of Nations is not a CIA front."

"C'mon, Professor. Stop lying. Bronson Tracy admitted everything to me. Call him if you like. If you level with me, I can rewrite this story so no names are mentioned."

"I'm terribly confused, Mr. Foxcroft. Jasmine was working for the CIA as a planner—then suddenly he wasn't at the Gaming Center anymore. There was some suspicion that he was 'insecure,' as they say."

Foxcroft did not like using intimidation as a weapon in journalism, but it produced results. "And what was the Ajax game?" he pressed.

"It was a plan to counter a Soviet coup in Iran," the Professor lied.

Foxcroft rushed off to the nearest pay phone. With this

ammunition in hand, he called Myles Smithline long distance.

"Have a heart, Foxy. I could lose my job if I told you about Jasmine. You need me as a source ..."

"You lied to me, Myles. You're not going to have much success as a press officer at State if you lie to the *Times.*"

"National security was involved."

"Yeah, 'I thought Ajax was just a game.' "

"We can't discuss this over the telephone, Foxy. Why don't we have lunch tomorrow?"

Foxcroft caught the evening plane to Washington. Since he was on an expense account, he took Smithline for lunch at the Sans Souci.

After three martinis and a bottle of claret, Smithline told him the story. Tracy had instructed him to feed Foxy. Jasmine did work for the CIA but he was compromised by an English girl and started stealing secrets. "The CIA only found out about Jasmine through a double-agent they have planted in Moscow—if you write a word of this, Foxy, you're signing his death warrant," Smithline finally blurted out.

Just as Smithline was getting up to leave, Foxcroft asked, "And who tried to blow him up?"

"Do you think they would tell me? Foxy, be reasonable."

"What's your guess, Myles?"

"The same as yours: No one tried to kill Jasmine," Smithline explained disingenuously. "You must have figured it out the same way. No one could miss with a telephone bomb. Christ, you don't detonate it until you hear the guy's voice." As Smithline fed Foxcroft the prearranged story, his admiration for Tracy grew. The bomb would only confirm to Foxcroft that he was on the right track.

On July twenty-ninth, Foxcroft ordered a first-class ticket to Teheran on his *Times* expense account. The travel agent told him the eleventh-floor suite he usually took in the Park Hotel had been booked for two months, but there was a smaller suite available on the tenth floor. He took it. If the Soviets were going to move on Iran, he wanted to be there—if only for the dateline.

Chapter XXVI

GAMES OF CHANCE

Nubar Gulbenkian placed a one-hundred-thousand-franc plaque on each of four numbers—1, 8, 9, 6. Those were the four numbers he always played at roulette. Four numbers he could never forget; combined they were his birth year—1896.

Darius Ali reached into the pile of chips in front of him with his bearlike hand and, moving back and forth across the board, dropped the thousand-franc chips in a dozen different places. He thought it unlucky to play single numbers, and thus chose combinations of two, four, and eight different numbers. In less than a minute, all his chips were transferred to the green-beige matrix of numbers.

The croupier looked at both men as he set the magnificently balanced wheel in motion. For the last three hours, they had been the only players in this private salon at the

Hôtel de Paris in Monte Carlo. He handed the ivory ball to Nubar. *"Votre jeu, Monsieur."* He had known Gulbenkian for twenty years, but never called him by name. A rule of the house.

Gulbenkian stroked his beard for a moment, fascinated by the spinning numbers. Then he dropped the ball, and listened with satisfaction as it bounced from number to number. It stopped for a moment in the one-slot, and he thought he had won, but it then rolled out.

"Zero," the croupier called as he raked in all the bets on the board.

Gulbenkian threw him a hundred-thousand plaque as a pourboire. It didn't matter to him that he lost. He always lost at roulette. He knew that the oil fields in which his father had a five-percent share were producing a million barrels a day in Iraq—and as long as Iran remained shut down, they would keep producing at that rate.

"Sometimes there are no winners," Darius said with a fatalistic sigh as they left the table. He was thinking that in less than three weeks the fate of his country would be decided by forces over which he had no control. This time he had gambled everything he had on the Shah and that made him uneasy. He preferred combinations.

They stopped in the public salon for a few minutes. Men in tuxedos and women in white evening gowns pressed themselves around kidney-shaped tables, and peered down at the clicking wheel as if looking into an open grave. How can they be so serious about gambling, Nubar thought. His eye settled on an American couple standing a few feet away. The man, short, thin, with silvery hair, was literally clawing the mahogany rail of the table with both hands and praying aloud, "God, if you ever cared, make it seven." His companion, suntanned down to her ankles and many years younger than he, was caressing her thighs with short strokes as she waited for the ball to come to rest. Her mouth was open. Her undisguised sexuality excited Gulbenkian. He moved closer.

Darius meanwhile was watching a Libyan prince lose a fortune. With each loss, he giggled, and threw some chips to a dark-haired boy standing next to him. It could have been his son, but Darius knew it wasn't. He recognized the bald-headed man with thick glasses behind the Libyan as William Caddy of El Dorado Oil. El Dorado, he also knew, was desperately searching for its own source of Middle East oil, since it had been cut off by the major producers when Iran closed down. A few gestures between the Libyan, the boy, and Caddy told the whole story. Darius guessed that Caddy had brought the Libyan to Monte Carlo to compromise him. He would provide him with as much money as he could lose, as much fine wine as he could drink, and whatever oriental delicacies his appetite craved. When the Libyan owed him more than he could repay and was hopelessly involved with the boy Caddy probably also provided, Caddy would make a few innocuous-sounding requests. Perhaps a letter of introduction to someone in the inner circle of King Idris' court; perhaps some information about the sexual dispositions of the assistants of Nessim, the Oil Minister; and perhaps for help in arranging a few discreet meetings in Tripoli. Caddy would then attempt to parlay those advantages into a concession for his company in the Libyan desert. Then it would no longer be a game of chance: as every geologist familiar with that area knew, if you pushed a straw into the sand, oil would gush out. The cartel had so far managed to keep this ocean of oil safely under the Libyan desert, but it was only a matter of time before Caddy or other independents would bribe, blackmail, or seduce a concession out of King Idris.

Gulbenkian could smell a cheap, fruity perfume on the

girl. Her café-au-lait tan still had traces of coconut oil on it from her afternoon on the beach. Nubar could see her fingers dig into her dress as the ball landed in the seven-slot. She gave a short, uncontrollable shriek of joy.

"Come, let's get out of here," Darius said. "I can put up with this sort of decadence only when I'm winning." He led the way past the baccarat, chemin-de-fer, and dice American tables. Gulbenkian followed.

The moment they were out the doors of the casino they were hit by the mistral winds. Even though it was July, the Mediterranean wind was cool and refreshing. They crossed the street and walked along the dock leading to the boat basin. In a moment, they were in a forest—a forest of masts culled from some of the most expensive trees in the world. Finally, they came to a long, ghostly white ship flying the Liberian flag.

"*Voilà*, the *Christina.*" Darius made the hand gesture of a head waiter offering a table. "You know it of course, Nubar."

"I've been on it twice." Gulbenkian took a cigar from his leather case and offered it to Darius, then lit it for him. Yes, he knew the *Christina*. It had been a Canadian destroyer until Aristotle Onassis bought it and converted it to his private yacht. Now it had everything: a tiled swimming pool whose floor rose, at the press of the button, to become a dance floor; a private seaplane; a collection of ninety impressionist masterpieces; a crew of a hundred and, on the last occasion he was aboard, Maria Callas. "Now that Onassis has rented a floor in the casino as his headquarters, he parks this bit of floating ostentation outside, so everyone can marvel at his riches."

"Some people say he's broke, but it doesn't matter." With both hands, Darius shielded from the wind the cigar Gulbenkian was trying to light for himself. In the flicker of light, he could see some pain in his friend's face. He knew that he had touched a nerve bringing him to Onassis' yacht. Onassis did not have a fraction of the wealth of the Gulbenkian family, but he used what he had to create the illusion of enormous wealth. And he knew that the illusion was a form of wealth.

"Of course his empire is a house of cards. It is held together with bank loans he can't pay, and he has to sink his own ships for the insurance." Nubar did not feel it necessary to elaborate. Darius knew, as well as he did, that Onassis had begun by recklessly gambling on the short-term tanker market. After the war he had made a killing, but then when there was a glut of oil on the market in 1950, and no one needed to charter his tankers, he'd gone broke—or would have if he hadn't had a few of his own ships scuttled and collected ten times their value from the insurance companies. Now he had invested all that money ordering supertankers from every Japanese and Scandinavian shipyard that could build them. And again, with Iran closed down, he was facing bankruptcy as soon as he accepted delivery of the first supertanker.

"Of course in theory, Onassis is in deep trouble, but in fact his gamble on tankers is going to pay off."

"How?" The competitive edge in Nubar was now showing.

"In three weeks Mossadeq will be gone. The oil companies are going to have to move a million barrels of Iranian oil a day to rebuild their reserves. How? The answer is supertankers, Onassis' supertankers."

Gulbenkian realized Darius was right. With Iran reopened, tanker space would be in demand, and Onassis would reap another undeserved fortune. "We're doing his work for him in Iran—is that the point?"

"No, the point is supertankers. The cartel is not going to last forever."

"I don't see your point."

"The cartel has managed to control the world oil business to date, not because it controls all the oil in the ground—they could never hold all the concessions—but because they control the only means of transporting oil across the oceans. What good did it do to Mossadeq to control a million barrels a day of oil in the Persian Gulf? Without tankers, it was as worthless as mud."

"Mossadeq might be in business today if there were a few more supertankers. Is that what you're suggesting?"

"Why talk about Mossadeq," Darius said. "He is the past. Finished. In three weeks, the Shah will nominally control Iranian oil."

"Only nominally?"

"Without tankers, the Shah is in no better position than Mossadeq. He will have to give the oil back to the cartel on their terms. But that is not the future, Nubar, is it? Someone is going to build a fleet of supertankers, then it will be a very different game?"

"If it's inevitable, it will happen—an old Armenian proverb."

"But a few years can make a difference to Iran, to the Shah. And to the Gulbenkian interest, especially if the Gulbenkians owned supertankers ..."

"I might even become as rich as Onassis," Gulbenkian quipped, afraid that the conversation was turning too conspiratorial.

"Nubar, imagine what the Middle East could look like if the Shah controlled Iranian oil. Iran is a country of forty million people—Kuwait, Oman, Abu Dhabi, even Saudi Arabia are populated by nomads. Some nation is going to have to dominate the Persian Gulf—why not Iran?"

"For one reason, there are still three divisions of British troops east of Suez."

"Think of the future, Nubar. When the British have withdrawn from Suez, when the Shah is no longer controlled by America, when oil is selling for many times a dollar-eighty a barrel in an oil-starved world, when the cartel no longer owns all the tankers."

"I'm too old and lecherous to think of any future more than a night away." But Gulbenkian was considering another possibility. He was thinking of striding into his father's office in Lisbon and taking command. He would then propose pulling the Gulbenkian money out of the arrangements they had in common with the cartel and putting it instead into a fleet of supertankers. He looked at the glistening white yacht as he thought of this course of action and wished he was a half-century younger.

"Nubar, it will happen with or without your help—but I wish it was you rather than him," he said, pointing to Onassis' ship. "Now that I've told you my dream, we can get down to the more practical matters of life—Mossadeq."

Gulbenkian wondered how Darius always seemed to know what he was about to say. "I've been asked to coordinate a few last details with you. Only two things are expected of the Shah—"

"You sound like Raven," Darius interrupted.

"They're his instructions." Gulbenkian smiled. "First, the Shah must issue the order dismissing Mossadeq—and second, after issuing the order, he must be ready on a minute's notice to board his plane and fly to Rome. That's it."

"All very simple. But don't you think it would be helpful if we knew a little more about the mechanics of this coup d'etat? What, for example, is going to happen to Mossadeq?

Is there going to be fighting? Military intervention? What's going to happen to the oil?"

"All very good questions—but unfortunately Raven has told me very little."

"But you have your own means of finding answers—you mentioned on the phone that you might have some 'context' on the event."

"Did you read about that professor at Harvard involved in the bombing?"

"The terrorist? Yes, I read about him in the *Herald Tribune.*"

"His name is Jacob Jasmine. He should be in London tomorrow. Thought you might like to see him."

"What good is a terrorist?"

"Jasmine is the person who planned the coup for the CIA. I thought he could fill you in on what you call the 'mechanics.' "

It took Darius a moment to digest what he had heard. "I see. . . . Does Raven know about this?"

"No. Made the arrangements myself."

"No matter what you say, Nubar, you are a friend of Iran's." Darius looked at Gulbenkian. He never ceased to be amazed at the Armenian's resourcefulness. "See you soon," he said, disappearing into the night. It was morning in Teheran and he had phone calls to make.

Gulbenkian returned to the casino. He quickly found the American girl. She was straining forward to watch the wheel go round. Her companion was still begging favors from heaven. He seemed too engrossed in the game even to turn around to talk to her.

"Excuse me, madame," Gulbenkian said, touching her lightly on the shoulder. "If you really want to see how roulette is played, there is a room upstairs without a limit.

In a minute, you can see a million francs won or lost."

"Sounds fascinating," she said. She looked first at the Odontoglossum orchid in Nubar's lapel, then at his beard, and finally at his monocle. She had never seen anyone so distinguished looking before. Possibly he was a prince, she thought.

He led her by the hand up the staircase and through a door marked "private." Croupiers bowed their heads as he passed. They had seen both him and his father lead women up the stairs before.

"This is just unbelievable ... wait till I tell Bob," she exclaimed as she took in the full magnificence of the private salon. The walls were covered in green silk brocade, the cut-glass crystals in the chandelier glittered like a thousand diamonds, and her bare toe could feel the deep pile of the carpet. There was only one gaming table and one croupier.

"One million francs, *s'il vous plaît,*" Gulbenkian ordered from the cashier. He then gave the ten one-hundred-thousand-franc plaques to the girl. "See what you can win."

"But I can't ... take ..." She looked up at him and took the money. She was more sure than ever that he was a prince.

He stood close to her as she played. He could feel every flutter of the warm excitement in her body. She trembled when the wheel began to pick up speed, froze when it stopped, and then released all her energy in a sudden burst when she saw she had won.

"I'm winning, winning, winning!" she cried out. He helped her stack her plaques in neat piles, and reaching over her, arranged her next bet for her. He was her croupier now—and with a wave of his hand, sent the house croupier out of the room.

She watched as he pulled the green cover over the wheel.

"You've broken the bank at Monte Carlo ... now we must make love right here on this table."

No one had ever been so direct before. No one had ever used the words before. It was like a dream. She didn't resist as her prince lifted her up.

Gulbenkian knew, even then, that he could never take charge of his father's company and begin building a fleet of supertankers. Not even for an alliance with the Shah. This was as much power as he ever wanted.

BOOK THREE

August, 1953

Chapter XXVII

THE ESCAPE

"Then what did you do?" Arabella asked, tilting her head forward so it rested on her knee. The bed she was sitting on was thinly disguised with four patchwork cushions to look like a couch.

Jasmine paced back and forth across the small room, his head nearly touching the eaved ceiling. He was afraid that if he stopped moving, he might crumple up on the floor like a rag doll. "I saw the cops coming in with McNab and ran out the back door. Kept running. There were sirens coming from every direction. All I could think of was getting away from McNab. Then I found myself in my car, driving across the bridge . . ."

"To where?"

"That's what I was trying to figure out. It was raining so

hard I could hardly see through the windshield. I just missed
running into a bus outside of Boston. I pulled over—thinking
I'd sleep for a few hours. Decide what to do in the morning.
Then I heard it on the radio. It was on the news: 'Harvard
Professor Identified as a Terrorist. Cache of Weapons Found
in Cambridge Apartment.' I had seen it all before in
Venezuela. They framed their victims before they killed
them. Now they were framing me."

"So you couldn't go to the police?"

"Not unless I wanted to be arrested. Who knows what sort
of accident McNab could arrange for me in jail. I don't
mean to sound paranoid."

"Go on." She wrapped both arms around her legs, forming the letter *A* with her body.

"Suddenly, I realized from the news report that they
thought I had been killed in the explosion. I figured that
gave me a few hours' head start before they came looking
for me. I started driving again. I remembered the air ticket
in my pocket to London. . . ."

"So you decided to visit me, your faithful tutee?"

"It was four A.M. when I got to the Canadian border," he
continued. "Just as I was about to cross, I thought they
might recognize the license plates so I made a U-turn."

"Functional paranoia," she commented. It was a phrase
he had used in his lectures to describe the behavior of
conspirators in a coup d'etat: Assume everyone is after you.

"I drove back to Plattsburg. Left the car at the station,
and caught the New York–Montreal express just as it was
pulling out."

"No problem at the border this time?"

"It was a breeze. They don't even check passports in
Canada. By nine o'clock that morning, I was headed for
Paris."

"Paris?"

"I took the first flight I could get. Fugitives from the CIA can't be choosy. I tried to get some sleep, but the hostess kept waking me to check that my seatbelt was fastened."

"I'll bet," she interrupted. Even with a five-day growth of beard, he looked very appealing. Those large sad eyes and thin delicate hands—she understood the hostess's interest in him.

"When I got off at Shannon to stretch my legs, I saw my photograph on the front page of the *Irish Times:* MANHUNT ON FOR HARVARD TERRORIST PROFESSOR. I couldn't go to Paris; Interpol might be waiting for me. I looked around. Air France was changing crews. My hostess was struggling with two plastic bags full of appliances she had bought in New York. *'Permettez-moi,'* I said in my best French. Grabbing one of the bags from her hands, and, keeping right in the center of the crew, I made it through the Flight Personnel Only gate. Luckily, the Irish are pretty lax."

"And you were born devious."

"I got a ride to the outskirts of Dublin with a farmer who didn't say a solitary word the whole time. Then I hitched a ride with a lorry driver. He was carrying a truckload of fresh haddock, and was in an awful hurry to get to Londonderry in Northern Ireland before they spoiled. As we got a few miles away, I took the driver into my confidence, and told him I was an American backer of the IRA, and my life depended on getting to Londonderry."

"A likely story. You look anything but Irish."

"I used the newspaper photograph to convince him I was a wanted terrorist. That was all it took. He said, 'God bless you, son,' and hid me behind a keg of haddock."

"Which you still smell from."

"Once in England, the rest was easy. I found two American tourists who were happy to change the few dollars I had with me into pounds. They even gave me a ride to London."

"Jake the Charmer."

"I couldn't afford to stay in London. I had a free room at the Dorchester thanks to Oxbridge Press, but couldn't take a chance on going there. I suddenly felt lost. I took the underground to the zoo, which is where I always go when I feel there's no place else to go. Then I counted the change in my pocket. I had just enough money left for a train ticket to Oxford."

"And here you are! Reeking of fish, flat broke, pursued by the police, but still scheming. What's your next move, Professor?"

"A bath. Then maybe some breakfast." By now, Jasmine hadn't eaten for two days.

"I'm not sure it will solve all your problems, Jake, but the bath is behind the kitchen." She pointed to a small door; then, thrusting her legs forward, sprang to her feet. "I'll see what I can do about breakfast while you're soaking."

He hardly fit in the cast-iron tub. There was just enough hot water to fill it up to his hips. Letting the cake of soap dissolve, he wondered what his next move should be. In just sixteen days, Mossadeq would be dead. Even then it might not be over. With his prior knowledge of the plot, and the memos in Raven's handwriting that he had, both the CIA and oil cartel would be out to silence him. He slouched down in the water, too tired to scheme.

He woke up when the front door slammed shut. There was a moment of panic, then he relaxed when he heard Arabella's voice.

"I got eggs, bacon, cheese, and six newspapers." She poked her hand holding the newspapers through the bathroom door. He took them from her and splashed back down in the tub.

He could smell the bacon frying in the kitchen as he raced through the papers looking for news about himself. There was only one story, and that was relegated to the back pages of *The Express.* The headline, TERRORIST PRO- FESSOR SURROUNDED, sent a shiver through him, but his anxiety was quickly relieved when he read the story itself. Under the dateline Plattsburg, New York, August 4th, 1953, it stated: "FBI and State Police believe Professor Jacob Jasmine is hiding out somewhere in this rural community in upstate New York. More than a hundred law enforcement officers, aided by a pack of bloodhounds, are searching the woods where he is believed hiding. Capture of the Harvard terrorist is expected momentarily." They had found the car, he concluded.

His anxiety was restored a moment later when he read the report in the *Times* by Fletcher Foxcroft from Teheran.

According to unimpeachable sources in this capital, there is increasing evidence of a Soviet campaign of intimidation and subversion directed against the gov- ernment of Iran. Despite official denials from the Soviet Embassy, reports from the border area indicate that a team of Soviet commandos have been infiltrating Iran. The search for these Soviet agents is being conducted under such top-secret conditions that no Iranian official will even acknowledge that the manhunt is taking place. Highly reliable sources have confirmed that the Soviet team includes two members of the Soviet Secret Police's Thirteenth Department, which is responsible for sabotage and assassination. American officials in Iran admit privately that they are concerned that

257

Premier Mohammed Mossadeq may not be able to cope with the threat. Despite this latest crisis, Mossadeq appeared at a press conference in his pajamas and openly wept. This did little to relieve the concerns that persist here.

"I wonder who's feeding Foxcroft this line—and what he's doing in Iran," Jasmine thought out loud as he reread the story. Then ne recalled that Option B had a provision for blaming the assassination on local Communists. "Tracy's behind Foxcroft," he concluded.

"Did you call me?" Arabella pushed the door open with the tray she was carrying. Averting her gaze from Jasmine, she set the bacon, eggs, cheese, and coffee down on the table next to the tub. She then scooped up his pile of clothes, holding them at arms' length.

"Where are you going with my clothes?" he called as the door slammed shut.

The front door opened. Halfway out, Arabella shouted back, "To the cleaners. Back in a jiff." Then the door clicked closed again.

Jasmine stepped out of the lukewarm water. Hands on his hips, he took a long look at himself in the full-length mirror on the back of the door. He felt even more naked than he was. For the first time in his life, he had no next move; no plan. Not even an idea where to turn. He had had a pretty good run—from New York to Cambridge to Plattsburg to Montreal to Shannon to Dublin to Londonderry to London to Oxford. But there was no place else to run. There were no more open squares in the mental chessboard he carried in his mind. All he could do was wait for the Smothered Mate.

He held the hand-shower over his head, splashing the soap off with cold water. That felt better. He saw Arabella's tiny razor on the sink and began methodically shaving off his beard. No need for disguise, he thought, as he cut long narrow roads through his tangled beard.

Arabella couldn't suppress a shriek of laughter when she walked in and saw Jasmine shaving with her petite razor. "Put this on, Jake," she said, throwing him a large terrycloth towel.

Embarrassed to see her standing there, he quickly wrapped the towel around him like a toga. In it, he looked almost noble—badly shaven as he was.

She handed him a fresh cup of coffee and waited for him to take his usual long strides across the floor as he plotted and schemed. Instead, he stood motionless. "Well Jake, where do you go from here?"

He sipped his coffee slowly, as if it were a substitute for an immediate answer.

She propped herself up on the desk. The afternoon sun glistened through her black hair. "You've had your bath, your breakfast—don't keep me hanging—what's your next move?" Her eyes opened with anticipation. She always loved to hear him spew forth scenarios.

"My next move?" He tilted his head downward as if the sun was bothering him. He could see she was beginning to be concerned. In a moment, she would see that he was lost, and would grow sad. That would never do, he decided. "I have to go to Iran, of course."

"Iran? Why Iran?" Her face perked up.

An answer was beginning to come to him. It just might work, he thought.

"For one thing, I have to reach Mossadeq."

"But will that help you?"

"If Mossadeq is killed, I'm the next domino to go—I can tell who did it."

He began to pace back and forth, his mind racing ahead to Iran. Of course, there was only a remote chance this line of play would succeed. But in an otherwise lost game, one seeks counterplay any place one can find it.

"So you think you can just pop into a strange country in the middle of a coup d'etat."

"Strange country? Remember, he asked all three questions rhetorically. It gave him time to think. Ajax, the country I invented. Remember my lecture on the labyrinth?"

How could she ever forget it. She saw him standing in front of three hundred awe-struck students, hands flailing high in the air, proclaiming in a whisper audible throughout the hall: "In the maze of government, whoever knows the floor plan ultimately holds the power. In this labyrinth, knowledge equals power." She nodded. "You were talking about situations in which there was total confusion. . . ."

"Right. Iran is the labyrinth I was talking about." His finger shot in the air: his old classroom sign for Eureka. "I planned every step of the coup, every option. I know the names of the participants down to the assassin; the sequence of events. I know enough to bluff my way right through the corridors of the palace, and I will." Even as he spoke he was arranging his final scenario. It involved Adams, Foxcroft, and Mossadeq.

"Aren't you forgetting that you're broke? And I only have twenty pounds to my name."

"Minor problem. Oxbridge Press offered me a thousand-pound advance for my book."

"That was before you were a terrorist. If you call them, they'll probably go straight to the police."

"Nonsense. I'm not wanted in England. Being a terrorist just increases the value of my book. Anyway, it's a chance I'll have to take." He began leafing through the M–Z phone book. "Oxbridge . . . here it is." He dialed the operator and asked for 589-9240 in London.

She watched him as he was shuttled between extensions,

knowing how he hated to be kept dangling on the phone. Suddenly, his whole face came alive. He began talking quickly to the editor, describing with great precision how they were to meet in Regents Park. "Tell him he'll recognize you because you'll be wearing a towel," she advised.

He glowered at her, then continued making a series of complicated arrangements for a rendezvous at the motor-boat station in Regents Park. It was a plan he had thought of the day before while wandering aimlessly around the zoo.

"Ah, intrigue," Arabella said as he hung up the phone. She kicked off one shoe, then the other. She could feel the tingling in the tips of her toes. Just like the first time she went to his office, his eyes glistened with excitement. "Your clothes won't be back until tomorrow. Can you wait?"

"Tomorrow?" He looked slowly around the one-room apartment. There was a chair, the desk Arabella was perched on, a stove, bath, bookcase, and a single bed. He decided not to ask any more questions.

Chapter XXVIII

RENDEZVOUS IN ZURICH

August eighth, Zurich. Allen Dulles paused momentarily as he stepped off the Pan Am stratocruiser. Zurich Airport looked familiar enough to him. So did the Swiss Intelligence agents, dressed in workmen's overalls and trying to look inconspicuous. He knew this territory well. It had been his espionage base during all of the Second World War. So they knew of his arrival. Swiss efficiency, he thought, as he slung his golf clubs over his shoulder and headed toward the terminal.

"Are you here on business or pleasure?" said the man behind the passport desk as if it were a routine question.

"Pleasure. Nothing like summer in the Alps." He smiled at the officer, recognizing him as the counterintelligence person who had tried to shadow him ten years before when he was secretly negotiating the surrender of Italy. It had taken him only a day to lose him then, he thought, remembering his younger days with a bit of nostalgia.

Outside the terminal, Dulles stepped into a Cadillac limousine. As it pulled away from the curb, the Mercedes behind it started its engine. When it reached the four-lane highway into Zurich, a small Citroën, with sides like iron washboards, cut in front of the Mercedes.

"Who's that in the Deux Chevaux?" Dulles asked the driver matter-of-factly.

"That souped-up Citroën? He's a new SDEC man, name's DeLamier, Pierre DeLamier."

So French Intelligence also knew of his trip to Zurich, he thought. He hoped they didn't know the purpose behind it. "And where are our Swiss friends?"

"They're in the Mercedes, two cars back."

"And the Russians?" Dulles asked, looking around as if for a missing guest at a cocktail party.

"They're doing a front tail." The driver pointed to the Peugeot directly ahead of them.

Dulles leaned back and relaxed. He knew by now that the Director of the CIA never traveled alone.

When the Cadillac pulled up in front of the Hotel St. Peter, the manager himself was waiting at the curb. Six bellboys unloaded the luggage while the manager personally escorted Dulles to his five-room suite on the top floor.

"Ah, the Alps," Dulles said, looking at the view. He walked into the living room. With its massive stone fireplace, rough-hewed beamed ceiling, and comfortable furniture, it reminded him of an Austrian hunting lodge. All it needs is a stag over the fire, he thought, as he finished his inspection of the room. In his thirty-five years as a diplomat, international lawyer, and spy, he had become a connoisseur of hotel rooms.

"I hope it meets with your approval, Mr. Dulles," the manager was saying as he backed out. "I can assure you it is utterly private."

"It is absolutely perfect, *Monsieur le Directeur,*" Dulles answered. *"Merci."*

The moment the door closed, his practiced eye surveyed the room. Utterly private? He knew that Swiss Intelligence had probably planted a dozen bugs. So, probably, had the French, Russians, and British. Luckily, McNab would be arriving shortly to ferret them out, he thought, as he lit his pipe.

A half-hour later, the phone rang. It was Tracy. "I'm downstairs with ... John."

"Come right up. Looking forward to seeing you both," Dulles boomed back.

A few minutes later Tracy and McNab arrived. Dulles waited patiently while McNab finished "sweeping" the living room with a device that looked like a small tennis racquet. Each time he found a miniature transmitter, he held it up proudly, like an exterminator whose trap had caught a mouse. "That's it," he said. "This room is secure." Just to be on the safe side, he plugged in the phonograph he brought with him, and put on a record—Cole Porter's "Anything You Can Do I Can Do Better." The music and lyrics would confuse any microphone that had escaped his search.

"Thanks, John," Dulles said, as McNab left to sweep the other rooms in the suite.

"Well, are we prepared?" He looked at Tracy through his rimless spectacles like a professor awaiting the answer to a difficult question from a prize student.

"Everything is set in Teheran. We only need your go-ahead, sir."

"The final briefing will be tonight?"

"At seven this evening. Here, if that is all right with you."

"Good. I'm still a little concerned about this Jasmine business."

"That's under control, sir. I think we've located him in England." He had in fact just had word from Raven an hour before, but he didn't want to worry Dulles with details.

"England? Last time you had him in Ireland. Sticky business." He clenched his front teeth at the thought that the Iran operation could be insecure. "What if he gets to Iran . . . ?"

"He won't, sir. He's just an amateur, in over his head."

"Don't be so sure, Tracy. Could be anything."

"But I . . ."

"No buts about it," Dulles overrode. "He got away from McNab, didn't he? He got the master list of agents?"

"Blind luck, sir."

"He got into England without a passport. Quality trade-craft, that's what it sounds like to me. Professional work."

"I promise, sir, he's not a professional. . . . I . . . er . . . recruited him myself from Harvard for the Ajax scenario. . . ."

"He did a brilliant job. Pity he's a defector, I was thinking of using him for Guatemala. Maybe we could turn him around. But take my word for it—he doesn't smell to me like an amateur. Did you read Foxcroft's story about Soviet spies in Iran?"

"I planted it, sir," Tracy cut in quickly so Dulles could change his tack before it was too late.

"Thought so. Sounded like rubbish to me."

At six that evening, General Schwartzkopf checked into the Hotel St. Peter under the alias Norman Normans. In his checkered sportshirt and straw hat, he hoped to pass for just another tourist in Zurich. The flight from Teheran to Wiesbaden had taken six hours on an Air Force jet, and the flight to Zurich on Swiss Air had taken another two hours. During those eight hours, he had gone over every nuance in the plan a dozen times. He checked the chronometer on his wrist: he had one hour before the briefing.

The chimes in the clock tower next door to the St. Peter rang seven times.

In Dulles' suite, the phonograph blared "Can you bake a cake ... I can bake a cake better than you." Schwartzkopf, the first to arrive, seated himself in a heavy oak chair at the table in front of the fireplace. He shuffled through the sheaf of papers he had brought with him, then looked at his watch, anxious to begin. Tracy sat next to him, a glass of port in his hand. "Would you like some port, General?" he asked genially.

"Never drink on duty," Schwartzkopf answered, more like a policeman than an army officer.

After a flurry of handshakes, the four men settled back in their chairs. Dulles tried a number of times to light his pipe, and finally succeeded. "Well, gentlemen," he began, then paused. "Is everyone comfortable with Ajax?" He looked slowly around the table and stopped at Schwartzkopf. "Well, General, can we assume that Kim has everything under control in Teheran?" He had wanted Kim to come to Zurich for the briefing, but understood his position in not wanting to leave Iran with the operation due to begin in four days.

Schwartzkopf leafed through the papers in front of him. "I have a full report on the situation; should I read it?"

Dulles nodded.

"Mossadeq's capacity for counterintelligence has been successfully neutralized. All key intelligence agents in the Iranian service are now effectively under our control."

"What about foreign agents, say Soviets in Teheran?" Dulles interrupted.

"Fortunately, Mossadeq looks with extreme suspicion on all foreign agents," Tracy cut in. "With the disinformation we're putting out, I don't think he'll believe a word the Soviets say."

"Continue, General," Dulles commanded.

"We have also established the capacity for generating disorder in Teheran, which will appear to be the work of Mossadeq's followers. Specifically, we have recruited sixty agents provocateurs to desecrate shrines and mosques in the name of Mossadeq."

"The idea is to neutralize Mossadeq's support with Moslem groups," Smithline said by way of elaboration. His specialty was provocation.

"Yes." Schwartzkopf resumed reading, "The private armies of General Zahedi and General Arfa are fully prepared to move into Teheran at a given signal. Tanks have already been airlifted in to General Zahedi so he can establish the necessary roadblocks."

"Let's not get too deeply into the nitty-gritty, General. I have full confidence in the Ajax scenario. What I want to know is: do you foresee any problems?" Dulles asked with an impatient edge.

"None whatsoever," Schwartzkopf answered, raising his head erect.

"No chance the refinery at Abadan will be blown up?"

"None whatsoever. Raven has arranged for private security guards to occupy all the key positions in the refineries. British paratroopers will also be standing by in Cyprus."

"One final point." Dulles pointed his pipe at Tracy. "Can we be sure that this will not embarrass the President?"

"Sir, I think there are enough cover stories built into the Ajax scenario to cover all foreseeable contingencies," Tracy answered.

"What about the unforeseeable ones?" Dulles muttered.

"In my opinion, the scenario will assure, no matter what happens, that President Eisenhower will have plausible deniability," Tracy continued.

Dulles again moved his eyes around the table. No one spoke up. "Well then, if there are no objections, we are in business. Tracy, I think it's time to wish Kim a happy birthday."

"Right." Tracy walked to the phone and asked the operator to get him room 919 in the Park Hotel in Teheran. He had waited nine months for this moment.

Dulles walked into the kitchen and reappeared a moment later with a magnum of vintage champagne. He shuffled over to the bar, and returned with five crystal-stemmed glasses.

"Can you fly to the sky ... I can fly ... I can do anything better than you," the phonograph continued.

"It's ringing, sir," Tracy called across the room. In his hand, he had a small card. "... Is the number I'm calling 71-00-17? ... Wrong number? ... Well, happy birthday."

"Happy birthday," Kim Adams replied on the other end of the line as he checked the code number. He had his Go signal. As he hung up, he could hear a cork popping five thousand miles away.

CHAPTER XXIX

THE ZOO

"Jake, I am going with you. . . ."

Jasmine could hear his name being called in the distance but he was still asleep. The "I" slowly undulated in his drowsy mind. Then it turned into a sort of inflatable life raft that slipped underneath him and floated him up toward the blurry red surface. Through his closed eyelids, he could see daylight.

"I've decided . . ." Arabella said.

He opened his eyes. She was lying next to him, her opened hand on his cheek. Pushing himself up, he looked at his watch. Ten o'clock. He tried to shake the grogginess out of his head.

". . . to go with you to London today." She punctuated her thought by kissing him on the neck.

269

He slumped back into bed and pulled her tightly to him. "I have to do this alone, Arabella."

"Just to London, Jake. I want to see this publisher. What's his name—David Allen?"

"No. I don't want you involved in any of this. And that's final." He felt her warm hands under the blanket.

"You don't want me as your co-conspirator, huh?"

"No. Not in this mess."

"Well then, how are you going to retrieve your clothes, my love?"

He sat up silently, adopting the pose of Rodin's "The Thinker."

"And who's going to pay for the train tickets to London?"

"O.K., London, and no further. But you're not going to meet Allen, and that's final."

An hour later, they were walking down Elizabeth Street, arms interlocked, headed for the Oxford station. "Promise, Arabella, when we get to Regents Park, that you'll keep at least twenty yards behind me. No matter what, we mustn't be seen together. For all I know, this Allen character might have called in the cops."

"I promise," she agreed. One of the reasons she insisted on going with him was that she also feared he might be walking into a trap. At least she'd be there to call a lawyer or someone.

"Perhaps you better take this." Jasmine handed her the worn attaché case he had with him.

"What's in it?" She recalled that he'd been clutching it for dear life when he stumbled into her apartment the day before.

"Raven's documents." Looking over his shoulder, he suddenly turned and gestured wildly for a taxi he thought he saw down the street.

"You fool, that's no taxi; it's a Rolls-Royce. If you're going to spend time in England, you'd better learn the difference." As she spoke, a black Silver Cloud Rolls slowly passed them. "Anyhow, we only have another block to the station."

The train from Oxford had arrived in Paddington Station in London at two o'clock. If nothing else, British trains run on time, Jasmine thought to himself as they began walking to Regents Park.

"Remember. At least twenty yards behind," he cautioned her again, when they reached the edge of the park.

"Twenty yards." She smiled. "Please be careful, Jake."

He walked briskly down a tree-lined path that circled a pond. He stopped and glanced back to make sure that Arabella was keeping her distance. He smiled to himself when he spotted her sitting on a bench reading a newspaper and trying, he presumed, to look inconspicuous.

He continued on into the Zoo. The hands on the clock above the monkey house showed it to be 2:45. He still had fifteen minutes to spare. After loitering by the elephants for a moment, he cut diagonally across to the lions, then back again to the giraffes. Finally, at the bear pits, he spotted a man holding his umbrella upside down, the signal he had suggested to his publisher over the phone. So that was David Allen. Despite his large bulk, he seemed to have a sympathetic face. Certainly, he didn't look like either a killer or a cop, Jasmine concluded.

Arabella followed Jasmine and Allen to the boat station, feeling faintly ridiculous. Anyone watching the three of them walking, stopping, looking around, and then walking again might assume they were all playing some child's game.

Darius Ali waited by the phone as he had been instructed. He had recognized Jasmine from his photograph in the

271

papers from as far back as the elephants, but kept up the pretense of being a somewhat absentminded publisher. Finally, the phone rang. "Mr. Allen: Please get on the boat leaving now. I'll meet you on it," Jasmine said, from the adjacent phone booth.

Darius shrugged and stepped onto the sixteen-passenger motor launch. Just as the boat was pushing off, he saw Jasmine leap on the back and make his way toward him.

The launch slowly chugged along the Regents Canal toward central London. It had only four passengers.

"Mr. Allen?" Jasmine said, introducing himself. "Sorry to put you to such trouble but . . ."

"No trouble at all, Professor Jasmine," Darius answered. "Many of our finest authors are persecuted by the police—or should be."

"My troubles all stem from the book I've written on coup d'etats. How, by the way, did you hear about me?"

"The Oxford-Cambridge grapevine. You know how word travels. Did you bring the manuscript, Professor?"

"It needs some updating, Mr. Allen. That's why it would be helpful to get an advance."

Darius paused for a moment, looking at the long-legged girl stepping on the boat at the Hampstead Road station. "We, of course, would finance your final research on the project."

Arabella tried to avoid looking at Jasmine as she sat down a dozen seats away. So far, so good, she thought, as the boat moved out of the station.

"The book might become a good deal more relevant . . ." Jasmine began explaining, then stopped.

"Is some coup d'etat in the offing?"

"Very possibly, Mr. Allen. If I had a thousand pounds for research, I think I could give a complete case history. . . ."

Darius looked at the once stately townhouses on either side of the Canal. Like everything else in England, they seemed to be collapsing—right into the Canal. Two passengers got out at the Kentish Road station, leaving only Darius, Jasmine and, at the other end of the boat, Arabella.

Darius reached in his pocket and counted out twenty fifty-pound notes. "A thousand pounds is no problem for us, Professor. . . . We are in the business of supporting research. But if you could tell me something about this expected event, it would help justify giving you the money under such unusual circumstances."

Jasmine looked at the money, then at Darius.

"You're not really a publisher, are you?" Arabella could hear Jasmine say. She wanted to see the expression on Allen's face, but, with great discipline, kept her head buried in the newspaper. Then she heard Allen begin to laugh. It was a very throaty laugh, almost a cough. "Not a pub-publisher? What do you think I'm doing here? You must be joking, Professor."

"Publishers meet authors in their office, not in canal boats. And they don't give money without manuscripts," Jasmine said.

"You might say I am not one of the more conventional publishers. Your story, Professor."

"Not until I have some idea who you are."

"I'm an Iranian. I know part of your . . . er . . . book deals with events that are going to take place in my country in ten days. I think your research—especially times, dates, individuals involved—would be of great interest to my . . . er . . . publisher."

"Who is your 'publisher'?"

"On that, you'll have to trust me. But consider this thousand pounds an advance on, say—twenty thousand pounds. And that would be only the beginning of my publisher's interest."

Jasmine took a long look at Allen. He had no doubt he was an Iranian. Why not tell him, he decided. "Where shall I begin . . ."

"Begin at the beginning."

Arabella put down her newspaper and pretended to look for something in her purse. Out of the corner of her eye, she could see Jasmine counting off points on his fingers, as he used to in his lectures. He was talking in a whisper, and she couldn't hear what he was saying. Just as she picked up her newspaper again, she saw Allen press the thousand pounds into Jasmine's hand.

The motorman cut the engines on the launch, letting it glide into Pancras Loch station. Suddenly, he saw one passenger, whom he had previously decided was an American, take a giant step onto the gunnels, and then leap onto the dock—one hundred yards before the station. "Damned Yankees," he said to himself, "always in a hurry."

Neither of the two remaining passengers looked at all surprised. Darius assumed Jasmine was simply playing it safe, getting off before the boat could be met by police or the others who were after him. He waved good-bye, even as Jasmine disappeared through the trees. He wished him well, thinking the Shah might someday be able to use someone with his capacity. In any case, he now had the information— the "context" Gulbenkian had promised him in Monte Carlo. In a few hours, he would be on his way to Teheran.

Arabella was more concerned. She assumed Jasmine had leaped off to get away from her. She knew he wanted to keep her out of danger. In bed that morning he had told her he loved her. And he did, she concluded. His plan to go to Iran was reckless. Now that he had some money, he could change his plans, and hide out for a while. As the boat tied up, she climbed off, anxious to catch up with him.

"Everyone's in a hurry, Gov'ner," the motorman said to Darius, as he guided the launch back into the Canal.

Taking her shoes off, Arabella raced up the long narrow street that ran parallel to the Canal. Just as she got to the corner, she saw a Rolls-Royce pulling away. It looked very much like the Silver Cloud Jasmine had tried to hail as a taxi in Oxford that morning. She got just close enough to see Jasmine's unmistakable profile through the back window. Then the Rolls turned a corner and disappeared.

CHAPTER XXX

100 FOLLOWERS

The hundred men were formed in a perfect square in the center of Zinenen Temple in Teheran. Facing them was a giant of a man, Haja Hassan. Haja slowly raised his arms upward and let his black robe fall off. So did the men in the formation.

The audience, seated along stone benches around the men, cheered wildly at the sight of their perfectly developed biceps.

"Jesus. All they're wearing are G-strings!" Red Murphy exclaimed. "What are we doing here, Kim?"

"Relax, Red. The Zinenen is a religious sect whose members believe in the perfection of the body. Stop fidgeting and enjoy the show," Kim Adams answered him.

Haja picked up two hundred-pound clubs and began

276

throwing them high in the air and then catching them. The men in the formation used smaller clubs, but the effect of hundreds of clubs tumbling through the air was hypnotic. When they stopped, there was complete silence in the temple.

Haja then handed his enormous clubs to one of his followers, and counted out loud the number of times he threw the clubs. Again, the crowd cheered.

"This place stinks of sweat," Red commented. He was feeling increasingly more uncomfortable.

"Be patient, my boy. It's almost over," Adams reassured him.

The hundred followers threw the clubs higher and higher into the air. Young apprentices ran onto the floor and tried their hand at throwing the lighter clubs. Haja worked his way up to two-hundred-pound clubs. The crowd was now in a frenzy, chanting its support.

"Wouldn't want to meet him in a dark alley." Red was beginning to get interested.

"Exactly the point, my boy."

Haja threw the clubs ten times, put them down gently, and bowed to his followers. They began filing out. The Zinenen ceremony was over.

"Are we going?" Red asked as the rest of the audience began leaving.

"In a minute." Adams was busy scribbling some notes on a sheet of triple-spaced typing. They were now the last two people sitting in the theater.

Red looked up. Haja was striding over toward them. He instinctively felt for his .357 magnum although he wasn't sure that even that would stop Haja.

"Keeem," Haja called out, stretching out Kim's name so it sounded Arabian. "What are you doing in Iran?"

Red relaxed his grip on his magnum. He realized by now

that Adams had a very strange collection of friends scattered around the world.

"I've come, Haja Hassan, because I need your help." Adams knew that the best way to handle men of power was to appear to be in utter need of their assistance.

"But Keeem, how could I, an Iranian without power or powerful friends, be of use to someone who has the strength of governments behind him?"

He's remarkably well informed about Adams, Red thought, still trying to figure out what game was being played.

"I need what you and you alone can provide ... the services of one hundred stouthearted men for about one hour." Adams decided it was best to come to the point.

"I have one hundred followers—but they would follow no one else."

"Exactly." Adams took the briefcase out of Murphy's hands. He reached in and took out an emerald-encrusted Koran. It had cost him ten thousand dollars. "A token of my affection."

"I couldn't accept such a valuable gift. It might be ... misconstrued."

"Nonsense. It's a donation to your temple." Adams reached again into the briefcase and pulled out a roll of one thousand-rial banknotes. He counted out one hundred. "Here, this is for your men."

"When do you want us?" Haja said in a businesslike tone.

"One week from Friday. Have your men in Majlis Square in civilian clothes—no black robes."

"I shall try to be of service to you—as you have been to my country in the past." He bowed his head, and quickly walked off.

"Now we can go, Red," Adams said, handing him back his briefcase.

They walked back to Red's jeep. "Now where?" Red asked as he cut in and out of the donkey carts on Shalimar Street.

"The palace.... The Shah has to sign this little declaration I prepared for him to get the show moving." Adams took another quick look at what he had pounded out on his typewriter that morning. It was an order from the Shah—dismissing Mossadeq as Prime Minister.

As the jeep approached the palace, Adams ducked down from sight. He thought it best that no one see him enter the palace on that particular day.

CHAPTER XXXI

STEP ONE

The BBC broadcast began: "A new crisis arose in Iran today when Shah Mohammed Pahlevi, issued a decree dismissing Premier Mohammed Mossadeq. Mossadeq denounced the Shah's decree as 'unconstitutional,' and arrested the messenger." The highly cultured voice of the BBC announcer seemed somehow out of place on a car radio.

Jasmine leaned forward to listen. So it has begun, he thought. Step One. He could visualize the screen in the Gaming Center flashing AJAX KING DISMISSES PRIME MINISTER.

"Fancy that," Sweeney said, as he reached out and put the barrel of his .45-caliber revolver against Jasmine's throat. Using it as a lever, he forced Jasmine's head slowly back until it was flush against the seat of the Silver Cloud.

280

"Is he getting restless?" Hummer chortled from the front seat. He turned around to see what was happening in the back seat. His face was covered with deep wrinkles that looked like crow's feet. His eyes were so bloodshot they appeared to be colored red. "We should be there in another hour."

Sweeney brought his gun back to his own lap, keeping it pointed all the time toward Jasmine. His white hair made him look much older than he was. His face was so gaunt that his massive cheekbones seemed to show through. His eyes were locked on Jasmine. They had no kindness in them.

Jasmine had seen that shock of white hair somewhere before, but where? He strained his memory. Suddenly, it came to him—the train down from Oxford. Then the rest fell in place. They must have been watching Arabella's apartment, waiting for him. That's what the Rolls was doing out front. Then they followed him to the station, Sweeney got on the train, and Hummer drove the Rolls down to London. Sweeney had probably seen him jump on the canal boat, and then they just drove from station to station waiting for him to disembark. Fortunately, he thought, he had given Arabella the briefcase with the papers in it. Then he wondered—had they seen the exchange?

The Rolls turned off the main road at a signpost that pointed to Loch Eddy forty miles away, and Inverness one hundred fifty miles away. The moors on both sides of the narrow road were covered with reddish-brown heather. So it's all going to end in Scotland, Jasmine thought as he watched the country grow more desolate with each passing mile. Sixteen hours had passed since Sweeney had stuck his gun in his stomach and forced him into the Rolls in London.

"Where did you find that nice girlie, Professor?"

Jasmine didn't answer. He knew Sweeney meant Arabella.

"Nice long legs, she had, didn't she? I'm asking you a question, Professor."

"Look, Mr. Sweeney—if that's your name. It's nice of you to give me a tour of Scotland, but I think you've mistaken me for someone else. I'm not a professor. . . . I keep telling you the name is Wilson, William Wilson."

Sweeney smiled as he dug the heel of his boot into Jasmine's ankle. "I asked you a friendly question, Professor."

Jasmine gasped with pain.

"Were they soft, Professor? The girl's legs, Professor? Hummer here loves long legs. He likes to pull them apart, don't you, Humm?"

Hummer opened his toothless mouth and grinned. "The name on the mailbox says she is A. Winchester. Is that right, Professor?"

Sweeney half-stood up to exert more pressure on the already swollen ankle. "Humm's asking you a question, Prof."

The pain was so sharp he could barely breathe. "Whatever her name is, she has nothing to say to you. She's just a student."

"Humm likes students," Sweeney said, relaxing the pressure slightly. "They like to talk to him. He has a way with them. He ties their hands behind their back. Works with the younger ones all the time." He laughed without moving his eyes.

"She's going to be lots of fun, isn't she, Sweeney?" Hummer said, laughing along with his partner.

"But first we're going to have a little talk with the Professor. Right, Professor Jasmine?"

"For the last time, the name is Wilson."

Sweeney's thin lips opened into a smile. Then he drove his fist into Jasmine's stomach, doubling him up.

The Rolls turned off the Inverness road toward Loch

282

Eddy. The macadam turned to dirt. The long silence was broken by the clap of gunshots from somewhere on the moor. With each bounce the car took, Jasmine felt sicker. He could see that his abductors were sadists, and knew it wouldn't take them long to get the information they wanted from him. Then they'd go after Arabella. There must be something he could do to divert them, some counterplay somewhere. He kept thinking hard.

The Rolls stopped in front of a log cabin on a totally desolate strip of land on the edge of the moor. Hummer got out first and opened the trunk of the car. He came back a minute later and handed Sweeney a leather dog's leash.

Sweeney looped the choke collar around Jasmine's neck. "Wouldn't want you to get any ideas about running away. And we wouldn't want to have to shoot you, Professor—not before we had our little talk." He pushed Jasmine out of the car, holding him at arm's length with the leash. Then, poking him in the back with his gun, he directed him toward the cabin. Hummer followed a few feet behind with a shotgun.

Once inside, Jasmine could see that the cabin was much larger than it looked from the outside. It had a fair-sized living room, kitchen, corridor, and ten small bedrooms that opened onto the corridor. From the collection of shotguns locked in the gunrack in the living room, and boxes of shells scattered all around, he assumed that the cabin was used for bird shooting. That might also explain the shots he had heard on the moor below while driving up. Of course. He almost snapped his fingers—the grouse-shooting season had just opened in Scotland.

Sweeney pulled him into one of the bedrooms. "Hold out your hands," he said. He took a long strand of thick rope from his pocket.

It had been in Houdini's book on magic, Jasmine recalled,

after racking his brain to reconstruct a trick he had read about as a child. He remembered, even as the rope was being lashed around his hands, the particular bit of logic of this legerdemain. It required expanding the muscles as much as possible at the point that the rope was being tied so as to provide a critical bit of slack when the muscles were relaxed.

"That'll do for the moment," Sweeney said, pulling the rope as tightly as he could and tying the strands into a braid of knots.

It took Jasmine's eyes a moment to adjust to the semi-darkness of the room. The one window was tightly boarded up, allowing only a sliver of light through an inch-wide gap in the boards. The only piece of furniture in the room was a chair.

Getting up on the chair, Sweeney tied the end of the chain leash over a beam, pulling it tight enough so that Jasmine could barely move without strangling himself. Then he walked out of the room with the chair. "Sorry to leave you hanging around like this," he chuckled.

Jasmine heard the door being locked from the outside. He realized he had very little time. The first problem would be to free his hands. Twisting his wrists carefully from right to left, he worked his way slowly and methodically out of the first strand of the rope.

Thank God for Houdini, he thought to himself, realizing at the same time that Sweeney was no master at rope tying. It took him only another minute to completely free his hands.

Now for the choke collar. Even with both hands loose, he couldn't prevent the chain from choking him when he moved. He needed something to block the sleeve of the collar.

Bending his foot backward and up, he pulled off the leather heel and extracted one of the small nails from his shoe. With his thumb he pressed the nail through the leather sleeve on the leash.

He reached down and pulled out a second nail. This time it was easier because the leash was no longer choking him. He worked the nail back and forth until he managed to lock the sleeve in place. Now at least he could breathe a little more freely.

Raising his hands as high as he could on the leash, he began to slide the top of it along the beam towards the window. It took him more than a minute to move an inch. Finally, he could see out the crack in the window. A rake was standing in a pile of leaves. He saw its prongs as a potential weapon.

Then he heard the roar of a car approaching. A Land Rover pulled to a stop next to the Rolls. It had a half-dozen dead quail tied to the backgate. So this was the grouse shooter, Jasmine thought, as he saw the door open.

Both Hummer and Sweeney ran out to meet the man in the Land Rover. Jasmine instantly recognized the large head emerging from the car. It was Raven.

Chapter XXXII

SWEENEY'S GUN

"You stole something from me, Jasmine," Raven began. He was still wearing the plus-four tweeds that he had been shooting grouse in an hour earlier.

Jasmine pointed with one thumb to the leash around his neck, and coughed. He didn't want anyone to know he had blocked the choke collar. Surprise, he had decided, was the only asset available to him in this game.

"Sweeney can untie you later. Right now I want those papers back."

"Then what happens to me?" Jasmine stalled, pretending to choke.

"McNab is coming to pick you up. From then on you're his problem, not mine."

"What will they do with someone who knows too much?"

"That's their business. They might not kill you. I understand that they've now perfected a nice technique for doing memory lobotomies." Raven pointed with his index finger to his temple. "If you were to tell me where those papers are, I might be disposed to give you a slight head start on McNab."

"Why are the papers so important?" Jasmine asked. As in chess, Jasmine decided to temporize until he found his next move.

"I jotted down the names of some friends in Iran. It could be embarrassing."

The telephone rang. Raven paused in midsentence to see if he would be called to the phone.

"I see. You don't want the CIA to get the names of all your agents . . ."

"Let's just say I don't want them to think me indiscreet. Now, if you please, where is the list?"

Jasmine turned toward the door. A shriveled old man was trying to catch Raven's eye.

"Excuse me, sir," Hugh Leigh-Jones called in from the doorway. "That was your pilot. He's just landed at Inverness and wants to know when you'll be ready to leave."

"Tell him one hour, Hugh."

"Don't you think a lighter suit might be appropriate for Iran, sir?"

"I'll change on the plane. You'd better get the Rolls ready, Hugh," Raven barked, somewhat exasperated by his butler-secretary.

"As you see, Professor Jasmine, I have no time to play games with you. You'll either tell me now where the list is or you'll tell Sweeney when I leave. You have no choice about that."

"If anything happens to me, copies of the list will be sent out . . ."

Even as he spoke, Jake knew the bluff wouldn't work.

"By your lady friend? No, I don't think so."

Jasmine heard a horn blowing outside. It was the Rolls.

"Before I say good-bye, do you want to tell me where the list is? No? Well, tally-ho, Jasmine. Give my regards to McNab..."

Raven shut the door as he left. Jasmine could hear him saying to Sweeney, "When you finish eating, get the list from Jasmine."

"It won't take five minutes," Sweeney answered, then gave a short laugh. It sounded like a donkey braying.

Jasmine began to inch his way back to the window. With the choke collar somewhat blocked, he could move much more quickly now. As he got to the window, he saw Raven getting into the Rolls with his secretary at the wheel. They drove off. Jasmine's eyes fastened on the rake in the pile of leaves. It was only about three feet away from him.

Sweeney and Hummer were laughing at each other's lewd jokes. They were only halfway through the excellent game stew that Raven had left for them, and saw no reason to rush. The Professor would present no problem.

Jasmine took off his belt. Forcing it through the opening in the window, he lowered the buckle until it dangled over the rake's head. Twice he missed, then he managed to hook it. He pulled the belt up until the metal bumped against the boards on the window. Now he had it within reach. But would it fit through the opening?

Hand over hand, he lifted the rake up the outside of the window until he could grab the handle. He slid it inside. Working the prongs first to the right, then to the left, he maneuvered the head of the rake in.

"I'd better get to work on Jasmine," Sweeney was saying in an intentionally threatening voice. He wanted Jasmine to hear him. "You do the dishes, Humm."

288

Jasmine heard Sweeney's footsteps approaching. Hooking the rake on the rafter overhead, he slowly succeeded in raising himself up. With the chain now free of his dangling weight, he could just manage to slip off the noose. The door creaked open. He kept the rake poised high over his head.

"What are you doing over there?" Sweeney demanded, squinting to see Jasmine in the darkness. At first he thought Jasmine was clutching at the leash over his head. Too late he realized that it wasn't the leash, and went for the gun in his belt.

Jasmine was a split second faster. He brought the rake crashing down. The deadly prongs smashed into Sweeney's forehead. Blood gushed from a half dozen stab wounds. Sweeney's gun hand wavered back and forth, as if it were searching for its target. Jasmine brought the rake down again and again.

With a groan more like that of an animal than a human, Sweeney toppled backwards against the half-opened door, the prongs of the rake now plunged into his head. The momentum from that final blow carried Jasmine forward. When he stopped himself he was standing almost on top of Sweeney. Sweeney held the gun pointed straight up, directly at Jasmine's stomach. Without thinking, Jasmine stomped on it with his foot.

The gun rolled out of Sweeney's hand and Jasmine grabbed it just as Hummer forced his way through the half-opened door. Hardly a minute had passed since Sweeney had come to the room. "Christ!" Hummer shouted, seeing Sweeney slumped on the floor. He raised the shotgun in his hands level with Jasmine's head.

The gun in Jasmine's hand fired first. The .45-caliber bullet tore into Hummer's groin. As he reeled back, Hummer tightened his fingers on the trigger of the shotgun. Both barrels exploded.

Jasmine felt the concussion from the blast as it whizzed past his head and knocked out the window boards. Through the opening, he could see the Land Rover still sitting where Raven had parked it. Across the moor, he could see a pair of headlights approaching the house.

Hummer had dropped the shotgun and was crawling down the corridor on his hands and knees like a crushed beetle. Sweeney's left hand was still twitching. Jasmine didn't wait to find out whether they were alive or dead. He leaped out the window, gun in hand, and made for the Land Rover.

The keys were still in the ignition. His fingers fumbled for the starter, then found it. The engine turned over just as the headlights turned into the driveway. He jammed the gears into first and let up on the clutch. The car shot forward. He was breathing so hard he could barely see the road.

McNab, in the approaching car, swerved sharply when he saw what looked like a truck coming straight at him. Only when it passed did he see that it was a Land Rover, driven by Jasmine. The sudden swerve took him into a ditch, and he tried to ease his car out of it, but it was no use. Lighting his pipe, he got out of the car. From the house, he heard a low moan.

First he found Sweeney, choking on his own blood. Lifting his head up by its white hair, McNab heard Sweeney say, "Jasmine."

McNab held his pistol less than an inch away from Sweeney's temple. That way he knew it would only take one bullet to finish the job. It was an electronically operated gun that the CIA had copied from the Soviets and it fired almost noiselessly.

Following the trail of blood down the hall, McNab found Hummer lying in a heap. His toothless mouth was emitting an almost inaudible moan. The electric gun moved down, then hissed. The moan ended.

McNab liked to do a clean job. His orders from Raven were "to dispatch" Jasmine—and the two men who had kidnapped him.

McNab picked up the telephone and asked the operator for the Hotel St. Peter in Zurich. He waited until he heard Tracy's voice on the other end.

"I was only able to deliver two of the packages ... I missed the Professor. But don't worry. There's no way he can leave the country." He hung up.

Tracy decided not to tell Dulles about Jasmine's escape. It would only confuse him further.

Chapter XXXIII

FLIGHT TO TEHERAN

"What seems to be the delay?" Raven shouted in an annoyed voice above the roar of the plane's engines.

"Well, sir, it seems that your Land Rover is coming across the runway," Hugh Leigh-Jones answered, looking out the window. He detested flying, and hoped that this might mean some urgent business of Raven's would result in the cancellation of the flight to Abadan.

"Damned idiots. They were supposed to wait at the cabin," Raven growled back. The only reason he could think of for Sweeney and Hummer to come out to the airport was that they had gotten hold of the list. "Don't waste any more time, Hugh. Open the blasted door and see what they want."

292

Hugh obediently began turning the crank controlling the passenger door.

It only had opened halfway when Jasmine stepped inside. In his right hand was Sweeney's revolver. "Close the door," Jasmine ordered.

Hugh obediently turned the crank in the other direction, his hands shaking visibly.

"What the hell are you doing here?" Raven tried to stand up, forgetting for the moment that he had his seatbelt fastened. Then he saw the .45. He slumped back in his seat.

"Tell the pilot to take off." Jasmine pointed to the telephone by Raven's right hand.

"What happened to Sweeney . . . and Hummer?"

"Pick up that damn phone." Jasmine sat directly across from Raven and pulled back the hammer of the gun with his thumb.

Raven realized that he had seriously underestimated Jasmine. He had outwitted two professional killers and the gun in his hands had a hair trigger. He said into the phone, "Take off immediately."

The plane's four engines revved up to a roar before he could even hang up the phone. A moment later, the Constellation was racing down the runway, then lifting into the air above the cold blue waters of Loch Inverness. The landing gear came up with a loud clang. The flight plan called for the plane to fly over France, Italy, the Mediterranean, Lebanon, Syria, and Iraq, before landing in Abadan.

At Abadan the plane would be met by security men from Anglo-Iranian Oil. They would know what to do with Jasmine, Raven thought, still staring at the lethal .45.

"Now I want you to write a few letters to your friends in Teheran," Jasmine ordered, passing Raven a sheaf of paper from the desk.

293

"Whatever you say, Jasmine—but please put that thing out of sight."

Jasmine lowered the gun, then slipped it under his jacket. He could see that Raven was a thoroughly cowed man. "The first is to your friend Savrenck in the Ministry of Information." He had memorized Raven's list of names. "You noted 'documentation' next to his name."

"Yes," Raven agreed.

"Write him to provide me with a full set of documents identifying me as an American journalist ... for the *Washington Post.*"

"Why not?" Raven said, scribbling out the note. Might as well humor him, he thought, until they land in Abadan. "So now you're going to be a journalist, Jasmine?"

"Next, I'll need a letter to your friend Phali."

"The Secretary to Mossadeq?"

"Right. The one on your list. He's to set up an immediate interview with Mossadeq for *The Washington Post* correspondent."

"As you like. But do you really think Mossadeq will believe anything you say?"

Jasmine waited for Raven to finish the second letter. He read it through and handed it back. "Add that he will be well rewarded for performing such a valuable service on short notice."

Raven shrugged and complied.

"Just one final note, Raven—to Colonel Ramses."

"I think that would be a very dangerous move, Professor."

Jasmine reached in his jacket for Sweeney's gun.

"No need for that, Jasmine. What do you want me to write?"

" '*Do exactly as the bearer of this note asks, no matter what previous instructions it contravenes.*' " Jasmine dictated. "Now sign it."

Raven signed it and, shaking his head as if a grave mistake were being made, handed it over to Jasmine.

Jasmine glanced out the window. The world below was an endless desert. They were over Iraq, according to the pilot's last report.

"Power is not something you study in a political science course, Professor," Raven said. He undid his seatbelt, rose, and walked to the storage compartment in the tail of the plane.

Jasmine followed him.

Raven pulled a white summer suit from the closet. "Power is the means to all ends; it is the essence, not the corruption, of politics."

Raven stepped out of his tweed plus-fours and into his linen slacks.

"In most places in this world, governments are just a fiction. Power is the control of the resources. It is that simple. Those who need the resources must pay the price. Look down there, Jasmine."

Below, Jasmine could see steel towers dotting the desert. He knew they were oil rigs.

"The Khoristan fields of Iran," Raven said, slipping on a raw silk shirt with epaulets on each shoulder. "Each well you see down there can produce ten thousand barrels of oil a day—four hundred forty thousand gallons. Just one well could light a city the size of New York, or provide the fuel to move a tank division across Europe. That is power. No government controls those wells; if they did, that government would control Europe, and the energy that lights a thousand cities all over the world. That's why Mossadeq cannot be allowed to survive."

Seven hours had passed since the plane took off from London. The pilot announced over the intercom that they would be landing in Abadan in five minutes. Hugh Leigh-

Jones, still cowering in his seat, fastened his seatbelt even tighter. Raven slipped on his white linen jacket. In white, he looked like a totally different person.

Below, Jasmine could see the huge metallic domes the oil companies had erected at Abadan for storage. They rivaled in size any mosque that Islam had built. The gantry cranes hovered over the empty docks like a ganglia of prehistoric beasts. On the airfield below he could see a tiny truck speeding down the runway; the men inside looked like toy soldiers. He looked up at Raven's smiling eyes and realized with a shock that it was a trap.

Raven confidently knotted his black knit tie. He also could see the airfield approaching and knew his security troops would be waiting.

"Pick up the phone, Raven. Tell the pilot we're not going to land at Abadan. We're going on to Teheran." Jasmine drew the gun out of his jacket as he gave the orders.

He's bluffing, Raven thought. If he could hold out for another few seconds, they would be on the ground.

The barrel of the gun moved toward Raven's heart. Bits of Sweeney's dried blood flaked off the barrel, falling on his linen jacket. Spots of moisture began to show through Raven's silk shirt. The phone was only a few inches from his hand, but he didn't move for it.

The landing gear clanged down.

"I've nothing to lose anymore." Jasmine held the gun in both hands and again pulled back the hammer with his right thumb. His face tightened as his fingers closed on the trigger.

Raven felt everything stop inside him. The fear of death was oozing through him. He suddenly realized that it was not Jasmine he feared, but Sweeney's gun! "Get this plane up into the air," Raven shouted into the phone, "Don't land here!"

As the wheels touched the ground, the pilot opened the throttle wide. The plane bounced up, gaining altitude. "Where will we land, sir?" the pilot asked over the intercom.

"Teheran," answered Raven. His shirt was drenched with sweat.

CHAPTER XXXIV

SNAFU

Zurich. August eighteenth. Dulles put down the phone. He looked down at his desk for a long moment, thinking, then turned and peered at Tracy, who was standing next to his desk.

"Kim says Jasmine is in Teheran," Dulles finally said. "Last I heard you had him ... er ... under control ... in England. Or was it Scotland?"

"Well, there's been a bit of a snafu in Scotland," Tracy began. A slight tremor of nervousness made him sway back and forth as he spoke.

MOORS MURDERER CAPTURED. Dulles pointed to the headline in that morning's edition of the Paris *Herald Tribune*. A photograph of McNab appeared on the front page. "Is that the snafu?"

298

CARTEL

"That's what I was coming in to see you about, Chief. McNab seems to have gotten himself into a muddle."

"Seems that way." Dulles paused, waiting for Tracy's explanation.

"Just as McNab was leaving the cabin where a couple of security men were holding Jasmine, the Scottish police and some news photographers arrived. When they saw the bodies..."

"Bodies?" Dulles repeated.

"Yes. Two oil company guards who were holding Jasmine were killed."

"The *Tribune* says 'brutally beaten, mauled, and shot,'" Dulles interrupted. "But do go on."

"Some girlfriend tipped off the police and reporters. Seems she saw the car that picked Jasmine up."

"Extraordinary. But what about McNab? Why suspect him?"

"The police found the murder weapon in his pocket."

"McNab? I'm afraid I don't really understand. What happened to Jasmine?"

"Got away ... McNab called me before the police arrived, told me."

"Got through the police dragnet, huh? Through all our security? Straight to Teheran?"

"It *is* shocking," Tracy said, shifting his weight back and forth from his right to his left foot. He could see Dulles was going off on a wrong track.

"Shocking is not the precise word, is it? His escape was almost predictable..."

"Don't see what you're driving at exactly, sir."

"Quite clearly. He had help. Help in high places. No other explanation. Don't you agree?"

"Possibly, sir. That girl in Oxford..."

"I'm talking about high places."

299

"It's a possibility but . . ."

"No 'buts' about it, Tracy. It's the only possibility. He managed to penetrate a major CIA operation in Washington. He obtained a master list of agents. He got away from McNab in Cambridge. Got away from two trained guards in Scotland. Moved through a half-dozen countries without proper travel documents. He's a pro."

"Jasmine admittedly has some almost animal-like cunning, but . . ."

"Who gave him the money for all this? Where did he get his fake passports? Disguises? Equipment? Someone is obviously behind him: the only question is who?"

"I'll try to look into these questions, sir . . . only . . ."

"Only what?" Dulles wondered why Tracy was resisting the obvious so consistently.

"Only I think this may be a case where there is less to the situation than meets the eye." He felt uneasy debunking one of Dulles' theories but he didn't want him to get too far afield. Jasmine undoubtedly would be picked up in Teheran.

Dulles leaned back in his chair. He could see that Tracy was exceedingly nervous about something. Could Tracy himself be insecure, he wondered?

Dulles quickly reviewed the case. It was Tracy who had recruited Jasmine, and thus provided him with the opportunity for penetrating Ajax. It was also Tracy who claimed to have Jasmine under control when others were worried about him. Tracy was the only other person who knew that McNab was sent to make the telephone "delivery" in Cambridge. Yet Jasmine had apparently been tipped off about the bomb. Tracy also knew that McNab would be picking Jasmine up in Scotland. And why had Tracy not told him of Jasmine's escape earlier? It all added up to one inescapable conclusion: Tracy could be hand-in-glove with

Jasmine. It was all circumstantial evidence but it added up in Dulles' mind. Tracy was probably a mole the Soviets had planted in the agency years ago, and now they had activated him to work under Jasmine. Obviously, Jasmine was one of their top agents. Brilliant. Too bad we don't have him, Dulles thought.

"I am reassigning you to Washington, Bronson."

"What?" Tracy's face dropped.

"There's a plane out of Zurich in an hour."

"An hour? But sir, we're in the middle of Ajax. It's going like a charm . . ."

"Sorry, Tracy."

"But I've worked on Ajax night and day for nine months."

"This other assignment is more urgent. Won't wait. The Embassy limousine will take you to the airport." Dulles looked at his watch. "Off you go. See you in Washington."

From his window in the Hotel St. Peter, he watched Tracy get in the limousine. I wonder if he'll defect en route, Dulles thought to himself. He must realize the game is up.

Chapter XXXV

TIME OF THE SHAH

Queen Soraya turned to take one last look at Iran before she stepped inside the DC-3. The wind from the propellers blew her long hair on both sides of her face. But her face never lost its calm. Her brown eyes looked down at her husband, splendidly dressed in his white uniform. The Shah.

"It's time, Your Majesty," Kim Adams said. He had never called him "Your Majesty" before.

The Shah nodded, a note of sadness in his eyes. Then he followed his wife aboard the plane. He wondered whether the American plan would really work, or whether he would spend the rest of his life in exile. The door closed, leaving him no more time for doubt.

Adams stood on the runway and watched the plane slowly lift off the ground. It flew out over the gray waters of the Caspian, then banked steeply, and turned west. In a few hours the Shah would be in Rome, Step 16 in the Ajax scenario.

Adams walked past the guard of Iranian soldiers, machine guns held on their hips, as they held their rigid salute to the Shah until his plane was out of sight.

Red started the engine in the jeep even before Adams opened the door. With the Shah safely out of the way, he knew they were ready to swing into action. "Queen's quite a looker. Why didn't you introduce me?" Red said, letting the clutch pop up. They were moving the moment Adams slid into the jeep.

"Knew you'd be in a hurry to see the festivities in Teheran, Red." Adams looked at his watch: it was 8 A.M. "Do you think we'll get there before your fireworks start popping?"

"I think we'll make it." As Red spoke he whipped the car around a hairpin turn, braking with his heel and simultaneously accelerating with his toe. "The incendiaries in the bazaar are timed to go off at one P.M." He had planted four of them, along with leaflets denouncing the Shah as a tyrant. "Does the Shah know about our little anti-Shah party?"

"The Shah knows all he needs to know: nothing." Adams was looking at the sheer drop on the right side of the mountain road as Red skidded through a sharp turn to the left. "The topplers are all set?"

"Yeah, picked out a half-dozen statues of the Shah for them to pull down. Hope the Shah doesn't mind my choice."

"He'll build taller ones. What about the painters?"

303

"Gave 'em thirty gallons of red paint. As soon as they see the smoke from the bazaar, they begin painting 'Down with the Shah. Long Live Mossadeq' on every mosque and shrine they can find."

"That should do the trick with the mullahs," Adams said, clutching the straps on the dashboard as if they were the reins of a bronco.

"You know, I'm ... I'm ... I'm sort of religious. I feel a little bad about desecrating their mosques—even if they are a bunch of Moo-slims," Red confessed.

"Don't worry. Tomorrow we'll give them thirty gallons of paint remover." Kim fell silent.

Red concentrated on driving. He liked the challenge of mountain roads, never knowing what he was going to find when he careened around a blind curve. A flock of sheep, an avalanche of rocks, or another blind curve. He turned the wheel sharply to the right as he began his thirtieth "S" turn, and hit the accelerator. He would skid through this one, he planned. He began twisting the wheel to the left—and then he spotted the shadow of the cannon. He stomped on the brakes with all his might. The jeep screeched to a stop inches from a hulking tank.

"Hello, Kim!" General Zahedi called from the turret of the tank. The roadblock he was manning was only thirty miles from Teheran.

"How do you like it?" Adams shouted back. He pointed to the tank. It was one of the twenty-four new Sherman tanks that the American AID mission in Iran had turned over to Zahedi. Step 13 in Ajax.

"It's a marvelous machine. Drives better than my Cadillac. I can't wait to get to Teheran," Zahedi said with enthusiasm in his voice. He hoped newsreel photographers would be there to take his picture standing in the turret of the tank, sword in hand, as he arrived in the capital to "restore order."

The tank slowly backed up and Red shot through the space.

"See you in Teheran!" Adams shouted back to Zahedi.

Red pressed his foot down on the accelerator, waiting to confront the next blind curve.

Chapter XXXVI

THE FINAL COUP

Jasmine dashed off a letter while waiting in the lobby of the Park Hotel in Teheran.

DEAREST ARABELLA,

One hour from now I have an appointment with Mossadeq. My run of luck still holds: I commandeered a jeep at the airport and, since I couldn't hold Raven a hostage forever, I handcuffed him to an oil derrick about ten miles from the airport. The cuffs were graciously supplied by an airport guard at Raven's own request. After I've seen Mossadeq, I'll tip the oil company off to his whereabouts. My pretext for seeing the Premier is that I'm a correspondent for the *Washington Post*—credentials that only cost me a hundred

306

pounds. It may or may not work. Everything, even luck, eventually runs out. In any case, I want you to know I love only you.

While posting this letter with the concierge, he felt a hand on his shoulder.

"Jake, what are you doing in Teheran?" Foxcroft asked, a puzzled look on his pudgy face.

"I'm doing a little writing for the *Washington Post,*" Jasmine answered. He wondered whether Foxcroft realized that the Ajax scenario he had read in New York was taking place before his very eyes right now. "Were you surprised to hear that the Shah had left the country this morning?" he asked, as a test.

"Everyone was. Never expected him to run away. Damn it, he was needed here—now the Commies can take over whenever they want." Foxcroft looked hard at Jasmine. If he were a Soviet agent, as everyone suspected, he certainly was playing it cool coming to Teheran.

"See you later, Foxy," Jasmine said, pushing his way across the lobby. "I've got an appointment downtown."

Jasmine told the taxi driver to take him to Majlis Square. On the drive there, he could see signs everywhere of the seventeenth step in the scenario. Fire engines raced by on their way to the bazaar. A statue of the Shah on Shah-en-Shah Square toppled over, breaking into a thousand fragments. Men with Mossadeq pictures on placards were sloshing red paint on the venerable shrine of the prophet. Oddly enough, most Iranians seemed oblivious to these acts of provocation. They sat in outdoor cafés, sipping black coffee and playing backgammon.

Jasmine asked the driver to turn on the car radio. The military music was unmistakable. "B" Team had seized the radio station. It was only a matter of minutes before an announcer would begin issuing appeals for help in restoring order in Teheran. The eighteenth step. Then Zahedi's tanks would move into the city. The nineteenth step.

When he got out at Majlis Square, he saw a group of one hundred powerfully built men, standing in almost military formation although they were wearing loose-fitting civilian clothes. A redheaded American was talking to one of them, who nodded slowly. The twentieth step, Jasmine thought, the storming of Mossadeq's residence.

He hurried for his appointment.

As soon as Jasmine had left the hotel, Foxcroft asked the concierge, whom he called Sammy, for the letter. Sammy hesitated until Foxcroft put a one-thousand-rial note in his hand. Then he shrugged and handed it over.

What Foxcroft read confirmed his suspicions. Jasmine was a Soviet agent and was operating with false credentials.

Why was Jasmine on his way over to Mossadeq? he wondered, crumpling up the note. Foxcroft first placed a call to *The Washington Post* to make sure that Jasmine really wasn't working for them. He wouldn't want to turn in another journalist—even if he were a spy.

His call to the *Post* finally came through. "Never heard of Jasmine," the foreign editor shouted over the weak connection.

Next Foxcroft called Smithline at the Embassy.

So Jasmine thinks he can block Option B? Smithline thought as he hung up the phone. Then he picked it up again and asked for Mossadeq's residence.

CHAPTER XXXVII

MOSSADEQ

The lights flickered on in Mossadeq's office, as the power was cut and restored again. Mohammed Mossadeq kept signing decrees. Decrees of amnesty, decrees of land reform, and decrees appointing his followers to positions in the provinces. He didn't need to read them, for he knew they would never be carried out. Still, he sat hunched over his chair in his blue pajamas and robe and finished the stack of decrees that would be the last official orders issued by his government.

"Show that reporter in now, Colonel," he said to his aide. It would be his last appointment; perhaps his last interview.

Jasmine stepped into the office carrying a manila envelope. Inside it was Sweeney's gun.

"This is not the best of times, Mr. Jasmine ... but I can

give you five minutes. What can I tell you that your paper would print?"

The lights flickered off for a minute. Even in the shadowy semidarkness Mossadeq maintained a very powerful presence. His small eyes seemed to generate their own light while his face remained absolutely calm. The lights from a car outside reflected through the window and fell around his bald head like a nimbus in a medieval painting. Then the light came on again.

"I can't oblige you with the sort of theatricality your newspapers love to print about me. I can't even weep for you, it's all too sad."

"I've come to tell you ..." Dr. Jasmine stopped speaking when he heard the phone on the desk buzz.

"Please excuse me, Mr. Jasmine." Mossadeq's long face seemed to lengthen as he heard the news. He hung up the phone. "It seems the only regiments loyal to me, rather than being returned to Teheran as I ordered, have been sent to Fars province. But it's for the better; they won't be butchered by the American tanks that Zahedi now has."

Jasmine realized this was Step 22 in the scenario: neutralizing all loyal units by controlling the Army Communications Center. All the moves that he had planned in the Gaming Center were now being played out in Teheran.

"Dr. Mossadeq. Part of the plot involves killing you ... "

"Thank you for trying to warn me, but my life is of little value. I'm nearly eighty, who would want to harm an old man who no longer has any power? It is the oil fields they want. See if your newspaper will print that. Ah, but they won't. They will talk about me as an hysterical, half-mad Communist. There is only one truth in the Middle East: oil. It is not I, or even the Shah, that matters. It is our oil they care about. Write that, Mr. Jasmine." He pressed a buzzer on his desk.

"But, sir—just hear me out." He couldn't help admiring Mossadeq's cool courage.

The aide came back into the room. He was a powerfully built man with an olive complexion that matched his uniform. He had faintly oriental eyes.

"Colonel, give Mr. Jasmine whatever facts he needs to write his story. There are things I must attend to . . . before we leave. Good-bye, Mr. Jasmine."

The Colonel escorted Jasmine out and into a smaller office. "I am Colonel Ramses," he introduced himself, smiling broadly. "You've heard of me, Mr. Jasmine?"

"I have a message for you, Colonel." He reached into his envelope and pulled out the note that he had forced Raven to write. "It is from Sir Anthony Raven."

"Ah, yes—Raven." The Colonel sighed. He looked up when he finished reading it, his eyes slanting into a smile. "So you know who I am?"

"You are to do exactly as I say. Raven wants you to drop . . ." Jasmine didn't finish his sentence. He saw Ramses was tearing the note into neat strips and throwing them into the wastepaper basket.

"So you know who I am?" Ramses repeated. "I also know who you are, Mr. Jasmine. While you were with the Premier, Mr. Smithline telephoned. He told me you had fake credentials and were a dangerous subversive, to be arrested on sight." He laughed softly, waiting for Jasmine's response.

"I have another message then." Jasmine reached again into the envelope. He was slipping out Sweeney's gun when he felt cold metal touching the back of his neck.

It was the barrel of a Czechoslovakian Ukian machine gun. The man holding it, Captain Bulbul, was squat and toadlike. With his left hand the Captain took the envelope from Jasmine. "What do we have here?" Bulbul croaked. He took out Sweeney's long-barreled .45 and handed it to Ramses.

"A dangerous subversive, eh?" Ramses said, still smiling. "Captain, it's time to escort our Premier to the van."

Option B. Jasmine remembered the shooting he had authored. He looked at the light, hoping.

Bulbul walked out of the room as quietly as he had come in. Now it was only the two of them, Jasmine thought. In the quiet of the room, he could hear the mob outside, rushing the residence.

Ramses checked the safety and the chamber on Sweeney's .45. With a menacing smile, he leveled the gun at Jasmine. In his intense preoccupation he failed to hear two men slip through the back door. Jasmine recognized one as the redheaded American he had seen outside, the other as Kim Adams. The redhead held a gun in both hands with a long silencer on it. The light flickered again.

Chapter XXXVIII

IN TRIUMPH

All of Teheran was alive with anticipation on August 20, 1953. The mullahs in the mosques, the hawkers in the bazaar, the coffee-sippers on the street, tribesmen on their camels, everyone in Teheran knew that the Shah was returning at high noon. At every corner, Army troops handed out photographs of the Shah; in every café, young cadets led the chant *"Zindabad Shah, Zindabad Shah"*—Long live the Shah; on every lamppost hung an Iranian flag. Schools, banks, and stores were closed. The crowd began to thicken along Shalimar Boulevard until it was impossible to see through it to the street. As the great mogul bell struck twelve, everyone was waiting.

313

Jasmine was also waiting. This was the thirty-sixth step in the scenario he had created: AJAX KING RETURNS IN TRIUMPH. He sipped coffee at a sidewalk café and leafed through *The New York Times*. Under the headline ROYALISTS OUST MOSSADEQ, the story reported "Iranians loyal to Shah Mohammed Reza Pahlevi, including Teheran civilians, soldiers and rural tribesmen, swept Premier Mossadeq out of power today ... Mossadeq, disguised as an old woman, managed to escape the angry crowd of loyalists and his present whereabouts is unknown." Next to that report was a longer background story by Fletcher F. Foxcroft. It began, "The Soviet plot to take control of this strategically vital country boomeranged today when Iranians rose up in support of their Shah...." Jasmine couldn't help smiling. Finishing his coffee, he, like everyone else in the café, stepped up onto a table to see the procession.

It was quite a sight. The Shah's black Mercedes was being carried down the street on the shoulders of a hundred powerful men in black gym suits—the Zinenen. The Shah and Queen Soraya stood on the front seat waving to the crowd, which was now in a frenzy. Darius Ali was seated in the back of the car. Jasmine instantly recognized him as his "publisher" in London.

From his balcony in the Park Hotel, Foxcroft watched the procession with Myles Smithline. "Being recalled to Washington, eh? Too bad, Smitty. Hey, look over there." He pointed to a tall man standing on a table on the street below. "Isn't that Jasmine?"

"Been meaning to talk to you about him, Foxy," Smithline began, then stopped short. He still couldn't figure out how Jasmine had escaped. He had given Ramses and Bulbul fair warning; now they were both dead. No sense putting that in his report, he decided. It never made sense to him to raise questions he couldn't answer.

"It's him all right. Still on the loose, huh?" Foxcroft squinted slightly, showing his suspicion.

"Exactly. Sorry to do this to you, Foxy, but you can't write about him . . . not yet."

"I see. He's part of something bigger?" Foxcroft relaxed his gaze slightly.

"Exactly, Foxy. I've always been straight with you in the past, haven't I?"

Foxcroft turned back to Jasmine. A redheaded man was sauntering up behind him.

Smithline was also watching Red Murphy close in on Jasmine. What is he doing with Jasmine? he wondered. It was another question without an answer as far as he was concerned.

Across the street, Jasmine, answer. He followed Murphy to the Park Hotel. Then patiently while Murphy banged on Kim Adams' door.

"Very thoughtful of you to call, Winston. Yes, I did what I could. Well, thank you," Kim Adams was saying on the telephone. He ignored the knock at the door until he finished the conversation.

Then Adams threw a silk bathrobe over his shoulders and asked, "Who's there?"

"Just me and Jasmine," Red answered and led Jasmine in. "Anything wrong?"

Adams wiped a splotch of shaving soap from his jaw. "I just want to know how you did it, Jasmine. Did you just sit down with a pencil and paper and write out thirty-six steps, without even knowing where they would take place?"

"Something like that. But it worked, didn't it?"

"Worked too damn well. That's the problem," Adams cut in. "Now everytime someone in Washington thinks something ought to be changed somewhere, he'll get in a Harvard professor to draw up a thirty-six-step scenario. Just

315

because it worked here, those bloody idiots are going to assume it will work anywhere. And if it doesn't, they'll blame the professor who drew up the scenario. This little success of yours might turn out to be an unmitigated disaster."

"I still don't understand, what happened yesterday?" Jasmine asked.

"No doubt you want to know what we were doing in Ramses' offices yesterday," Red interrupted.

"I thought Ramses was your man," Jasmine said, still trying to figure out why Red had shot him.

"Well, he had done odd jobs for Raven, but ... we couldn't have him shooting old Mossy, could we? No real point to it ... it would annoy the Shah." Adams shrugged, as if the explanation were so obvious as to be unnecessary.

"But Option B was part of the final scenario ..."

"Never liked it to begin with. But we left it in to please Raven. We needed the agents he had in place there. Except for Red ... we didn't really have any assets to speak of in Iran." Adams looked at Murphy as he spoke.

"And now you have the Shah," Jasmine added. It was becoming clear to him why the CIA had done the coup for the cartel.

"I have to get back to Washington. I'll try to clear things up for you—but it might be a bit sticky." Adams threw his clothing into a small suitcase as he talked. He had a plane to catch. "Going back to Harvard, Jasmine?"

"No."

"New horizons then. Good luck."

Jasmine left with a smile. He had no idea what he would do. He was finished at Harvard after the bomb incident and presumably Yale would withdraw its offer. There was only one thing he could do: rewrite his book on coups d'etat.